AN IRISH LULLABY DEPICTS HUMANITIES' SEARCH FOR RELEVANCY AND FULFILLMENT, SET AGAINST THE BACKDROP OF ONE OF THE MOST CONTROVERSIAL, MORAL, AND BURNING SOCIAL/CULTURAL ISSUES OF OUR TIME, ABORTION.

As Father O'Connor, an aging priest at Saint Aloysius Parish, contemplates his legacy, Angela Sanchez, a troubled teen, sits in an abortion clinic awaiting her procedure. She is comforted by Aubrey Fitzgibbons, who is married to the church deacon but also serves as a leader in the local Planned Parenthood. Aubrey is conflicted between her obligations to the church and her responsibilities to Planned Parenthood. More complications arise when Aubrey becomes pregnant herself, triggering a serious medical condition that threatens her life. Doctors recommend abortion, but something incredible is about to happen.

"In the halcyon days of Hudson County, the Catholic Church's priests and nuns shaped an ethic of respect for both church and society. Louis Manzo's "An Irish Lullaby" captures that spirit and the ways in which benign authoritarian voices insured a civil society where people learned to get along with each other. Those were the days."— *Fr. Alexander M. Santora, Faith Matters columnist for THE JERSEY JOURNAL and pastor of Our Lady of Grace & St. Joseph, Hoboken*

"In my hometown, a priest in the twilight of his priesthood inadvertently intertwines past morays with the present culture, revealing personal decisions best left in the past."—*Pat O'Melia, Host of the Jersey City Show and Television Producer*

FROM REVIEWS POSTED ON THE *ONLINE BOOKCLUB* and *READER'S FAVORITE:*

"...It is so well written that you can hear the Irish brogue, taste the Irish whiskey, feel the deep-rooted bonds of friendship..."

"...The dramatic story portrays a balanced perspective of the politics and religious views pertaining to abortion."

"...Father O'Connor's endearing mannerisms captured my heart at the onset and never let go."

"...Louis Michael Manzo shows great skill in storytelling, weaving a tale that will keep readers enthralled.

"*An Irish Lullaby* sings a timeless song; a memorable melody that will keep you humming and pondering its truth for a lifetime."

"...Manzo also has an aptitude for drawing emotion out of the readers; I found myself laughing out loud at times and shedding tears at other times."

AN IRISH LULLABY

Louis Michael Manzo

Moonshine Cove Publishing, LLC
Abbeville, South Carolina U.S.A.
First Moonshine Cove edition May 2018

ISBN: 978-1-945181-412
Library of Congress PCN: 2018952041

Book cover design by Moonshine Cove Staff, Cover Images public domain

About the Author

As Chief of the Jersey City Department of Health,
Louis Manzo exposed corporate greed—an

 unscrupulous company trying to cover up
chromium contamination affecting
children and city neighborhoods. His
efforts led to health studies for the
residents and culminated in the country's
largest chromium contamination
remediation project.

As a New Jersey Assemblyman, Louis Manzo sat on a
special legislative committee that sponsored legislation
producing the largest property tax rebate in New
Jersey's history. He also cosponsored some of the
toughest anti-gang and gun violence laws in recent
history. In a Resolution of tribute passed by the entire
New Jersey General Assembly, Manzo's colleagues
proclaimed, "Louis Manzo is an individual of
remarkable character and exceptional determination."

Manzo now resides in Belmar, New Jersey, where he is
dedicated to writing. He previously authored *God's
Earth Also Cries,* a novel based on the chromium
contamination crisis of the 1980s, and *Ruthless
Ambition: The Rise and Fall of Chris Christie,* a semi
biography of the New Jersey Governor and Manzo's
experience with him.

https://anirishlullaby.com/

For the families and friends of the old neighborhood

"Life is made up of meetings and partings. That is the way of it."

—Charles Dickens

An Irish Lullaby

Chapter One

Angela Sanchez reclined on a gurney in the preparation room of the Hudson Family Planning Center's clinic. The clinic was stationed in the east wing of the Medical Arts Building at the Jersey City Medical Center complex, located in the city's Downtown ward, just across the Hudson River from New York City. The room was drowned in a sterile white décor from the tile floor and walls, right on up to the ceiling panels. The aroma of alcohol antiseptic, emanating from instrument basins throughout the clinic, laced the air of the preparation room. Angela's caseworker, Cindy Stone, was by her side and had driven the teen to the center each day.

"Is she here yet?" Angela asked, looking up at the ceiling. The "she" that Angela referred to was the President of the Board for the family planning center, who had taken a shine to the girl throughout her ordeal — ever since Angela's condition was thrust onto the facility's doorstep during the course of the past few weeks. She promised to stand by Angela as she underwent her procedure.

"She's on her way," Cindy replied.

Resting on a chair, across from where Angela lay, were the clothes that she shed for a hospital garment: blue dungarees and a powder blue shirt. The teenager's high school letter jacket — a maroon woolen vest with attached white leather sleeves — was draped around the back of the chair. It was a dead giveaway that she attended Jersey City's Dickinson High School. Pompoms and a megaphone straddled a huge Old English "D" chenille varsity letter on the jacket's front, shouting out to the world that the teen was a cheerleader. Beneath the chair, her tan loafers rested on the tile floor.

The dreary and rainy Monday morning seemed to suit the mood for Angela's scheduled dilation and evacuation procedure — sanitized medical terms used to categorize an abortion. She had been asked to arrive several hours before her procedure, so that the clinic staff could administer her Misoprostol — a medicine that helps to soften the cervix. The girl already had a busy weekend — she was examined both Saturday and Sunday at the clinic, having an opportunity to meet the medical team that would be performing her abortion procedure. They briefed Angela on what to expect and answered her questions. It was then that they inserted laminaria sticks — a sea plant extract — into her cervix to help it begin to spread.

The seventeen-year-old was terrified, depressed, and just about ready to breakdown. Mere moments away from the start of her procedure, the consequences of some very heavy decisions were finally settling in. The tears that slowly welled up in Angela's eyes timed their escape and streamed down her beautiful face, streaking the dark-beige hue of her soft skin. On cue, she lifted her left arm and, alternating it from eye to eye, wiped away the streams of misery with the smooth undersides of the limb. Her open right hand and wrist were positioned resting atop her swollen abdomen, entwined by a set of black Rosary Beads. Those Rosary Beads seemed to perturb her caseworker Cindy, who was waiting for the optimum time to snatch them away.

Angela had been stewarded by her grandmother in the Roman Catholic religion and culture.

Angela was religiously devout, but in a weak moment, simply fell to temptation as all mortals do, and made a mistake for which she now was paying the price. As she felt movement inside of her womb, second thoughts began creeping into the girl's mind. When she thought about the shame of her predicament — having to face friends and neighbors and forgo what remained of a teenage girl's normal high school years — Angela cancelled her reservations. Yet, she continued to pray to the God that she knew she was disobeying, almost as if seeking a Divine Intervention.

Not today.

The door leading to the procedure room swung open. The head nurse stepped inside to announce, "We'll be ready any moment now." The veteran caregiver on the procedure team was a soul filled with sunshine, someone with a knack for handling patients expecting to go through such a traumatic event, bestowing charm like a PEZ dispenser whenever she could. She lured patients into a calming demeanor with a more-or-less spider and fly technique. This morning, the nurse's sunshiny personality was quickly eclipsed by the somber mood cast by Angela's circumstances, and which now hung over the clinic like a cloud. Nurse Sunshine had met her match.

The nurse's declaration filled Angela's gut with butterflies, crowding the unborn being.

Cindy Stone seized the moment to grab the Rosary Beads out of Angela's hand and stuff them into the pocket of the teen's high school letter jacket, setting the Bead's five decades back centuries.

Angela's caseworker wasn't the only one concerned about her. The President of the Board for the facility and the family planning center psychologist were apprehensive about how she would handle the aftermath of her abortion. Angela's fragile mental state gave them pause as to whether she would be able to cope with the depression that often accompanied a late-midterm abortion. They knew that Angela would need plenty of post-procedure counseling. It was a guessing game as to how severe the aftermath would be for the teen.

Angela began cramping badly. The fetus inside of her was kicking about furiously, not accustomed to the recent changes it sensed occurring to the perimeter of its environment. That environment was about to change again as one of the gynecologists entered the room to remove the laminaria sticks. He replaced them with a standard cervical dilator to help further open the cervix. The center scheduled two gynecologists for her procedure, uneasy about the youth of the mother and the lateness of the pregnancy. Stone continually tried to keep Angela's spirits up, almost sounding at times as if she was giving the girl a pep talk.

As promised, the President of the Board finally arrived. She greeted Angela, who was ecstatic that she had finally made it to her side. The teen's nervousness began to slightly quell.

One of the gynecologists whisked the Board President aside for a moment, trying to dissuade her from observing the procedure. He reasoned that once Angela went under, the teen would not know whether or not anyone was with her or not. He suggested that once Angela awoke in the recovery room, she could then be there for the teenager again. The Board President wasn't backing down, and the doctor wasn't about to get into it with the person who was paying his salary. He did forewarn her to prepare herself. She had never seen an abortion performed live before, but she knew what they entailed...*at least she thought she did.*

"After what this poor girl's gone through already, I'm standing right by her side till this is over with — I'm not taking any chances," she said to the doctor. "You do know about what's already happened to her, don't you?"

The puzzled look on the doctor's face indicated that he hadn't a clue. "I haven't any idea what you are talking about. All I know is that this isn't the ideal timeframe for the procedure on someone so young. Why wasn't she administered Methotrexate? I'm very uncomfortable — "

"Stop," she cried. "This is another royal screw-up, courtesy of the West Side Neighborhood Health Clinic. Months ago, she went there for an abortion. The doctor made a notation in the file to refer her to our facility. The file was placed on the desk of an office clerk, who ironically left that very day for a maternity leave. All this time later, someone finds the file still sitting on the desk and makes contact with the girl. Meanwhile, Angela thought she had been turned down and was too embarrassed to check back with the clinic. By then, all hell broke loose. She lives with her drugged-out mother and her grandmother — who is really her guardian. The family was thrown into turmoil: the poor girl demanding an abortion; her mother was approving and her grandmother was opposed. Then, they all arrive on our doorstep and, unfortunately, now on your doorstep. You're right, Doctor, Methotrexate would have been the right solution, but how can anyone account for such bungling by the clinic?"

"*Obamacare* will never cure that," the doctor quipped. He then retreated back to the procedure room to rejoin his colleagues who were preparing for the procedure. He filled them in on why a girl so young was getting an abortion so late in term.

A short time later, the Board President was led into the medical procedures staff prepping area by a medical technician. There, the procedure team — the two gynecologists, the nurse, and the anesthesiologist — washed up and garbed before the procedure. She was instructed to do likewise and was then handed a set of pale blue scrubs, a surgical gown, mask, and slippers that the nurse helped her to suit up in. Once dressed, she followed the abortion team into the surgical procedure room. Through the other door of the procedure room — connecting to the patient prep room — two attendants rolled in Angela Sanchez's gurney. The other gynecologist, who would not be performing but assisting the procedure, had already administered an antibiotic to Angela while she waited in the preparation room. The medication was for guarding against infection. The teenager was pale and looked frightened to death. She smiled a bit when her friend, the Board President, approached and reached out to take hold of her hand. Despite her being covered over with surgical garb, Angela could tell who it was by the unmistakable hazel eyes peering back at her from just above the surgical mask that the Board President wore.

The Board President told Angela to relax.

The two attendants transferred Angela from the gurney onto the operating table. They elevated her legs and secured them into the surgical stirrups attached to the sides of the table. The gynecologist who was to perform the procedure adjusted the stirrups to how he wanted them positioned. "Put her under," he said.

The anesthesiologist squeezed a needle that he clutched in his hand and which was attached to an intravenous tube, the other end of which was inserted into a vein on the underside of Angela's arm. He asked her to begin to count backwards from one hundred. The Board President, standing to the side of the operating table, was lined up with Angela's upper torso. She could see the teenager's cervix spreading in the overhead mirror that was attached to the surgical lamps above the table. A ceiling camera focused its lens on the mirror from which it would record the procedure — the center's insurance company required documenting every procedure in case of inevitable law suites. The doctor stepped onto a button protruding from the floor, switching on the surgical lamps to the desired brightness level necessary for him to conduct the procedure.

The nurse rolled a surgical tray beside the operating table and close to the doctor. She peeled off a sanitized cloth covering, revealing an assortment of surgical instruments sitting beside several empty sterile silver metal pans stacked atop each other. The pans and instruments glistened and reflected the light cast by the surgical lamps. On another surgical tray, stationed a bit below the height of the operating table, sat an aspirator pump attached by a tube to the threaded lid of a large sterilized glass jar. Another tube also extended from a second attachment atop the jar, it connected to an instrument known as a *cannula*, which was used for insertion into the uterus to vacuum out its contents. From the ceiling extended a metallic arm holding a huge computer screen that hovered over the instrument tables and displayed the information fed to it by sensors positioned on Angela's body — her vital signs.

The doctor checked out the wall clock in the room — it was ten minutes past eleven. He glanced down at Angela mumbling a countdown, eyed the anesthesiologist, assessed the condition of the cervix again, and gave one last look over at the tray of instruments. He peered over at the screen displaying her vital signs. He was now waiting on the anesthesiologist.

"She's out," the anesthesiologist said. "She only made it to seventy-five."

The Board President felt Angela's grip on her hand loosen. The other gynecologist hit a switch on one of the walls in the room — music then boomed out from speakers imbedded in the ceiling tiles. It was classical music. The Board President recognized it — *Schubert's 'Unfinished' symphony. How appropriate.* The music seemed to cue the procedure as the gynecologist conducting the abortion stepped to the end of the table between Angela' spread legs. The nurse placed one of the metal pans adjacent to Angela's buttocks and below her vaginal opening. The doctor inserted a speculum into the vaginal cavity — a device for spreading it apart, in order to provide further easy access to the cervix and the uterus. The Board President watched the procedure's every move through the mirror attached to the surgical lamp.

"Forceps," the doctor said.

From off of the instrument table, the nurse proceeded to pick up a long and slender scissor styled, needle-nosed instrument with serrated tips on its jaw. She slapped it down and seated it firmly in the gynecologist's palm. The doctor clenched the instrument, hunched forward a bit, and then slowly, carefully, and gently began inserting its tip into Angela's vagina. He carefully moved it forward through the cervix to the mouth of the uterus. As the closed forceps pierced the amniotic sac entombing the fetus, a gooey reddish-brown fluid was expelled — spewing through the cervix and out the vagina, into the metal pan that had been positioned below the opening.

As the forceps made its way into the sac, it brushed alongside the unborn being. The being's nerve endings could sense the cold, hard metal probe. Instinct and reflex caused the being to retract from the forceps, slamming into the side of Angela's uterus and kicking its legs and feet about wildly. From years of practice, the skilled gynecologist could get a feel from the forceps as to what part of the fetus he was probing.

The Board President's mouth fell open, watching the amniotic fluid drip down the long stem of the forceps and onto the doctor's gloved fingers and wrist. She almost cringed as she watched him push the probe up into Angela's cervix, imagining how it was colliding into Angela's never to be born baby. The Board President was breathing through her mouth now, sucking in the surgical mask between her lips each time that she inhaled. She squeezed Angela's hand.

The doctor sensed that the still closed forceps were positioned on the being's abdomen and then chest. He pushed and pinned the being to the side of the uterus, planning to next move in for the kill. His thumb and index fingers were secure in the eye openings of the forceps handle; the skilled gynecologist slowly extended them apart. The serrated teeth on the instrument's clamp end opened. The doctor slid the implement further up the being, sensing that he had each blade shank of the instrument aligned on opposite sides of the being's head — about the size of large walnut. Then he slowly closed his fingers together again, forcing the serrated teeth of the instrument to secure its grip on the skull. He paused a second to make sure the clamp was secure and would not slip. Years of practice told him that he had a death grip.

The being sensed the pressure and felt excruciating pain filling its head — *imagine the worst migraine ever.* The being opened its mouth and expelled a silent scream that no one in the world would hear. The gynecologist squeezed tighter, collapsing the skull onto the being's brain and causing it to slip into a semi-conscious state. Blood leaked out of the openings that had been punctured through the skull by the serrated edges on the clamp ends of the forceps. The blood poured out of the uterus, cervix, and vagina; spilling into the metal pan below. It signaled to the doctor that he had made the kill — a humane act considering what was to follow.

By habit, the doctor looked up at the computer screen to check Angela's vital signs. Then he looked over at the Board President, whose eyes were glued on the overhead mirror. He could sense that she was becoming overwhelmed. "Miss…Miss…Oh, Miss," he called out, finally getting her attention on the third try. She looked over, acknowledging him. She focused on his voice. "Are you all right? Why don't you wait in the recovery room?"

"I'm okay, doctor. I'm okay. I am not going anywhere. Please continue."

You asked for it, lady.

The unborn being wasn't actually dead as the doctor had thought, it had merely slipped into a semiconscious state. The being had lost all control of any motor functions — the result of the trauma to the brain. It could still sense pain. The doctor had no way of knowing that the unborn being was still alive and had survived the usually fatal collapsing of the skull into the brain.

The doctor spread open his fingers, loosening the clasp of the forceps. The jaws of the instrument responded, relaxing the grip on the unborn being's skull. When the serrated teeth lifted out of the puncture holes that they had inflicted, more blood began to gush forth from the being. The doctor closed the forceps' jaws and slid the instrument back down the body of the being — chest, abdomen, legs. The doctor probed and opened the teeth of the forceps again, then closed them to grab more of the being's tissue. The doctor tugged, snipped, and then retracted the instrument out of the cervix. A perfectly formed foot, about the size of a crayon tip, was clutched in the teeth of the forceps. The doctor expelled it onto the metal tray. More blood poured out of the cervix, this time spurting from the being's severed limb. Slipping into a soon to be fully unconscious state, the being felt a muted sharp pain and let out another final, silent scream. Then the being bled out and died.

The Board President breathed more rapidly through her mouth now, nearly gagging at the sight of what appeared to be a doll's foot lying in a puddle of amniotic fluid and blood in the tray. She didn't notice that the doctor inserted the forceps back into the uterus. This time, to snag the upper thigh of the deceased being, severing the remaining leg limb from the abdomen and pulling it through the cervix to plop it down onto the tray. The Board President gagged this time and began to perspire and feel woozy.

The doctor moved with precision speed now, hacking away at the remaining parts of the corpse inside of Angela. He pulled it apart in sections. The arms — small enough to extract intact from the fingertips up to the armpits. The abdomen — its contents of intestines and body organs, making for the most horrid of spectacles. When the section of the pelvic area revealing the sexual identity was withdrawn, the nurse spoke up, announcing, "It was a girl."

Finally, the head was delivered — in two half sections to facilitate its easy passage through the narrow body openings leading to the tray. A frontal section, extending from the forehead to the chin, landed on the tray face up. The Board President stared at it, visions of her own children, just after their birth, consumed her thoughts. She contemplated a *what if it were them'* moment. She then fantasized that the closed eyes on the being's head had opened and were staring back at her. She panted now, falling into a trance. She was out cold, eyes wide open — having fainted on her feet.

The gynecologist performing the abortion did another check around the room, noticing the Board president. "Grab hold of her and then get her the hell out of here," he said.

The other gynecologist clutched the Board President's arms. She was frozen in shock; her body was rigid. He told the nurse to have the attendants bring in a wheelchair. The nurse made a beeline for the doors leading to the prep room, seconds later she returned rolling the wheelchair into the room. She assisted the gynecologist to seat the Board President in the chair, then rolled it back toward the prep room door where the attendants took hold of the chair. The gynecologist exited and followed them out the door, intending to attend to the shocked observer.

Back inside the procedure room, the doctor performing the abortion signaled for a curette, an instrument with a long metal rod with a one-inch in diameter, eyehole-shaped implement at its end. It was used for scraping the uterus clean of the placenta and any remaining tissue. He scooped out the tissue residue onto the same metal tray, but kept it segregated from the expired being's remains. Once finished, he asked the nurse to hand him the cannula. He inserted it into Angela's cervix, as his foot pressed down upon another button on the floor near the base of the operating table. The vacuum pump's motor sounded, and the doctor used the powerful sucking instrument to void any still remaining tissue from the uterus.

Meanwhile, the nurse placed the tray containing the contents of the abortion beside the instruments tray. With a pair of dull tipped forceps, she began reassembling the being, almost like working on a jigsaw puzzle — standard procedure to make sure that no parts were missing and potentially left inside of the uterus. Everything was accounted for. The remains were then poured into a medical bio-waste container in which they would be transported for incineration.

The doctor next removed the cervical dilator and speculum that were spreading open Angela's vagina and cervix. The nurse began cleaning and swabbing the intruded area with antiseptic. After a little less than an hour, the abortion was completed and Angela Sanchez was transferred back onto a gurney and wheeled into the recovery room where she would awaken in about a half-hour — groggy, sore, and cramping.

That would be the least of her worries.

Chapter Two
Approximately one week earlier...

At half-past ten in the morning, the breakfast rush finally subsided at Lee's Luncheonette & Old Fashioned Soda Shoppe — just a short respite before the brunch and lunch crowd would begin to pile into the popular eatery. A whiff of the recently cooked breakfast bacon still lingered in the air, working overtime, still whetting the appetites of patrons as they entered.

Lee's was a popular spot at about the midpoint of West Side Avenue — the main thoroughfare in the center of Jersey City, New Jersey's West Side Ward — otherwise known as the Saint Aloysius Parish neighborhoods. New Jersey's second largest city sat less than two miles across the Hudson River from New York City. A huge Roman Catholic population once thrived in Jersey City during its earliest days, and neighborhoods were typically identified by the numerous churches that were strewn throughout those vicinities to service the expanse of the Catholic populaces in each of the city's districts. Those districts would later evolve into the latter-day city's six wards. The city's Irish Catholic population settled in the neighborhoods surrounding Saint Al's. Time and the city's decay saw the decline of that once leading population — it was a mixed neighborhood now, and no longer predominately Irish Catholic, although they still maintained a staple presence in that part of Jersey City.

Located a mere block and a half away from Saint Aloysius Church, Lee's was now a Jersey City, as well as New Jersey, landmark. Stepping into Lee's was like stepping back into time. The owners had preserved the eatery's décor just as it was on the day that Lee's first opened. The stainless-steel restaurant fixtures still sparkled and shined. Even the original booths and wall jukebox stations remained and were functional.

The walls were adorned with framed photographs taken throughout the decades. The photos typically depicted customers over the years, and several local and national celebrities whom happened by to sample some of Lee's famous homemade ice cream. The crème de la crème of this gallery was a blown-up picture of President Kennedy sipping down a Lee's milkshake, surrounded by the establishment proprietor, Lee Burke, and his family. When the then Senator Kennedy campaigned for the presidency in 1960, a motorcade celebrating his candidacy was held in the strongly Democratic, Irish-Catholic bastion of Hudson County, New Jersey.

Then elected officials, New Jersey Governor Richard J. Hughes, Hudson County Democratic Chairman John V. Kenny and Jersey City Mayor Charles Witkowski hosted the event, which winded its way along the then Hudson County Boulevard and culminated at Journal Square. From Journal Square, the Jersey pols escorted the soon-to-be President to Lee's for a taste of ice cream. The youthful and charismatic Kennedy passed through the entire establishment shaking hands with every one of the patrons.

A red top lunch counter ran half the length of the eatery, terminating a few feet away from a set of swinging kitchen doors that separated the rear dining room from the front counter area. The shoe bottoms of the breakfast crowd scuffed the shiny red and white checkerboard tile floor of the establishment that was mopped down nightly.

Lee's front door swung open as the local beat cop, Patrolman Bernard McCarthy, burst into the establishment, dragging in along with him a gaunt, scruffy looking teenager with a mop top head of hair. The youth was handcuffed. McCarthy guided him over to the cashier counter of the restaurant, which was set apart from the lunch counter. The cashier's station was positioned at the front end of the restaurant, almost abutting Lee's huge storefront windows, which offered a grand view of the bustling West Side Avenue.

McCarthy guided his forlorn prisoner by pushing and pulling the hood of the youth's sweatshirt, which the cop's hand clutched in an almost death grip. Red bruises were apparent on the cop's knuckles, seeming to match up with the welt that was welling up under the right eye of the teen, along with a split in his upper lip. The boy dabbed up the blood leaking from his cracked lip by sporadically running his tongue over the wound.

Behind the cashier counter stood Lenny Burke, the manager and the son of the proprietor.

"Is this him?" McCarthy asked.

Burke recognized the young troublemaker right away. Hours earlier, the youth ordered a breakfast sandwich special, pretended to be groping through his pockets for money, then swiped the already bagged food off the counter and hightailed it out the front door. "That's him. That's the punk," Burke said.

"That's all we needed — a positive ID. Don't you worry none, Lenny, his cellmates at the county youth house will teach him some manners," the cop continued, twisting the sweatshirt hood with his hand so that it began to choke his prey.

"And just who is it that'll be learnin' ye some manners of your own, might I ask?" a voice laced with a distinct Irish brogue blurted out from behind the cop and the teenager.

The voice seemed to shrink the mountainous cop down to the size of a molehill. McCarthy recognized the voice right away. He turned around to greet the priest whose voice he knew. "Good morning, Father. Just taking care of MY BUSINESS, if you don't mind," he said.

"Then I'll just be doin' my business…if ye don't mind."
The just under six-foot tall, lean and elderly reverend then
stepped forward with all the swagger of Moses approaching
the Red Sea. The priest's full head of white hair added to his
distinguished appearance. The cleric had been sitting at the
end of the lunch counter closest to the cash register podium,
staring into the mirrored wall behind the luncheonette's
counter. He fixated on the mirror while reflecting on his aging
face, lost in a daydream between the space where he sat and
his reflection. He pondered where he had already been in life,
and where he was heading. He contemplated how so much
time had flown by and whether or not he was relevant
anymore…or if he had ever been.

The boisterous entrance of the cop and his prey snapped
the priest out of his trance. He began to eavesdrop on the
commotion. The fear of irrelevance had gotten the best of him
and he decided to get involved. Father O'Connor looked the
cop and the teenager square in their eyes, as if he were almost
reading their minds. Then the priest glanced down at the
airtight handcuffs digging into the youth's wrists. "He seems
to be a mighty dangerous criminal yer luggin' about. Are ye
sure that he mighten be needin' leg irons?"

Officer McCarthy just frowned, not wanting to confront
the old codger.

Father Sean O'Connor was once the Monsignor of Saint
Aloysius Parish, some twenty years prior. As is typical in the
Catholic Church, no assignments are permanent, and after his
stay as Saint Al's pastor for some good many years, Father
O'Connor was then shuttled about from archdiocese to
archdiocese and parish to parish. Now seventy-five years old,
O'Connor was semiretired and back residing at Saint Al's,
supplementing the pastoral staffing there. The parish was
O'Connor's sentimental favorite. As a close friend of the
Archdiocese of Newark Archbishop, Mario Scaponi, landing
this assignment, which would probably be the last call of his

priesthood, was a breeze. But O'Connor dreaded the specter of the inevitable call that he knew would come one day soon — a call that would land him at a semiretirement community for priests at the Jersey Shore.

O'Connor clung to the hope of somehow becoming relevant in the world again. A world that, at least he felt, seemed to have passed him by. Though, as was customary, O'Connor still retained the honorary title of *Monsignor,* when he returned to Saint Aloysius, he insisted that everyone just still refer to him as *Father* — a title that he found to be endearing throughout the years, and one that seemed to make him feel young again.

"I was by the gramma school today, and I stopped in to see Misses McCarthy's classroom, I'll have ye know," the priest said, referring to the cop's wife with whom he was very friendly. "Wonderful woman that ye have there, if ye don't mind me sayin' so, McCarthy. She seems to be much too good for the likes of a blockhead as yerself, though."

Behind the cashier counter, Lenny Burke became impatient. "Now see here, Father," he said, pointing towards McCarthy's prisoner. "This punk robbed me earlier this morning!"

The priest turned towards Burke, a look of *'I didn't appreciate your butting in'* filled out his face. "My Lord, and how many thousands did he make it outta here with?" The priest's sarcasm was meant to be apparent.

"He ordered a sandwich than ran off without paying."

"Oh, me heavens, what was the weapon — a hungry belly?"

The priest then looked back into the face of the frightened teen, who trembled in fear each time that McCarthy tightened the hold on his hoody — weary of being cracked in the face again by the burly cop. "Son, what might yer name be?" Father O'Connor asked.

The kid looked up at the cop, as if to seek permission to answer the priest.

"Answer Father O'Connor," McCarthy said, jerking back on the youth's sweatshirt hood.

"My name is Griffin Reilly, Father."

"IRISH! Right after me own heart," O'Connor said.

McCarthy and Burke rolled their eyes, sensing that what was about to ensue would be more agonizing for them than for Griffin Reilly.

"Griffin's a beautiful Irish name, Lad," O'Connor remarked. And where might ye be from?

"Boston, Father," — that explained the dialect with which the youth spoke.

"Boston!" Ye don't say. That'd be me own hometown as well."

"Jackpot," McCarthy muttered under his breath.

O'Connor began to regale the youth with remembrances from his own childhood growing up in South Boston. Born in the harbor city to first generation Irish immigrants, O'Connor was raised in a modest home that included his grandparents. A nearby neighborhood tenement house hosted several aunts and uncles and was inhabited with plenty of cousins for playmates. That childhood experience explained the priest's distinct Irish brogue, occasionally laced with his very distinguishable Bostonian accent. It also explained the priest's witticisms — his grandparents were always flowering their conversations with an Irish maxim a minute. The priest, at times, was steep in proverbs when he spoke. O'Connor's philosophical jargon was further complemented by his fondness for quoting the scripture. On occasion, he would sometimes mix the maxims with scripture, muddling the distinctions.

The O'Connor clan was a musical tribe as well. His father was an accomplished accordion player and singer. His mother, a pianist and singer. Under his mother's tutelage,

O'Connor learned to play the piano. Both his parents helped him hone his music skills at a young age. The priest's singing voice was pure gold, carrying not a hint of his brogue or Boston accent, except when singing Irish folk songs and ballads. It was his beautiful crooning voice that O'Conner eventually became renowned for — parishioners loved hearing him entertain them at Masses, his pleasing voice often drowning out the choir's singing of church hymns. They also loved O'Connor's renderings of some Irish ditties and selections from the American Songbook, which he often sang at parish events and functions.

As O'Connor continued along his trip down memory lane, McCarthy and Burke stood by fidgeting, shaking their heads from side to side. Their faces were plastered with expressions that registered their frustration and impatience.

"Father O'Connor," McCarthy said, stepping all over the priest's reminiscences, "I have police work to conduct here, if you don't mind."

"And I have the Lord's work to conduct here…if ye don't mind," Then O'Connor turned to look kindly into Griffin's sad face. "Do yer parents know that ye're here? What's yer story, Griffin?"

Feeling a bit more comfortable because of O'Connor's presence, Griffin Reilly began to unload his tale of woe — almost as if he were more than happy to get it off his chest. The fragile youth explained that he was from a broken family. His dad skipped out on him and his mom when he was but three years old. Mom was later swept off her feet by another suitor by the time that Griffin was seven. The heel wanted no part of the boy. Griffin's mother married the cad and took off for the West Coast and a new lifestyle, leaving her son behind with her mother.

Griffin adored his grandmother, the only good soul to enter his life. But he felt as if he was becoming a burden to the woman. He took notice of how she would scrimp and save in order to provide for him. As the years went on, more and more money was required to keep pace with caring for a growing boy. With the exception of his grandmother, Griffin felt that to the rest of the world he was unwanted and useless. Running away was his way of relieving his grandmother of the burden that he felt he was to her.

O'Connor soaked it all in, empathizing with the crisis in the youth's life. He continued his interrogation. "How long have ye been away from home, Lad?"

"Three days, Father," Griffin answered, explaining that he had been camping out in the back of nearby Lincoln Park.

"Me son, is yer Grandmother Irish?" O'Connor asked.

"Yes, Father."

"Then ye are her pride and joy — not a burden. She lives fer ye, Lad — trust me on that. And, trust me on somethin' else — she's broken hearted and worried sick about yer leavin' home, she is," O'Connor told him. He could read the youth's face — Griffin wanted out of his predicament in the worse way. "Are ye Catholic, Lad?" O'Connor asked.

"Yes, Father — I used to be an altar boy at Saint Patrick's Church."

"Trifecta!" McCarthy muttered, rolling his eyes again and adjusting the uniform cap that sat atop his head. "Good night, nurse!"

"An Irish altar boy from good *ould* Saint Paddy's in Boston — what's there not to like about the boy, McCarthy?" the priest commented.

Griffin was starting to feel more at ease.

"When was the last time that ye've eaten, before that sandwich that ye bought *on account* this morning?" O'Connor asked.

"Two days ago, Father," Griffin answered. "I brought some candy bars with me, but I ate them all the first night in the park."

"Wait! What do you mean, *'bought on account?'"*Lenny Burke said.

"I meant it was *'bought on account'* because I'm gonna pay ye fer the sandwich now," O'Connor answered.

A scowl formed on the manager's face.

"How much was the sandwich?" O'Connor asked Burke.

"That was the breakfast special — four dollars."

O'Connor slipped his hand into his pants pocket and pulled out his wallet. He unfolded it and slid out a five-dollar bill.

"But!" Burke began objecting, seemingly expressing the sentiment that he preferred that Griffin be arrested rather than he be reimbursed for the breakfast sandwich.

"But nuthin, Officer McCarthy, you'll be kindly escortin' Griffin over to the high school and droppin' him off at the guidance counselor's Office, please. I'll call over there and tell them to be expectin' ye both." O'Connor was already working out a plan for returning Griffin back to Boston. He placed the money down on the cashier counter between Burke and him.

"Now see here, Father O'Connor," McCarthy spoke up, "he committed a crime, and — "

"Ye know, McCarthy, I just might be havin' to walk over to the gramma school and plead me case to a higher court — Misses McCarthy."

"What?"

O'Connor grabbed hold of the cop's free arm and pulled him aside. The priest gave a quick jerk of his head, indicating that he wanted to tell McCarthy something on the sly. The cop leaned back to listen, but kept his other arm, still clutching Griffin, fully extended — attempting to keep the teen out of earshot of whatever O'Connor was going to say.

"Ye know, McCarthy, 'twould be a real shame if Misses McCarthy were to find out that ye've been fibbin' to her about bowlin' on Thursday nights, and have instead been out playin' poker with the boys. Especially when she tries so hard to stretch every penny of the family budget to make ends meet," O'Connor told the cop in an Irish whisper, the likes of which Griffin and Lenny Burke could hear every word.

"See here, Father — I confessed those misgivings to you at church." McCarthy was visibly perturbed. "It's God's word that confessions shall not be revealed."

"Yer confession is safe with God, McCarthy — just not me. God will keep his word, but as for me — that's another story. So, what's it gonna be, flatfoot — are ye dealin' with me, or am I dealin' with yer wife?"

O'Connor knew he could never reveal the cop's confessions to his wife, but he also knew how much of a sucker that McCarthy was for a bluff, which explained most of the cop's poker losses. The priest's gambit was to merely bluff the cop into submission.

"Do you know that you're breaking the law — extorting me like this?"

O'Connor didn't miss a beat. "I look at it as if I'm upholdin' God's laws — feed the hungry."

"If you weren't a war hero, I'd be running you in."

"Hey," O'Connor turned another shade of serious at the remark. "My war record is off limits — ye know better than that."

"Sorry, Father, I got carried away," McCarthy said. He knew how sensitive the *Medal of Honor* winner was about his war exploits. McCarthy had ventured into territory that O'Connor had always warned those who knew him to dare not tread on. "Oh, well..." At this point, the cop was completely perplexed and ready to cave. O'Connor had him over a barrel. McCarthy made one last play. "But, Mister Burke, will have to agree to not press any charges."

O'Connor stepped back towards the cashier counter.

"I don't go to confession, Father, and I don't play poker either — you've got nothing to hold over my head," Burke said, shocking McCarthy, who dropped open his jaw upon learning that the manager overheard his private aside with O'Connor.

Burke's resistance didn't faze O'Connor at all. "Ye know, Lenny, I suppose that I could take the matter up with yer father...then come back to watch ye cower when he starts ballin' ye out. But let me put it to ye a bit more matter-of-factly: it was back when I was Monsignor of this parish — some twenty years ago — that I interceded and told the high school principal to permit the students to come to lunch here if they wanted. Yer Dad asked me to do him that favor."

Now Burke's jaw dropped. "What are you saying?"

"Ye've been doin' a pretty good lunch trade here, thanks to the Saint Aloysius High School students. I could just as easily persuade the high school principal to suspend that lunchtime privilege granted to the high school. I remember when I hired Sister Joseph Eleanor as the principal — we're tighter than Saints Peter and Paul, ye know."

O'Connor had effectively tied Burke and McCarthy in knots.

"I'm not pressing charges, McCarthy," Burke muttered, frustration evident in his face.

Griffin exhaled a sigh of relief, relishing his reversal of fortune, but attempting to maintain a stoic posture and avoiding to appear to be gloating. McCarthy let loose his grip of the boy's hoody, then reached down and removed the handcuffs. Griffin rubbed his wrists where the metal rings had dug into his skin and left bruise marks.

"Griffin, did ye get yer juice and coffee as part of the breakfast special?" O'Connor asked.

"No, Father," the boy answered. *Is he kidding?*

O'Connor gazed over at Burke. "Now, Lenny, 'tis not wise to be shortchanging the customers." The priest played it dead serious. "Tell ye what — the lad will settle for a milkshake."

"But — " Burke began to object.

"But nuttin,' If I give the say-so to Sister Joseph Eleanor, this joint'll be as empty as a hermit's address book."

Burke pondered the priest's words, having second thoughts. He turned and looked towards Griffin, then asked him, "What flavor milkshake would you like?"

"Chocolate, sir, thank you."

"Better fetch a coffee-to-go fer Officer McCarthy as well," O'Connor added. He looked over at Griffin's swollen eye and cracked lip, then glanced down at the cop's swollen knuckles. "He'll be needin' something to keep his hands occupied while he escorts young Griffin over to the high school guidance counselor."

Burke headed behind the lunch counter to make Griffin's milkshake. He directed the waitress stationed there, Mrs. McNish, to retrieve the coffee-to-go for McCarthy. O'Connor made small talk with McCarthy and Griffin while waiting for Burke to return. He also made use of the phone beside the cash register — calling the high school guidance counselor to announce Griffin and McCarthy's soon-to-be arrival and explain the teenager's circumstances. Burke returned and handed McCarthy his coffee and Griffin his milkshake.

"Will you be needing me for anything else, Father?" McCarthy asked. "There aren't any bank robbers you might be wanting to have me release — are there?" McCarthy enjoyed ribbing the priest with his sarcastic remark, a sort of getting even.

"Not at all. You'd have to catch them first, and seein' how yer so busy huntin' down dangerous criminals like Griffin, 'tis certain that ye wouldn't have the time to nab any bank robbers. Now stop yer actin' the maggot with me, McCarthy."

McCarthy shook his head and looked up towards the ceiling, as if he was asking God for help. He was overmatched. "Let's be on our way, Son," he said to Griffin, heading for the door.

"Griffin," O'Connor called out, distracting the teen from his milkshake. "I have a bit of sorcery in me, ye know. I can look into someone's eyes and see right down to their soul. I see a good person with a big heart inside of ye, Son. Ye matter. Yer not insignificant — yer somebody. Ye damn well matter. Don't ye ever forget that. Make sure ye understand what I said, Griffin — Ye are a somebody."

O'Connor's words struck a nerve in Griffin — it triggered a tear to stream down the teen's face. O'Connor mouthed the words that the youth longed to hear from a mother or father for all the years he was without one. Griffin handed off his milkshake to McCarthy and made a beeline towards the priest. He threw his arms around O'Connor, burying his face in the priest's cleric jacket and sobbing uncontrollably. "Thank you, Father. Thank you," he repeated over and over. Griffin finally knew what it felt like to have a dad or an older brother to go to bat for you.

Griffin hugged the priest tighter and tighter, as if he were squeezing out the past thirteen years of pain from his life — the angst of a life without a father to turn to when he needed one. The keen O'Connor sensed the youth's condition right away. The priest knew firsthand how hard it was for the kids who came from single parent homes, or were being raised by a grandparent, courtesy of his experiences with them at Saint Al's grammar and high schools.

"I'm somebody. I'm somebody. I matter," Griffin repeated over and over again, still holding tight to the priest who understood it all. Griffin would remember this day and that significant moment for the rest of his life. He would consider it the single most important event that turned him around — the moment when he lit up inside like a Christmas tree, beaming with meaning for his life and a belief in himself. The day he came to understand that he was somebody.

The scene had tears welling up in McCarthy's eyes as well.

"That's all right, Lad. This is what happens when we come to realize that we do matter after all," O'Connor said, placing his hand atop Griffin's mop top head of hair and patting it. Then he reached down and peeled the boy off of him and tilted Griffin's chin up with his hand. "We'll talk later. I'll be over to the school in just a bit to see how ye made out with the guidance counselor. Ye can call yer Grandma from there — she'll be happy to hear from ye. Then we'll arrange to get ye back home to good ould Boston."

Griffin ran his sweatshirt sleeve across his face, wiping away the tears. He thanked the priest again and moved back towards the door. McCarthy handed the teen back his milkshake, then they both exited Lee's, heading down the block towards Saint Aloysius High School. O'Connor slogged back to his space at the counter, marked by a half-finished, now cold, cup of coffee and a half-eaten cheese Danish. He moved with a barely noticeable gimp to his gate. He ordered a fresh cup of coffee and another cheese Danish from the waitress. The other patrons at the counter buried their noses back in their own business, the entertainment provided by the commotion of Griffin's near arrest was over. Sitting on his stool, O'Connor leaned back and glanced towards the rear of the eatery, peering above the swinging panel doors and into the dining room area.

"Looking for someone, Father?" Misses McNish asked, setting a fresh cup of coffee and another cheese Danish down in front of him.

"Hmmm — yes, yes. Has Misses Fitzgibbon been in yet?"

"Aubrey? She usually stops in closer to the lunch hour."

O'Connor dove into his cheese Danish and coffee. He began pondering over the grave matter that he wanted to discuss with the woman who wasn't there and plotted out his next move.

Chapter Three

Monsignor Timothy Norton gently tilted the wine glass that he clutched in his hand from side to side, swirling about the red wine that it captured, appreciating the spectacle of the liquid's body and texture. The wine had accompanied his supper moments earlier, just before he departed from the dining room of the Saint Aloysius rectory and the company of Father O'Connor. The Monsignor poured himself a second glass, then retreated to the second-floor den of the rectory.

The Saint Aloysius rectory was a modest, originally constructed three-story Victorian home that was built extemporaneously with the church. The rectory once hosted four resident priests, but as their numbers declined, two of the structure's bedrooms were converted into a chapel and a den. The rectory was seated some fifteen yards directly behind the church, which served as a buffer to the traffic noise of West Side Avenue, where the church sat. The south side and rear of the rectory paralleled Lincoln Park — Hudson County and Jersey City's largest park.

Monsignor Norton sat in a cushy, oversized leather easy chair that rested across from a twin of itself, both positioned in front of the room's welcoming wall hearth that was currently unlit. The chairs were situated on an oversized area rug and they seemed to swallow up anyone who settled into them. The den was where the resident clergy usually relaxed, caught up on reading, watched television, played board games or cards, engaged in deep conversations, or just simply listened to the rectory's music collection or the radio.

In his other hand, Monsignor Norton clasped a letter that he opened earlier in the day and which he continued to peruse while awaiting the presence of Father O'Connor. Norton's attention to the letter was abruptly suspended by the entrance of the priest. The elder O'Connor carried a freshly poured after dinner drink, Irish whiskey — *Jameson* on the rocks. It was his own brand of medicine in moderation, approved by his doctor, for the treatment of an ailing heart. The after-dinner sojourn to the den was a ritual for both Father Norton and O'Connor — their *R & R* time.

Norton was uneasy — he knew the abruptly postponed conversation which O'Connor attempted to engage him in at dinner was about to resume. O'Connor had begun to report on his intended dealings with a prominent congregant of the church, Aubrey Fitzgibbon, whom the priest intended to bump into at Lee's Luncheonette, earlier in the day. The monsignor was hesitant to discuss the sensitive personal matter at the rectory dining table — not within earshot of the rectory's homemaker and cook, Misses Cavendish. Monsignor Norton suggested to O'Connor that they discuss the matter after dinner — upstairs in the den. O'Connor concurred.

As the Board President of the Hudson Family Planning Center, a nonprofit healthcare facility that housed Jersey City's only abortion clinic, Aubrey Fitzgibbon became *a parishioner of interest* just a day earlier — that was when Maria Ramos, the grandmother of Angela Sanchez, turned up at the rectory pleading for the priests' help. Maria Ramos had a suddenly pregnant granddaughter who wanted to have an abortion.

The grandmother lived with Angela and the girl's mother — her daughter — in a housing project many blocks below West Side Avenue. The *'projects,'* as they were aptly nicknamed by the community, were located on Duncan Avenue, which intersected the ward's main thoroughfare. Angela's parents were separated, and her father lived in Puerto Rico. Angela's mom battled demons of her own — drugs and alcohol. Angela's grandmother, affectionately referred to as *Abuela,* was the girl's true caregiver for the time being. The makeshift family were Saint Aloysius parishioners.

When Angela told her mother and grandmother that she refused to carry the baby to term, a crisis gripped the unconventional family. Angela's mom encouraged her daughter to opt for the abortion for purely selfish reasons — currently back on a drug binge, she did not want to be saddled with any more responsibilities. She further did not need another mouth in the household competing for meager resources, especially when some of that money was siphoned off to the side for her recreational drug use. Conversely, Angela's grandmother, a devout Roman Catholic, was solidly against Angela considering the abortion. The conflict flamed passions and kept all in the household on edge as tempers frequently flared in the midst of this family predicament. Complicating the calamity, under New Jersey law, neither adult could interfere with Angela's decision to have an abortion, even though she was a minor.

It was Aubrey Fitzgibbon and the Hudson Family Planning Center — ready, willing, and able to facilitate the abortion — that now stood in the way of the grandmother. The wise *Abuela* knew all too well about Aubrey Fitzgibbon's prominence and connections to Saint Aloysius Parish, which is why she addressed the matter to the priests.

Norton braced himself for the discourse that he anticipated would flow from the frank discussion that he and Father O'Connor were about to engage in, relative for determining how best to deal with the Sanchez matter and Aubrey Fitzgibbon. But O'Connor wasn't prepared to bring the matter up just yet, having decided to engage in a bit of playful banter.

Monsignor Norton was merely half the age of the senior O'Connor. Norton was initially uncomfortable with the elder priest's appointment to Saint Aloysius — he was leery about the close relationship between O'Connor and the Archbishop. In time, however, he realized that O'Connor could be trusted and was a useful tool in church matters because of that relationship. O'Connor became somewhat of a mentor to the younger monsignor. The two priests were of diverse church philosophies. O'Connor was more of a conservative and church traditionalist, not too fond of the practices, transformations, and the partings of the church from its *Latin* traditions — ever since *Vatican II laid* a path leading to the modern-day church. O'Connor's disdain also included the continuing prominence of the roles for church deacons, which he vehemently opposed, making for a very unpleasant experience for any deacons serving at Saint Aloysius — they avoided O'Connor like the plague.

Norton was more liberal and felt that the church needed to change and modernize even more. Despite a bumpy start, the two priests gradually developed an affinity and great respect for each other, which in turn nourished a worthy friendship between the two.

"I see that the *Tullamore Dew* bottle is still sittin' by its lonesome self — collecting dust in the kitchen cubby now, Father Norton." O'Connor was once again needling Norton about the bottle of *Tullamore Dew,* a cherished Irish whiskey that Norton received as a gift from relatives in Ireland, and which still sat unopened in the kitchen cabinet since the day that it had arrived. *Tullamore Dew* was a favorite of Father O'Connor.

Norton knew that O'Connor liked the libation and was playfully teasing him along by not opening the smooth Irish whiskey that he discerned the priest was longing to sample. The brand was sold only in *Erin.* "I was planning on giving it up for, Lent," Norton said — the liturgical season was more than nine months away.

"Why don't ye really do yerself some penance and just gift it on over to me now," O'Connor shot back.

"Besides, if the church collections fall off any more than they have, I might be forced to raffle it away."

"Ahhh! We could always fix the raffle and let me win, we could. Now, don't be troubled by the collections, me young Monsignor — they are down in every church in the archdiocese. Either, we Catholics seem to be on the decline, or we're becoming notoriously cheap."

"Maybe I should try your tact — shorter sermons. The parishioners seem to be coughing up more in the collection baskets at your Masses. Maybe, it's the shorter sermons," Norton said.

"Tis nothin' to do with shorter sermons, me young Monsignor — 'tis me good looks that's got them coughing up the dough, 'tis all."

Monsignor Norton did a double take.

"Maybe ye should urge the parish council to throw some fundraisers — ye know: a night at the races, Las Vegas night, Bingo and the sort. Ye can always call on me ould friend Sal Panetta to come through. The man's a living saint — always settin' some time aside to run and chair the events that help the church come up with a few extra bucks. When I was Monsignor, Sal raised the parish a small fortune. Ye just give good ould Sal a call."

"Races? Las Vegas? BINGO? Father, we're a church — not a floating crap game. Besides, I've been meaning to tell you — Mister Panetta is not doing too well of late."

"Oh?" O'Connor was caught off guard by the news about his longtime friend.

Monsignor Norton gently elaborated about how Panetta recently underwent a bout with cancer and that his prospects were not that good. He could see the old priest was taken aback by the news. O'Connor thought about the last time he saw his old friend — it seemed as if it were only yesterday, but then he realized that yesterday was almost ten years ago.

Panetta's illness explained why the priest hadn't seen nor heard from his friend since his return to the parish. O'Connor had mistakenly just shrugged it off, assuming that Panetta was just not wanting to be bothered — back when he was Monsignor, the priest really overworked the man on behalf of the church. Panetta not showing his face to the priest had been misinterpreted as *"leave me alone."*

The news about Sal Panetta gave O'Connor pause, causing him to realize how the good old days were gone, and how it now seemed that each tomorrow only served to kick to the curb some more of those cherished memories. The priest's eyes welled up as he fondly reminisced about his friend. Then he committed to paying a visit to the *'saint'* of a man, as he mumbled a prayer on his friend's behalf.

The news of Sal Panetta put a damper on O'Connor's mood and crimped his playful banter — melancholy sat in. He spied the letterhead on the piece of paper and envelope that Norton clutched in his hand — the seal of the Archbishop of the Archdiocese of Newark, one of O'Connor's dear friends since childhood days, Mario Scaponi. "What might that be that I see yer reading there now, if ye don't mind me prying — is that a letter from the Archbishop?"

Norton frowned while waving the letter in the air. "*His Excellency's* annual denial of my request for a sabbatical to complete my theology doctorate. I'll never get that degree," Norton lamented, elaborating further about his lifelong ambition to achieve the doctorate degree, which would improve his chances of being elevated to a dwindling pool of church hierarchy such as a Bishop or Archbishop. The Catholic Church offered scholarships for qualifying clergy to attend Georgetown's well-established theology courses that satisfied the curriculum for achieving the advanced degree. Norton always qualified but could never secure Archbishop Scaponi's blessing for a sabbatical. This was the third year in a row that he was turned down by Scaponi. Norton was almost taking it personally.

"He's probably hindered by not being able to find a suitable replacement for ye here at Saint Aloysius, 'tis all," O'Connor said. "This is the second largest parish in the archdiocese next to where he sits at Saint Michael's Cathedral in Newark. He just can't be stickin' any Tom, Dick, or Harry in here to replace ye, might I add."

"I suppose so," a seemingly much chagrined Monsignor Norton agreed.

"Would ye mind if I spoke to him about the matter?" O'Connor asked.

"No. No thank you, Father. It's kind of you to offer, but no, please, that would make me feel uncomfortable." Norton didn't like playing church politics to get what he wanted — it wasn't his style.

O'Connor sensed the firm resistance to his offer and decided to change the subject. "Father, I'm attempting to pay a visit to young Misses Fitzgibbon. I tried to bump into her at Lee's earlier in the day, but she didn't show up," he said, reengaging the conversation that he had attempted at dinner. O'Connor knew that the monsignor was sensitive to matters involving Aubrey Fitzgibbon, who was a prominent fundraiser for many of the church's yearly functions. O'Connor also knew, because of that fact, Norton would cut Aubrey some slack for her affiliation with the Hudson Family Planning Center.

"The Sanchez problem?"

"Indeed, indeed. The Sanchez family drama of life and, let us pray, hopefully not death."

The two men discussed the subject long past the time that it took for the ice in O'Connor's rock glass to melt. Several attempts by O'Connor to try and talk with Angela Sanchez were rebuffed — Angela's mother forbid the priests to contact the girl. The only avenue now open to them for stopping the abortion was at the source — the Hudson Family Planning Center and its President of the Board, Aubrey Fitzgibbon. O'Connor had visions of sugarplums — namely, glory and a ticket to relevance — dancing in his head. He elaborated to Monsignor Norton about his plan to take on the Hudson Family Planning Center. The social agency was a longtime thorn in O'Connor's side, and his sermons often times took shots at the facility's abortion clinic and birth control advocacy.

When the thought for establishing the abortion clinic first reared its head while he was Saint Aloysius' pastor, the then Monsignor O'Connor was able to defeat its attempted formation through the action of local activists that he rallied to the church's side. He considered the facility pure evil. The popular Monsignor carried a lot of weight in the city back then, and he used his juice at town hall as well, in order to kill the planned project. Seven Roman Catholics sitting on the city council and an Irish-Catholic Mayor, certainly, helped to grease the skids.

However, when the outspoken priest was eventually summoned away to another assignment, the planners of the facility took advantage of his absence, moving ahead again with a second attempt to found the center. This time, they cloaked the abortion clinic with other health clinics addressing women medical issues that the center would facilitate — providing free mammograms and additional health screenings to women who could not afford them otherwise. The strategy was successful — the changing, more liberal, political winds were now at the backs of those attempting to establish the facility.

The center's founders also chose an important resident of the Jersey City community, Aubrey Fitzgibbon, to spearhead that second drive. Not only was Aubrey an outspoken progressive for women's issues, but she was a prominent Roman Catholic parishioner from Saint Aloysius as well.

Aubrey took advantage of O'Connor's mild-mannered replacement, who didn't have the connections in the city like O'Connor, and who thus lacked any significant clout. At the time, Jersey City's prominent Roman Catholic population was about half of what it had been at the turn of the twentieth century.

Norton cautioned O'Connor about the city's dwindling Catholic population and its new populaces with more liberal social mores; which, he felt, would make any attempt to take on the Hudson Family Planning Center extremely difficult. He warned O'Connor that the support he had in the past for defeating the center could not be counted on again from the changed Jersey City community. Gradually, the monsignor convincingly led O'Connor to the conclusion that he was better off fighting a battle vis-a-vis the Angela Sanchez situation, rather than waging a war against the Hudson Family Planning Center. O'Connor realized that Norton's solid reasoning was right. He decided to take on Aubrey Fitzgibbons as a Saint Aloysius parishioner instead. He did have a stake, after all, in guiding the flock of the church.

"We're victims of the very church that we've be tryin' to help," said O'Connor. "After I left here, they replaced me with too weak a pastor. He paid no mind to the goings on in the city — when the center raised its ugly head again, there was no resistance. 'Twas a big mistake."

"Agreed," Monsignor Norton said. "But that's a mistake we're now saddled with."

O'Connor sunk back in his chair, retreating in thought. The specter of irrelevance haunted him again. He told the monsignor that he concurred with his suggestion to focus on Angela Sanchez and Aubrey Fitzgibbon rather than the Hudson Family Health Center. Then the elder priest confided to the monsignor what his approach to Misses Fitzgibbon would entail. "I'm no longer pastor here, Lad, but if I were, as sure as there is tomorrow, I would be restricting Misses

Fitzgibbon's privileges as a communicant." O'Connor advocated that Aubrey's right to receive Holy Communion as a practicing Catholic be suspended for as long as she was affiliated with the Hudson Family Planning Center. "Ye will come to learn, me young Monsignor, that ye cannot play favorites with the people who fill the pews. 'Tis a cancer that could spread throughout the entire congregation here, it is."

Monsignor Norton fidgeted in his chair. He knew O'Connor offered sage advice that he did not have the stomach to heed. He let his elder peer vent, but he thought to himself that suspending Aubrey Fitzgibbon's Holy Communion privileges was a reaction too extreme. "Let's tread lightly there, Father. That's a bridge for us to cross another day."

"And what about our church deacon? Shall I talk to him?"

"No. No!" Monsignor Norton knew the elder priest's disapproval for the vocation. "I will handle the deacon." In his observation of the relationship between Father O'Connor and the church deacon, the monsignor sensed tension a plenty, mostly driven by O'Connor's disdain of the church policy to involve deacons more and more in the work and rituals that had been historically carried out by priests. Norton knew that O'Connor resented the expanding new role that had been carved out for deacons in the modern-day church, almost as if the elderly priest was personally threatened by the intrusion. "I'll talk to the deacon once you've raised the topic with Misses Fitzgibbon — she deserves to hear it from us first."

A grandfather clock, stationed in the dimly lit foyer outside the den, chimed the nine o'clock hour. Norton rose from the easy chair, stretched and yawned, and then bid O'Connor goodnight. Before turning in for the night, Norton retired to the rectory chapel for prayer. Later, falling off to sleep, he contemplated the rough going over that Misses

Fitzgibbon would be getting from Father O'Connor the next day.

Chapter Four

It was a half-hour before the noon lunch hour and the tables of Lee's Luncheonette & Old Fashioned Soda Shoppe were already full. Some of the spillover crowd began to opt for seats at the long, red top lunch counter that spanned half the length of the eatery. The pleasing aroma of a roasted brisket of beef, a roasted turkey, and a baked ham — fresh out of the oven — drifted from the kitchen, triggering saliva flows from the taste buds of the patrons.

"I did not appreciate being caught off guard by a late addition agenda item…and neither did the other Board members. You know, they elected *me* the President of the Board because they were counting on *me* not to allow this type of bullshit to happen. And, when something as unbelievable as this does happen, then they think that I am in on it." Aubrey Fitzgibbon angrily asserted herself to the source of her anger, her lunchtime companion, Cindy Stone. They were sharing one of Lee's smaller lunch tables at the back of the eatery.

"But…" Stone tried to get in a word in the middle of Fitzgibbon's lecture, but it was to no avail. Aubrey continued her rant, ignoring Stone's attempt to *butt in* before she could finish. Aubrey then stopped in midsentence, obviously distracted by something. She caught herself, having completely lost her train of thought, and then she apologized to Stone for the confusion.

"Are you okay?" Stone asked. "You don't seem to be yourself. I don't want to pry, but is something bother — "

"I'm fine. I'm fine," Aubrey said, quick to interpose.

But there was something eating away at Aubrey. She was distracted by a matter concerning her marriage. Something that dropped down on her doorstep that very morning. She did not yet know how she would confront it. The problem consumed her, prompting more thoughts about it to capture her attention like an incoming tide laying claim to a beachfront — evident from her loss of concentration during her conversation with Stone. Its presence would not ebb away. Aubrey attempted to block it out of her mind for the time being, trying to focus on the issue at hand, instead.

"You were talking about the Angela Sanchez agenda item," Stone said, cuing Aubrey to pick up where she had left off.

"Yes. Thank you. Not to mention the gravity of that agenda item. The Board was stressed out, and they only went along in voting for it out of deference to me," she said, recalling the uncomfortable moment at the board meeting that they were discussing.

As President of the Board for the Hudson Family Planning Center, Aubrey Fitzgibbon was troubled by the item that appeared on the agenda of the previous day's meeting, prompting her to summon Stone to the hastily put together lunchtime chat. Stone worked at the agency and was responsible for the item appearing on the agenda. The matter dealt with a teenager late into her second trimester pregnancy who wanted an abortion — Angela Sanchez. It was a series of screw-ups of epic proportions that brought the girl to the doorstep of the family planning facility. The situation made most of the center's board members uncomfortable, until Aubrey — just as uncomfortable — convinced them to approve funding the teenager's abortion by tying certain caveats to the agenda item, and then giving the board her personal guarantee that she would implement those stipulations.

As the teenager's caseworker, Stone rushed the item onto the meeting agenda, without the usual screening, and without the typical notification that was always provided to the board members by means of their meeting packets. The packets were normally mailed out to the board members at least a week in advance of their monthly sessions. The surprise of a last-minute agenda item caused as much of a hullabaloo amongst the board members as the girl's predicament itself.

Aubrey opted to share Angela Sanchez's lurid tale of woe with the board members, making a play for sympathy. The circumstances, as embellished upon by Aubrey, were upsetting as much as the lateness of the planned abortion. The teenage girl thought she'd met the boy of her dreams while spending the Christmas and New Year's holidays at her Dad's home in Puerto Rico. Because of her outstanding high school grades, Angela was granted an additional two weeks off from school in order to extend her holiday visit with her father. Angela's parents had split from each other, and she now lived with her mom and grandmother in their Jersey City Housing Authority apartment on the city's West Side. Her mother agreed to let Angela visit her father over the holidays, since he could not spend as much time with his daughter during the rest of the year because of their geographical separation.

While shopping in a San Juan mall, the young, real looker caught the eyes of a teenage *Romeo,* who then fed her line after line until reeling her in and winning over her trust. They spent practically every day of Angela's extended vacation seeing each other, including a few discreet teenage drinking parties and love fests on the beach. Five weeks later, upon returning home from her trip, Angela missed her period and bought a drugstore pregnancy test kit to find out that she had just hit the baby lottery.

Choosing not to tell her mother and grandmother, Angela headed to the West Side Neighborhood Health Clinic where she opted for an abortion. After a newly hired clinic doctor examined her, the young internist was reluctant to perform the procedure, and he then told Angela that she should seek assistance from the Hudson Family Planning Center. He promised to have the clinic arrange for her procedure there, but then Angela fell through the cracks of a healthcare bureaucracy and the referral was somehow lost.

Angela kept the news of her pregnancy to herself while she tried to figure out what to do. She struggled to conceal her evolving condition from her mother and grandmother. Keeping things from her in-and-out of drug rehab mother was easy, but her guardian grandmother noticed that Angela was starting to show about the fifteenth week into her pregnancy. Ironically, the only one that Angela shared her plight with she couldn't reach anymore — *Romeo's* cell phone was no longer in service since she told him about her pregnancy. Her being played by the boy whom she fell for, depressed her as much as her condition.

The clock was ticking, and with Angela's pregnancy fast approaching the third trimester, her options for having an uncomplicated procedure, or any at all, were fast expiring. As Angela's caseworker, Cindy Stone quickly moved to intercede — abruptly placing the item on the agenda of the board meeting.

"So, what can I tell Angela?" Stone asked, pushing to the center of the table the empty plate that a few minutes earlier hosted the juicy rare cheeseburger she consumed.

"I promised the Board that I would talk to her first and explore other options, given her age and the term of her pregnancy," Aubrey answered, referring to the caveats she assured the other Board members that she would carry out — seeing if she could persuade the teenager to bring the pregnancy to term and opt for adoption as an alternative.

"I did counsel her, Aubrey. She wants an abortion," Stone said, practically cheering. Stone was a zealot for feminist issues, known for sometimes going a bit overboard in her passion for fighting for women's rights. That zeal would have some characterize her as a battle-axe for the movement. She was a gruff woman whose crude personality could curdle a glass of milk.

"I know you did, Cindy, this has nothing to do with your competency. It's what I had to promise the Board that I would do in order to get the resolution passed." Aubrey sensed that Stone was becoming territorial. "In the meantime, I want you to immediately lineup a date for a procedure as quickly as possible…so that we are at the ready if, in fact, it is a go. I don't want this lingering any longer than it already has." If the girl was having the procedure, Aubrey wanted it done before the twenty third week of the pregnancy. After such time, even she was uncomfortable with having the center administer an abortion at such a late term, unless for the sake of a health emergency in order to save the life of a mother.

"Trust me, it's a go," Stone said, a morbid grin of satisfaction filling her face.

As their waitress swooped by to drop off the check, Aubrey looked up to notice a figure heading down the aisle between the lunch counter and tables. "Oh Lord, here comes Father O'Connor."

Stone turned around and looked back over her shoulder to see the lean and elderly priest stepping his way towards them. She quickly turned back around. A scowl consumed her face — her discomfort obvious.

Wherever he went, Father Sean O'Connor carried a powerful presence. Approaching their table, the priest said, "Top of the morning, Ladies. Busy at the task of planning families for society, are we? Certainly, the Good Lord could use all the help that he can get."

Aubrey and Stone caught onto O'Connor's sarcasm. Because of her affiliation with a center that offered birth control and facilitated abortions, as a congregant of Saint Aloysius Church, Aubrey seemed headed on a collision course with a priest whom she once held in great respect. O'Connor had baptized Aubrey, administered first Holy

Communion to her, confirmed her, and presided at her wedding. But then a strain in their relationship began to develop over the distinct philosophical differences between the church and the Hudson Family Planning Center agenda. In due time, Aubrey came to consider O'Connor too old fashioned. She was not appreciative of his blunt tact and was now merely tolerating his presence out of her dwindling respect for the clergy.

As for the relationship between Stone and O'Connor, a mutual, very special disaffection for each other existed. Since Stone was the advocate and activist in the community, who was doing the actual promotion of birth control and the final solution that family planning offered for woman with unwanted pregnancies, she remained O'Connor's most notable adversary.

"How are you, Father?" Aubrey responded to the priest, not letting her displeasure show. "What a coincidence seeing you here."

Stone said nothing, her silence radiating her disdain. One could almost sense the milk in the table dispenser starting to sour.

"Nothing is by coincidence, Misses Fitzgibbon. Sometimes God chooses to put us in the most extraordinary places at the most unordinary times. Not that this is one of them now, I only came by to wolf down one of Lee's famous Cheese Danish for brunch," he added, before cutting to the chase.

Aubrey rolled her eyes at the adage. *I hope philosophy class is short today,* knowing the priest's penchant for citing axioms and witticisms at the drop of a hat. *Nothing is by coincidence...Sometimes God chooses to put us in the most extraordinary places at the most unordinary times.* O'Connor's particular words stirred Aubrey, who harbored a dark secret of her own related to her marriage.

"I hope ye'll excuse me, Misses Fitzgibbon, but when I was getting up from me seat at the counter, I just so happened to spy ye at the table over here. I thought that I might spare myself the quarter fer a phone call, and just ask ye in person if I might be able to happen by and see ye regarding a personal matter?" O'Connor took notice that Aubrey did not seem to be her normal perky self. Like Stone, he too sensed that something was troubling her. He noticed that her lunch — a tuna salad on toast — sat untouched on the plate before her.

This can't be good. Judging from past practice, Aubrey knew that *personal matter* meant the priest wanted to see her about something in which the Hudson Family Planning Center was involved. She wondered if Angela Sanchez's grandmother, Maria Ramos — the angry woman who disrupted the center's administrative offices a few days ago — found her way to Father O'Connor's doorstep. Dissatisfied with the center's decision to assist her granddaughter's intention to abort her fetus, the woman threatened that she would be taking her case to the church. *Did he find out already?*

"Why of course, Father. Would you like to come by the day after tomorrow — say around noon?" Aubrey typically hosted meetings at her home office.

"Around noon it is, Misses Fitzgibbon, thank ye." O'Connor caught the look of displeasure on Stone's face from the corner of his eye. "Permit me," he said, reaching down and sliding an ignored glass of water that sat on the table towards him. He mumbled a blessing while crossing the air above the glass with his hand. Then he plunged several fingers inside of the glass and swished them about in the water before withdrawing them. He then crossed his hand through the air above Aubrey's and Stone's heads, splashing them with droplets of the water that flew off his fingertips. He mumbled another prayer. "A blessing for you both," he said, a sly grin spreading across his face.

They didn't know if he was being sarcastic or sincere. Visibly annoyed, Stone grabbed a napkin from the old-fashioned dispenser on the table and dabbed up the droplets of water that landed on her. She peered back at the priest in utter contempt. O'Connor sensed her displeasure...it was a good thing that he couldn't read minds.

"Tis not burning ye now, is it, Misses Stone?" the priest deadpanned, winking an eye towards Aubrey — letting her know that he was only teasing the caseworker. Then O'Connor quickly turned up his wrist to eye his watch. "Indeed. Indeed. Where does the time go, indeed? Must make haste — I'm due back at Saint Al's. I'm serving *the one,*" he said, turning to depart.

Aubrey knew what he meant — O'Connor was celebrating the midweek afternoon Mass at Saint Aloysius. Coincidentally, she intended to catch the Mass on her way back home.

Chapter Five

Aubrey Fitzgibbon steered the Ford Taurus right, turning off of West Side Avenue and into Lincoln Park — its main thoroughfare directly bordered the southern side of Saint Aloysius Church and rectory. The wide roadway in the park allowed for curbside parking by church congregants. As Aubrey pulled the car over and parked, the music background to *We Are Family* sounded out from the *iPhone* in her pocketbook, which rested on the vacant front passenger seat beside her. The melody signaled a call from Nicole Spencer, Aubrey's lifelong chum and best friend. She reached over and retrieved the phone from her bag.

"Nikki. Hey, girl," she greeted.

"And…was I right?" Spencer asked.

Nikki and Aubrey had shared their deepest secrets with each other since grade and high schools — they attended both Saint Aloysius Parish parochial schools. They were really more like sisters than friends. In fact, they each met their future husbands while attending Saint Aloysius High School — they hung out in the same clique of friends. Both couples courted each other as high school sweethearts. That young love turned out lasting a lifetime. Through the years, the couples' lives and families became inseparable — they double dated together, vacationed together, and their children played together.

"I'm on a break before my next class — it's the first chance I've had to call," Nicole continued. She was a drama professor at Jersey City State University, situated on Kennedy Boulevard in the city's southernmost section — also known as the Greenville neighborhoods of Jersey City.

"I was his first appointment this morning. I swear you are a witch, Nicole Spencer," Aubrey answered. "You were right — Doctor Friedman said I'm pregnant. He's referring me back to my old obstetrician, Doctor Thompson," she further reported, sensing a rare and awkward uneasiness begin to envelop the conversation about the matter. She wondered, *did Nikki suspect?*

"Oh Aubrey, I'm so happy for you. I guess that weekend away with me and Matt worked wonders for you and Mike." Nicole referred to Aubrey and her husband's weekend stay, a short while back, at the Spencer's shore house. The Fitzgibbons helped the Spencers prepare the home in advance for the Jersey Shore's coming summer season. Nikki thought that weekend might have been the time of Aubrey's conception. "Now I know why you guys retired so early to bed that Saturday night."

If only she knew the 'wonders.'

"When are you going to tell Michael?" Nikki asked.

A silent pause, one that seemed almost endless, befell the conversation. In the lingering dead silence, Nicole sensed that something was wrong. She braced herself. Aubrey now knew that her friend hadn't suspected, and she prepared to drop a bomb on Nicole.

"Nikki, I need to confide in you, and I have to ask that you keep this news to yourself. Michael doesn't know yet. I…I…I am thinking about having an abortion."

"Oh my God. Oh my God. Aubrey, what are you thinking?" Aubrey's words landed on Nikki like a ton of bricks. She knew that her friend was ecstatic about her recently resurrected career and newfound standing in the community. There was even talk that Mayor O'Dea wanted to run Aubrey for city council on his slate in the next election. But would Aubrey go to such an extreme just for the sake of maintaining her new status in life?

"Please, Nikki, I'm not sure...but I don't want Mike to know, at least not until I know, for sure, what course I'm going to take. My God, I'm thirty-nine years old. I have a reactivated career. I don't know if I'm ready for *Motherhood Two.*"

"But Aubrey...given Mike's position...don't you think you have to let him weigh in — one way or the other? You're not thinking of not tell — "

"Nikki, I have to go. I need to think. Let's talk this over later." Aubrey noticed on her dashboard that it was a minute before one o'clock — the Mass was about to start. She hit the END button. *My God, if Nikki only knew.*

She stashed the phone back in her bag, exited the vehicle and cut through a park path that wound around trees and shrubbery. The path led to a set of stairs setoff to the side of the park, which rose up to the side entrance of the church.

Saint Aloysius was the largest church in Jersey City — enormous. A life-sized marble statue of the church's namesake, Aloysius Gonzaga, stood in the church corridor. Every one of the parishioners knew the story of their church's patron saint. An Italian aristocrat who gave up everything — including his inheritance — to become a member of the *Society of Jesus* in the latter half of the sixteenth century. While still a student at the Roman College, he died as a result of caring for the victims of an epidemic. He was beatified in 1605 and canonized a Saint in 1726 by Pope Benedict XIII, who later declared him the patron saint of young students. In 1926, Pope Pius XI further declared him the patron of Christian youth. Because of the manner of his death and his courage and compassion in the face of an epidemic, he was conferred as the latter-day patron of AIDS sufferers and their caregivers.

Aubrey pulled open one of the bronzed outer doors of the church, emblazoned with a raised emblem of Saint Aloysius upon it. She whisked through a foyer and then pushed open an inner bronzed glass-paneled door, finally entering the church itself. Spontaneously, her hand reached into one of the many half-moon shaped basins of holy water adorning the walls to the side of the church doors. She blessed herself.

The midday sun pierced through the vast assortment of stained glass windows adorning the walls of the church, bathing the interior in a dim fuzzy hue. The pleasing scent of incense was everywhere. An altar boy jangled the bells that hung from the sacristy's entry way onto the altar, signaling the Mass was about to begin. The altar boy led the procession for the Mass onto the altar. Following the altar boy were a deacon and then Father O'Connor, both adorned in green vestments — signifying Ordinary Time in the calendar of the Roman Catholic Church. The trio paraded over to the altar. The priest and deacon kissed the altar top which was covered with a white cloth. The altar boy clumsily genuflected. Then all three retraced their steps back towards a collaboration of presidential church chairs stationed along the wall that adjoined the altar just outside of the sacristy. They performed under a magnificent mural — religious figures and events depicted on the high oblong ceiling that seemed as if it were miles above the altar.

As Aubrey made her way up the side aisle, the eyes of the deacon fell upon her. She noticed his familiar face and smiled.

Deacon Michael Fitzgibbon, her husband, smiled back.

"Let us begin," Father O'Connor said. Then the priest led the congregation in the Sign of the Cross.

Chapter Six

Father O'Connor retired to his bedroom shortly after Monsignor Norton left the den. The night's topic was O'Connor recollecting his encounter with Aubrey Fitzgibbon at Lee's earlier in the day — reporting on his success in securing a meeting with her.

Stepping just inside his bedroom door, O'Connor stretched out his arm and groped along the wall till he found and hit a light switch that turned on a floor lamp in the room. He then strode towards a dresser bureau and lifted up a wooden box that sat on top. He retreated towards the bed with the box and plopped himself down on top of the mattress. The lid of the box was secured by a hinge and held closed by a fastener and eyehook. O'Connor slid open the clasp and then lifted open the lid of the box. He moved the chest around so that the beams of light from the bedroom floor lamp would shine inside on its contents. Lying inside, resting atop a pile of yellowed and disintegrating old newspaper clippings, sat a collection of army medals. O'Connor reached in and lifted out the medal at the top of the pile. Setting it on his open palm, he began staring at it. A rush of sentiment overcame the priest, overwhelming him nearly to the point of tears. It happened practically every time that he clutched the medallion. It was the Medal of Honor, awarded by Congress and presented by the President.

The medal was suspended from a blue ribbon that was hung around the neck of the recipient. The blue ribbon blended into an eight-sided cloth pad of the same material to which it was attached. The cloth pad bore thirteen white stars arranged in the form of three chevrons. Immediately suspended below the cloth shield was an eagle with its wings spread and clutching olive branches and arrows in its talons. The eagle sat perched upon a slim, oblong metal bar with the word 'VALOR' inscribed upon it. Suspended from the metal bar was a gold five-pointed star, each point tipped with trefoils. On each ray of the star was a green oak leaf that represented strength. The gold star sat overlaid upon a green laurel wreath, which represented victory. In the center of the star was the head of the Roman Goddess of wisdom and war — Minerva. The words *"United States of America"* surrounded the head of the goddess.

On the other side of the medal, a simple inscription was engraved, "THE CONGRESS TO CHAPLAIN (CAPTAIN) REVEREND SEAN O'CONNOR."

Father O'Connor reached inside the box again, this time lifting out one of the folded up and wilting newspaper clippings. He unfurled it, revealing a *New York Times* front page story from yesteryear. At the top right of the page, beneath its banner, a headline trumpeted, "Hero Priest Awarded the Medal of Honor." Below the caption, a black and white photo of O'Connor dressed in his priest's garb was published. He was surrounded by five soldiers attired in their Army dress blues — appearing dark gray in the photo. Below the photo ran its caption *"Father O'Connor's Miracles."* Smaller print below the caption listed the names of the soldiers and the priest — Private Barry Freeman, Private Mike D'Andrea, Private Larry Johnson, Chaplain (Captain) Reverend Sean O'Connor, Private Tyrone Williams, and Private John Santoro. Williams and Johnson were two African American kids from Newark, New Jersey. Freeman was a Jewish kid from Brooklyn. Santoro and D'Andrea were two Italian American youths, both Roman Catholics, who also hailed from O'Connor's hometown of Boston.

O'Connor received his draft notice just as he was about to be ordained into the priesthood. He requested and received permission from the church to join the Army Chaplain Corps, and then received permission from the Army to put off his enlistment until the completion of his ordination. After attending a basic officers' leadership course, O'Connor was classified as a 2nd Lieutenant — a commissioned officer — and then shipped to Southeast Asia to serve army congregations fighting in the Vietnam conflict. He was assigned to part of the 199th Infantry Brigade. It was after his display of heroism in battle that he was promoted to Captain.

O'Connor then began to recall a December day back in 1967, shortly after his arrival in Vietnam. He was convoying with a Company of men on a search and destroy operation in Phouc-Lac, near Bien Hoa Province. Simultaneous to his recollection, he started to read the copy of the story that ran beneath the photo — announcing how he was selected to be a recipient of the Medal of Honor. The news story gave a brief depiction of the priest's glorious deeds. Then he reached into the box again and pulled out a folded parchment. He opened up the stiff paper, revealing a photocopy of the citation that accompanied his Medal of Honor — the original citation was framed and now hung in the lobby of a veterans' hospital in Massachusetts.

O'Connor read the words of the citation that were sandwiched between a facsimile of the Medal of Honor at the top, and the signature of President Richard Nixon at the bottom. O'Connor felt tears welling up in his eyes. They soon began cascading into a steady stream, rolling down his cheeks and off of his face, blotting the parchment as he read it.

Citation: "Chaplain O'Connor distinguished himself by exceptional heroism while serving with Company A, 4th Battalion, 12th Infantry, 199th Light Infantry Brigade. He was participating in a search and destroy operation when Company A came under intense fire from a battalion size enemy force. Momentarily stunned from the immediate encounter that ensued, the men hugged the ground for cover. Observing 3 wounded men, Chaplain O'Connor moved to within 15 meters of an enemy machine gun position to reach them, placing himself between the enemy and the wounded men.

O'Connor elicited the scene in his mind, as vivid as the day that it occurred. He could see the faces of the three men whom would later become his lifelong friends — Freeman, Williams, and Santoro. He reflected upon the look of hopelessness that consumed each one of the men when he first made contact with them. He read on.

When there was a brief respite in the fighting, he managed to drag them to the relative safety of the landing zone. Inspired by his courageous actions, the company rallied and began placing a heavy volume of fire upon the enemy's positions. In a magnificent display of courage and leadership, Chaplain O'Connor began moving upright through the enemy fire, and despite being pelted by fragments of shrapnel, he continued administering last rites to the dying and evacuating the wounded.

The priest began to breathe heavily, almost as if he were reliving the event and experiencing its exertion again. He reached down and ran his free hand over the back of his legs, where he'd been hit with the shrapnel — the explanation for the barely noticeable limp in his walk. As he envisioned the scene of what happened next, the face of the hulking Larry Johnson came to mind. O'Connor read on.

Noticing another trapped and seriously wounded man, Chaplain O'Connor crawled to his aid. Realizing that the wounded man was too heavy to carry, he rolled on his back, placed the man on his chest and through sheer determination and fortitude crawled back to the landing zone using his elbows and heels to push himself along.

O'Connor let out a sob. His emotions were overwhelming him now. Then he envisioned the face of Mike D'Andrea. He remembered how frightened he looked — wounded and tangled up in the thick Asian underbrush, thinking that he had reached the end of the line. O'Connor took a deep breath and read some more.

> Pausing for breath momentarily, he returned to the action and came upon a man entangled in the dense, thorny underbrush. Once more intense enemy fire was directed at him, but Chaplain O'Connor stood his ground and calmly broke the vines and carried the man to the landing zone for evacuation. On several occasions when the landing zone was under small arms and rocket fire, Chaplain O'Connor stood up in the face of hostile fire and personally directed the medevac helicopters into and out of the area. With the wounded safely evacuated, Chaplain O'Connor returned to the perimeter, constantly encouraging and inspiring the men.
>
> Upon the unit's relief on the morning of 7 December 1967, it was discovered that despite painful wounds in the back and leg, Chaplain O'Connor had personally carried over 20 men to the landing zone for evacuation during the savage fighting. Through his indomitable inspiration and heroic actions, Chaplain O'Connor saved the lives of a number of his comrades and enabled the company to repulse the enemy. Chaplain O'Connor's actions reflect great credit upon himself and were in keeping with the highest traditions of the U.S. Army.

O'Connor slid down off of the bed; his knees gently hit the floor. He knelt down beside the bed, rested his elbows atop the mattress, then looked up at a crucifix mounted on the wall above the headboard of the bed. He interspersed prayers for his friends and their families with a friendly monologue to his God — thanking the Lord for saving them and asking the Almighty for his blessing. It was during that traumatic Vietnam battle that O'Connor found the meaning of "faith in

God" and how to mouth a prayer that would land a payoff. All through the battle and the rescue of his companions, Sean O'Connor was constantly talking to God, beseeching his help in keeping himself and the men that he had rescued out of harm's way.

When he finished praying, Father O'Connor thought about the last planned reunion the six men had since the medal ceremony, during the Christmas holiday week in New York — just about the turn of the century. Since then, the group had only gotten together twice more — to say farewell and bury Johnson and Santoro; a heart attack took the former and cancer claimed the latter. Santoro was the most recent to pass — about seven years ago. Now, Christmas and Birthday cards, and an occasional email and phone call sufficed in place of get-togethers.

The melancholy ritual of rummaging through his keepsakes was performed by O'Connor several times each month, whenever he was feeling down — which was a lot lately. Whenever he yearned for significance. Whenever he needed to step out from the shadows of irrelevance that he felt were continuing to envelop him.

Chapter Seven

Angela Sanchez sat trembling, desperately gasping for breaths of air between sobs, as she recounted to Aubrey Fitzgibbon her holiday visit to San Juan, Puerto Rico. The teen saw her plight as the end of the world. Hurt beyond repair when the boy, whom she had a head-over-heels crush on, disappeared just as suddenly as he had entered her life. Right after she called him to share the news about her pregnancy, he ditched his cellphone number. That was the last Angela would ever hear from him. She felt humiliated and used.

Aubrey Fitzgibbon took it all in, seated across the table from Angela in the Hudson Family Planning Center's brightly lit conference room. She reached out and grasped the distraught teenager's hands, expressing her empathy for the girl. In the back of her mind, she pondered how her role in all of this would play out when her husband, the deacon, found out.

"I was so happy, when I first found out…and I thought that Jamie would be just as happy." Angela sobbed, recalling her ill-fated notion of her and the hit-and-run lover actually sharing a life together. "I was even thinking about names for the baby — *Jamie*, after his father, if it was a boy; or *Estefani or Stefanie* if it was a girl. I couldn't wait. I fell so much in love with Jamie in just the short time that I was in Puerto Rico. I thought he loved me too. I thought we would all be a family." Angela was merely living in fairytale land. Aubrey Fitzgibbon knew all too well how little a chance Angela's expectations had of playing out. "Then, when I told Mama and Abuela, they made me feel so guilty and dirty. They said I was a tramp."

Angela also said that her *Abuela* brought the matter to the church, since she knew that Aubrey's husband was the deacon there. The revelation reminded Aubrey that she had yet to address the matter with her husband. As the church deacon, Monsignor Norton and Father O'Connor would certainly tell Mike. *I should have told him after Father O'Connor confronted me at Lee's.* She was setting her own husband up to be blindsided. Another unpleasant item on the list of things that she would have to deal with.

The girl balled her eyes out a bit more, then Aubrey asked her if she understood the complexity of the medical procedure that the doctor explained to her the day before. Aubrey also arranged for a psychologist to examine Angela and to speak with her as well. The girl was adamant — she did not want the baby. Her resentment for the child that she carried was being driven by her having been used by the *Don Juan,* compounded by the callous way that she was being treated at home. These displaced sentiments were motivating her choice for an abortion. The psychologist diagnosed as much. Angela felt that by aborting the fetus all of her problems and all of her hurt would just go away, along with the unwanted pregnancy.

Aubrey tried another route. "Have you thought about bringing the baby to term and putting it up for adoption?" This was the final caveat that she promised her Board to put forward. Angela resisted the suggestion. She saw abortion as the solution to her problems.

Through the little more than the two-hour session, Aubrey and Angela developed a trusting bond with each other. At the conclusion of the meeting they exchanged cellphone numbers. Aubrey made it clear that Angela could call her at any time, sensing that the poor girl had no one else to talk to and nowhere else to turn.

***

"Honey, how could you not tell me? Even after all of our arguments about your work at the center — despite my feelings about it — still you should have told me," Mike Fitzgibbon said to his wife, trying the best he could to calm his excited voice and hold it to a low enough volume that would not be heard outside of their bedroom. The Fitzgibbon children's bedrooms were located at the back of the house, just down the hall from the second-floor master bedroom.

Monsignor Norton broke the news to Mike about the Angela Sanchez abortion matter. Once the monsignor knew that Father O'Connor set up a meeting with Aubrey Fitzgibbon, Norton decided it was time for him to give the deacon the heads-up. After his discussion about the matter with Father O'Connor, Norton wanted the deacon prepared for O'Connor's intended intervention. Monsignor Norton was astonished to find out from Deacon Fitzgibbon that Aubrey had yet to tell him anything about the situation.

"This is the same issue that we argue about every time something that the Family Planning Center is doing comes to the attention of the church. It is none of the church's business."

"When a grandmother comes to the rectory door and tells the monsignor that the deacon's wife is providing the means to have an abortion for her seventeen-year-old granddaughter, it is church business. And, since I'm the deacon, it's my business." Mike Fitzgibbon stared right into his wife's eyes, who lay no more than two feet across from him on the mattress of their bedroom's king-size bed. The only light illuminating them came from a small lamp on the nightstand adjacent to Aubrey's side of the bed.

Aubrey rose her head up and then planted her elbow joint into her pillow to serve as a makeshift base. She then lowered her head on her open hand for support. Mike was getting feisty and she was not going to take his guff while lying down. "You told me that you would not interfere. You promised me, when I supported your call to become a deacon, that nothing would change between us...but it has."

"Do you not see the magnitude of this? It isn't about dispensing contraceptives; this is about a teenager's abortion."

"You know, I resent the fact, with all due respect to your, Father O'Connor's, and Monsignor Norton's church titles, that three men want to insert themselves into the personal and private matters of a woman."

"A teenager, not a woman. And a Catholic teen at that."

"Please. You know we suggested that she consider adoption as an alternative."

"But —"

"But nothing. You, nor the church, have a feel for the tragedy of unprepared teenagers raising unwanted children — both lives get destroyed. After she ruled out adoption, allowing an unfit mother to raise an unwanted baby is senseless. Why not give this kid another shot at life? She's certainly learned her lesson."

"At the expense of another life?"

"The church would have been just as upset if I encouraged a teenager to use contraceptives so that something like this was less likely to happen. But either way, they are quick to point the finger of blame. No disrespect to Father O'Connor and Monsignor Norton, but celibate men should not be telling women what to do with their bodies. ...And how about the new leaf that you've turned over in your life? If I ever told you back in our college days that I felt that we both should abstain from sex until we were married, I truly believe there'd be another Misses Fitzgibbon lying beside you in this bed. One of a man's best friends is always his lover's birth control pills."

Mike could sense that Aubrey was getting hotter by the low ball she pitched at him. He looked into that dreamy face of the woman whom he was still so devoutly in love with and he knew not to press the matter any further, lest an already unpleasant situation turn ugly. He waited a moment as some much-needed silence consumed a pause in the argument. "Brey," he called to her softly, almost in a whisper. Brey was his pet nickname for her. "Let's not talk about it anymore. Just know that, even though I'm upset, I love you."

When Aubrey heard him call her Brey, she knew that he had caved. *He's is still crazy about me.* Mike extended his arm and gently stroked her soft hair with the back of his hand, pushing back a few strands that were partially covering her face. She laid back down on her opposite side and slid her backside over and into him — spoons position. She felt his lips press against her cheeks as he aroused her with a bevy of soft kisses. Mike's other arm reached around her midriff softly stroking her side before coming to a rest and draping over her hip. His hand then gently rubbed her abdomen.

Aubrey loosened her body into the comfort of her husband's embrace. She mused about the fetus forming in her womb within inches of Mike's hand. She felt that she had made the right decision in not telling him about her pregnancy and her plans to have an abortion. *That would destroy him.* She loved him too much to ever subject him to such hurt. They fell off to sleep, Aubrey and the fetus growing inside of her, locked in the arms of Mike's loving embrace.

Chapter Eight

"Father O'Connor! Father O'Connor!" Sister Joseph Eleanor's shrill voice carried across the courtyard between Saint Aloysius Church and the parish school. The high school principal was an institution in the parish, serving in her next to last school year before retirement. It was Father O'Connor, in fact, who lobbied the archdiocese for her appointment — when he served as monsignor there many moons go.

Treading across the courtyard towards its West Side Avenue exit, O'Connor froze in place and spun around, instantly recognizing the voice. He had just served a ten o'clock Funeral Mass and was about to hoof it over to the Fitzgibbons' home, which was within walking distance of the church. His eyes settled upon the nun, still sprite for her elderly age. Sister Joseph Eleanor was adorned in her more traditional Sisters of Charity's habit, and she was towing a slightly chubby student by his ear lobe as she made her way towards O'Connor. The boy's uniform shirt's tail hung out from his pants and flapped in the breeze with each pace he took. The high school freshman's conduct was reported to the principal by her counterpart in a Jesuit Catholic high school located in the city, Saint Peter's Prep. The frosh, Jason Nealon, pummeled one of the prep school's students in a fight.

Catching up to O'Connor, Sister Joseph Eleanor filled the priest in on her prisoner's exploits. Whenever there was a serious discipline problem with any of the students, such as fighting, it was O'Connor whom the principal always sought out — he would always nip the problem in the bud. She didn't appreciate the more lax and liberal admonishments that were typically handed down by Monsignor Norton.

"Fighting, is it? Well now, Sister Joseph, ye better leave this young scalawag with me — so that I might be straightenin' him out a bit." O'Connor placed his hand on Jason's shoulder and guided him in the direction of his walk. He was hoping that his words would begin to intimidate the student. He noticed the bright red throbbing earlobe of the youth, which the nun had squeezed between her fingertips. "Not to worry about anything, Sister, I'll send the lad back around when I'm done with him."

"Thank you, Father. He bloodied the other boy's nose." She turned to head back to her office in the high school.

"Fighting, aye? So why don't you explain yerself to me, young man. What's this all about?"

Jason delivered his tale of woe, explaining how the Saint Peter's Prep sophomore called him a "pussy" for attending Saint Aloysius High School.

"Mind yer language, Lad. For the sake of the story, let us agree that he called ye a *'wuss'*…shall we?"

"A what? Is a 'wuss' worse than a …"

"Now, now," O'Connor said, before the youth could utter the distasteful word again.

"Those Prep kids are always razzing us, Father. They think that we are all puss — I mean, *wusses* here at Saint Al's." Jason regaled the priest with his story of how he pummeled the agitator with a few roundhouse wallops, done for the purpose of attempting to defend the integrity of Saint Aloysius High School and its students.

"Is that what those heathens think of us, now? Leave it to the Jesuits to instill such poor manners on their breed. But why be hittin' him so close to the last few weeks of the school year — what are ye thinkin', Lad? Ye should have waited a couple of weeks for summer vacation…and then walloped the rapscallion. Now we'll have to deal with it. …Well, I suppose we can give you a pass fer yer behavior — just this one time, of course — since, after all, ye did uphold the honor of Saint

Aloysius. Let's call this a confession, and as for yer penance — ye head straight on over to the church and pray three Hail Marys, Our Fathers, and Glory Be's each. Ye did well, Lad."

"Sister Joseph Eleanor said that *'we should do unto others as we would have them do unto us.'*"

"Aye...but she might be forgettin' in all of this hullabaloo that yer just a freshman."

"Huh?"

"Ye see, that's the New Testament that the good sister cited, Lad, and you're still but a freshman...so instead, I think we should be guiding you by the Old Testament: *'an eye for an eye and a tooth for a tooth,'*" O'Connor deadpanned, pulling the confused freshman's leg.

"But I hit him in his nose, not his eye or tooth, Father."

"Aye, not to worry — it's covered. The nose is between the eyes and the teeth." O'Connor motioned with is hands. He read from Jason's face that the naive youth was buying it all. Then the priest reached into his pants pocket and pulled out his wallet, sliding out a crumbled one-dollar bill. "Now, don't be telling Sister Joseph what we spoke about, and take this dollar to go and be treatin' yerself to a nice milkshake at Lee's...after school of course. Saint Aloysius would be proud of ye, he would." He grabbed Jason's hand and smacked the bill down into his open palm.

The youth was further confused — was he being rewarded or punished? Jason had the idea that he was being let off easy because, somehow, Father O'Connor had a distaste for Saint Peter's Prep or, at the very least, the Jesuits.

"Father O'Connor, milkshakes cost three dollars at Lee's."

O'Connor frowned, reaching inside his wallet again to pull out two additional dollar bills, handing them over to Jason. "Three dollars...now...is it? The Jesuits must be pricing the menu there. Move along with ye now, and don't forget — not a word about this to Sister Joseph Eleanor."

They both departed in separate directions — Jason headed to the church for penance, and O'Connor headed to see Aubrey Fitzgibbon for a frank discussion.

***

Aubrey Fitzgibbon lifted up the picture frame that was seated atop the mantelpiece of the hearth in her home office — a black and white portrait photograph of her parents. Aubrey was an only child. Her parents were now both deceased. Cancer claimed her Mom early in life — Aubrey was but a middle-age teen when she passed. Much later on, Aubrey's Dad passed, but it was sudden — a brain aneurism, just two years ago. Today would have been her father's birthday, and she was still carrying a bit of a heavy heart. Aubrey navigated a sudden gush of emotion before setting the picture frame back on the top of the mantelpiece. She smiled at the portrait of her parents, as if they could somehow acknowledge her.

A former career journalist, when it became time to raise a family, the media corporation that Aubrey worked for offered her a job that she could do at home — an associate editor who read manuscripts to determine their potential for the organization's publishing arm. The cozy home office had an orderly desk with a foot-high stack of the latest book proposals that she was slated to review.

Aubrey stepped to her right and picked up another picture frame that rested at the opposite end of the mantelpiece. She smiled at the images in this photograph as well — a picture of her fourteen-year-old son, Justin, and her sixteen-year-old daughter, Tracy. How proud Aubrey was of her children. How she loved them so — her personal pride and joy in life.

She rewound the discussion she had just earlier that morning with Justin, before he headed out for school. The boy was melancholy as he pleaded his case to his mom. Justin needed a signoff from a parent in order to try out for the Saint Aloysius High School freshman football team in the fall. He made the mistake of misreading his father's sentiment for allowing him to play football in high school. Justin's heart had been set on it. Dad let him down hard with a firm, "No way!" Now Justin was taking his case up to mom on appeal.

"How many times do I have to tell you, Justin, on stuff like this, you should always see me first. Now it creates a problem," Aubrey said. She took the permission form and signed it. "Not a word about this until I talk to your father. Do you understand, young man?" After handling the Angela Sanchez drama, Aubrey felt comfortable that she could also work her magic on Mike for Justin.

Aubrey then focused on her daughter Tracy's image in the photo, pondering to herself where the time went. It seemed to her that it was almost yesterday when Tracy was born. She flashed forward through the events in her daughter's life in a matter of seconds — baptism, baby's first Christmas, the toddler years, the first day of school, Holy Communion, Confirmation, grammar school graduation, her first high school dance and date, and her recent sweet sixteen birthday party. The little girl who once wanted to do everything with mom, now had little time for mom as she grew up and began to involve so many other people in her life. A sense of remorse overwhelmed Aubrey as she contemplated the growth of her daughter, and the fear of losing her child's sweet innocence to the world.

"Are you ready for your visitor?" a voice sounded, startling Aubrey for a second. Then she remembered it was her husband's day of the week to work late, which meant that he wasn't due at his office until later in the morning. Mike Fitzgibbon interrupted his wife's trip down memory lane. Though the Sanchez matter was settled between Aubrey and him, Mike was aware that she was expecting Father O'Connor, and was none too pleased about the meddlesome priest's butting into his wife's personal affairs. Despite being tipped off about O'Connor's intentions by Monsignor Norton, Mike resented O'Connor's nerve in confronting his wife without consulting him first. Mike felt disrespected, but he dared not say anything — he too feared the relationship between O'Connor and Archbishop Scaponi. Devoutly Catholic, Michael treasured his position as one of Saint Aloysius' first deacons, and he would not make any waves that could jeopardize it. He gave O'Connor a wide berth.

"I'm as ready as I'll ever be," Aubrey answered, checking out her better half as he walked into the office. She reached over and straightened Mike's necktie. "As ready as anyone can ever be for Father O'Connor, I guess."

"I'm outta here — I'll see you tonight." He stepped closer towards Aubrey, delivering her a peck on her cheek. His gestures always served as a testament for how he remained so madly in love and adoring of her, as he had always been since they first met back in high school. Aubrey knew it as well, and at times she took advantage of her hubby's limitless love for her.

"Thanks, Sweetie," she said, acknowledging the kiss. "Good luck in court," Aubrey wished him well. *I'll tell him about Justin trying out for the football team after dinner.*

Mike made a living and supported his family as a lawyer. He and another Jersey City attorney formed a practice and opened an office in downtown Jersey City. Mike was a damn good attorney, though it was rather an odd career choice for a man who was also a Roman-Catholic Church Deacon. Mike rushed out the door and dashed down the backstairs of the front porch, which led to the driveway where his car was parked. He was making sure to leave before the arrival of Aubrey's expected company, wanting to avoid any chance of bumping into Father O'Connor. He backed the car down the raised driveway aside the house, and then out onto Gifford Avenue. Before pulling away, he glanced into the rearview mirror and noticed the head and then the upper torso of O'Connor ascending the hilled street from below. He shook his head, pressed his foot down on the car's accelerator and sped off. *Perfect timing.*

***

Father O'Connor peered up at the house from the bottom of the concrete staircase that led up to the front porch. He prepared himself for the climb, a bit out of wind from his trek up Gifford Avenue. The pristine tree lined block was located in one of the city's most prestigious neighborhoods. The block began at its intersection with West Side Avenue at the bottom of the hill, seated across from the midsection of Lincoln Park, which extended along the western side of the main thoroughfare for several blocks. The Fitzgibbon home was just a short two blocks from the church and O'Connor enjoyed the stroll.

As O'Connor ambled up the steps, he felt his angina kick in — a sharp pain running across the center of his chest. He halted a few steps from the top of the porch and allowed the nitroglycerin transdermal patch that he wore to likewise 'kick in.' O'Connor had coronary artery disease — a narrowing of the blood vessels that supplied his heart. He already had suffered two mild heart attacks. Doctors suggested procedures to clear the arteries, but the old-fashioned priest refused, opting to "Leave me fate in God's hands and not the doctor's," as he so aptly put it. The nitro patches were the limit for what he would allow the doctors to do for him. He wore the patch on his nearly hairless chest, over his heart. His hand reached up and pressed his jacket down over the patch, as if it would help in squeezing out faster relief for his pain.

Ascending the remaining steps to the top of the porch, Father O'Connor caught his breath and then pressed the doorbell, pondering how *Father Time* had caught up with him. Aubrey greeted the priest at the door, exchanged pleasantries, and then led him into her home office — a converted first floor sitting room. As he passed through the house, the pleasant odor of fresh baking brought on a rush of memories, back to his childhood days in Boston, when the same aroma would fill the house on Sunday mornings as his mother baked pies for after Sunday church and brunch.

As they entered Aubrey's makeshift office, she seated the priest in one of the two leather accent chairs stationed in the front of her desk. A ceramic teapot and accompaniments were stationed on a rolling serving tray that Aubrey earlier pushed into the room. An assortment of finger sandwiches, neatly piled on a plate and covered with clear plastic wrap, sat beside the tea pot. Another plate of uncovered raisin scones sat beside the plate of sandwiches, the steam still rising out of them. O'Connor surmised them to be the cause of the pleasant baking aroma.

The conversation shifted from pleasantries to the Fitzgibbon children, whom O'Connor complimented to their proud mother, eyeing their photograph on the mantelpiece. Aubrey poured the priest a cup of piping hot tea. A dense steam rose up from the cup, signaling that the brew was too hot to sip just yet. Father O'Connor's eyes scanned over the room and settled on a miniature cactus rose plant sitting on the windowsill. Two of its flowers were completely bloomed — a brilliant yellow bud with a scarlet inner center. "Aye, that's a gorgeous flower, now what might that be called?" he asked.

"A cactus rose, Father. I ordered it from a garden shop in Texas." She then explained that she had a dear aunt who lived in Texas, and when she was a young girl, her parents would take her along to visit her Aunt Mindy. Aubrey took notice of the plant in her aunt's garden and it grew on her. "It's my favorite flower."

O'Connor's eyes continued scanning the room as if he was still searching for something.

Aubrey took notice. "Something you need, Father?"

The humbled priest glanced right and left, as if checking to see if the coast was clear, then he leaned forward and, in a soft voice, he whispered across to Aubrey. "Misses Fitzgibbon, excuse me for asking, but *mighten* you have a wee bit of the creature *lerkin'* about the house?"

Aubrey laughed aloud, knowing exactly to what O'Connor was alluding. "Why certainly, Father," she acknowledged, then Aubrey exited the room to return seconds later holding a bottle of rye. She remembered the priest's usual routine whenever he visited and was served tea. She handed him the bottle, mimicking in a brogue, *"A wee bit of the creature,* Father."

"One never knows when a cold draft might be *'lerkin'* about and ready to take us down." O'Connor opened the bottle and poured a bit of the rye into his tea. The *'cold draft'* excuse was but O'Connor's little white lie to cover for the fact that he knew the rye would help to settle his angina discomfort. A personal matter that he kept to himself.

"Today seems a bit too warm for any cold drafts to be lurking about."

"Me mother use to say, *'ye can never be too prepared.'*" He went on to thank Aubrey for agreeing to see him, and also for her warm hospitality, as evident by the treats that she had prepared for their meeting.

Over more small talk, they snacked on a few of the finger sandwiches. Father O'Connor wolfed down two of the scones, to boot. O'Connor felt a bit of an ingrate for where he knew he would take the conversation next, so he prefaced himself. "Misses Fitzgibbon, yer much too kind and have been all too gracious towards an old pain like *meself.* Especially, when what I have come to talk to ye about is something that might not be all that pleasant. I hope ye'll forgive me, but it's not my intention to hurt ye — I genuinely like ye."

The conversation turned to a darker shade of serious as O'Connor raised the subject of Angela Sanchez's planned abortion. He strongly condemned the actions of anyone, including the girl's mother, who would persuade or enable the teen to abort the *"child"* that she carried. Aubrey normally could not discuss a patient's case with anyone, but she felt comfortable in breaking the law to discuss the matter with a man of the cloth. She explained her own displeasure with Angela's decision, and how she tried to convince her to opt for adoption, but to no avail. She explained to him how the center's psychologist felt that Angela's bringing the fetus to term could possibly leave deep psychological scars in the fragile girl. O'Connor was unmoved and remained resolved in his conviction — the planned abortion had to be stopped.

Aubrey insisted that, at the end of the day, the decision ultimately rested with Angela — it was her choice. That practically sent O'Connor through the roof. "Life is a gift from the Lord almighty. It is his alone to decide to give or take, not the Family Planning Center or a confused teenager." O'Connor paused a second to compose himself before he exploded, and then cited scripture to sum up his thought. "In his hand is the soul of every living thing, and the life breath of all mankind. ...Job, chapter twelve."

The deeper into the politics of the argument that they delved, the more upsetting it became. They were pulling further apart from any point of reasoning or resolution. No one was going to change anyone's mind. O'Connor several times reminded Aubrey that she was a practicing Roman Catholic. Aubrey countered that she was also a liberated and free woman in twenty-first century America.

O'Connor fired off another retort, "Render to Caesar the things that are Caesar's, and to God the things that are God's: *creation and life,* Misses Fitzgibbon — the wonders found in Genesis."

"Please, Fath — " Aubrey tried arguing to no avail. The priest cut her off.

"Me dear Misses Fitzgibbon, the foundation of our religion is founded on faith. Jesus Christ's life, death, and resurrection are a source of hope for all the world. Abortion is a wanton, hopeless act that is contrary to our faith in Christ. It presupposes a negative life situation for a child who has yet to be born. It denies hope and it is seeded by doubters. That is a slap in the face to Christ, himself, who has told us that *'through God all things are possible.'* Abortion flies in the face of all of that. It is a godless, desperate act of a maleficent person who hasn't a clue what faith is all about."

"The church could have won the battle on abortion, Father, had it not waged the war against a woman's use of contraceptives. Sometimes, you have to pick your battles."

"I'm afraid, we don't have the option of negotiating with God, or compromising his laws. As Catholics, we are obliged to follow his commandments — not as we see fit, but as he sees fit to give us. Ye know, back in the day of me grandparents, the purity of a woman was honored. The respectful courting ritual and the anticipation of the wedding night helped to make the relations between a man and woman dignified. Today, it's been turned into a social sport."

"That's the argument that has lost the church a lot of its following, Father — harping back to the *good old days.* Women once did not even have the right to vote. We were second-rate citizens. Today, we have evolved. The church's message threatens a woman's new-found freedoms. It renders the ugly image of a Neanderthal dragging his mate along by a handful of her hair, hauling her back to his cave for a date." Aubrey's insolence was only getting the priest even hotter under the collar.

After they exhausted themselves in a good half-hour more of heated quarrel, a solemn silence befell the room. Each of them came to realize that they were not going to change the mind of the other. Stalemate. O'Connor lifted the saucer and empty teacup that rested on his lap and sat it down on the serving cart beside the desk. He leaned forward and looked Aubrey sternly and squarely in the eyes. He took a deep breath and then began to slowly expel it. The crafty priest was about to lower the boom.

"Misses Fitzgibbon, please don't take what I have to say next in the wrong way. I cannot force ye to practice yer faith as the church sees fit, but neither can ye force me to ignore my obligation to uphold church doctrine. Me young Lass, this pains me as much as, I know, it will pain ye." O'Connor took a breath and paused, as if almost contemplating whether or not he should continue. He knew that telling Aubrey what he had to say next would not be easy.

Aubrey leaned forward, hanging on the edge of her seat. She nervously grasped the arms of her chair at each side. *Where is he going with this?*

"Misses Fitzgibbon, forgive me, but I must ask that you refrain from the sacrament of the Holy Eucharist. I will not administer the sacrament to ye at any of the Masses that I serve. Ye may come to the altar in the communion line and I will bless ye, but I cannot consent to yer partaking of our Lord's sacred body and blood while ye're in the throes of mortal sin. …Ye must choose between the creed of the church and your position at the center. I am truly sorry, Lass, but I will not allow the teachings of Christ to be compromised."

O'Connor was saddened, and Aubrey could tell that he was feeling just as bad as he had made her feel. Deep down, judging by church doctrine, she knew that he was right and declined to argue the point or appeal her sentence, as much as she disagreed with it. Even though she firmly resented and defended the attacks against the Family Planning Center and a woman's choice, she knew the priest was just as committed to defending the laws of the church. But O'Connor's imposed sentence knocked the wind out of her. Totally unexpected. Aubrey was stunned that he decided to carry things that far. She was almost ready to cry but managed to maintain her composure.

O'Connor cleared his throat. He thought for a second, then made an attempt at mitigating the punishment he had already meted out. "I suppose ye could always attend Monsignor Norton's Masses, as I'll not broach the subject with him." He hung his head low, not wanting to see the pain that he caused to register in Aubrey's pretty face. Sometimes, being relevant was painful.

"I would not do that, Father. I'm upset by this, but not with you — I understand your position. Besides, I really love your sermons, and I love hearing you sing at the high Masses. *Telling him the truth won't help.* "But, I must tell Mike. He'll be wanting to know why I'm not receiving communion, especially whenever he is assisting you at one of your Masses. I have to let him know."

"I understand, Lass. I think that I'm now starting to feel *worse* off about this than *yerself.* How kind ye are, after all of this, to flatter me as you did…I dare say that I'm embarrassed. I will pray for ye."

Is he kidding? "And I will pray for you, too, Father." Aubrey was bitter and confused, feeling as if she had misplaced her admiration for the priest.

Notwithstanding their bitter argument, Aubrey and Father O'Connor at least wrapped up their rancorous disagreement civilly. They each downed another cup of tea, as if to wash away the taste of any bitter words that still might have lingered from their discussion. Aubrey then escorted the priest to the door and extended her hand. Father O'Connor clasped it and shook. Aubrey noticed his beautiful ring, a fourteen-karat white gold band with an emerald stone that was emblazoned by a Celtic cross affixed to it. Aubrey recalled him wearing it ever since the first time that she could recall meeting him. "I always meant to ask you, Father, where did you get that gorgeous ring?"

"Oh," me own mother gifted it to me on the day that I became a priest. I've been wearing it ever since. Over time, it's brought me much good luck, it has. Do you really like it, Misses Fitzgibbon?"

"I love it, even more than today's sermon," she said, as she opened the front door.

The ruffled priest bid Aubrey, "Good day," and walked through the open doorway onto the porch.

"Good day, Father."

O'Connor thought to himself a second, then turned back towards the door and pushed it back towards Aubrey. "Misses Fitzgibbon," he said, watching as Aubrey peered out from behind the half-closed door.

"Yes, Father?"

O'Connor looked her dead in the eyes and spoke. "Please, allow me to bless ye."

Aubrey was shocked — she hadn't anticipated the priest's actions. She nodded her head, consenting to the blessing.

Father O'Connor lifted his right hand and rested his palm on top of Aubrey's forehead, his slightly trembling fingers extending over the top of her head. He pronounced distinctly, "John, Chapter One," as he proceeded to quote scripture. "In the beginning was the Word, and the word was with God, and the Word was God. He was in the beginning with God. All things came to be through him, and without him nothin' came to be. What came to be through him was life, and this life was the light of the human race; the light shines in the darkness, and the darkness has not overcome it." He then murmured a prayer in Latin, and finally capped off the blessing by saying, "The Lord bless and keep ye. May he shine is face upon ye and be gracious to ye. May the Lord look upon ye kindly and give ye peace." O'Connor lifted his hand off of Aubrey's head and crossed the air above it. "In the name of the Father, the Son, and the Holy Spirit," he said, as Aubrey made the sign of the cross.

A silent pause followed O'Connor's blessing. Once again, he stared into Aubrey's eyes and told her in a calm soft voice, "Where God breeds life…there will always be hope."

Aubrey took in his words and said nothing more. She slowly closed the door and leaned back against it, reflecting on the priest's visit and his departing words, cradling her abdomen and the life therein with her hands.

Chapter Nine

Doctor Kyle Thompson's office was located on the fourth floor of the Medical Arts Building, situated in the Jersey City Medical Center complex. The building was an expansive four-story structure with four wings that intersected each other at the center, forming a cross. A number of doctors, specialists, dentists, and psychiatrists rented office and clinic space in the edifice that was very accommodating to the needs of the medical community — just across the street from the Jersey City Medical Center, in Jersey City's Downtown section. The same office block also hosted the Hudson Family Planning Center's abortion clinic. The building was within view of the New York City waterfront, which lay just across the Hudson River.

"All that I'm asking, is that you just sleep on it over the weekend — a few more days is not going to complicate the procedure," Doctor Kyle Thompson said to the office patient who was trying his patience. They were sitting in the doctor's private office, where he would usually consult with the patients that he just examined.

Aubrey Fitzgibbon remained insistent. Her mind was made up — she wanted to abort her pregnancy. She knew a few days would not change her mind. Then she thought to herself, *is my haste going to make him suspicious?* She decided to cave, after all, it was Friday — nothing would happen on the weekend. She conceded to her obstetrician's point — two more days would not make a difference. "Okay, I'll think about it for your peace of mind, but I want my meds on Monday." Aubrey referred to the Methotrexate tablets she would take.

Methotrexate is a cancer drug used in chemotherapy because it attacks the most rapidly growing cells in the body. In the case of an abortion, it causes the fetus and placenta to separate from the lining of the uterus. Using the drug for that purpose is not approved by the FDA, but physicians and abortion clinics used it for that purpose anyway. Five to seven days later, the patient would then be given a Misoprostol tablet to take at home. This medication would trigger uterine contractions that would cause the body to void its contents.

"I want my meds on Monday," Aubrey said again, wanting to make sure her doctor understood.

"Monday sounds much better than 'now'. And, please, consider talking it over with Mike."

"Let's be clear about this. It is my decision, my choice, and my privacy. The consequences of his knowing are far graver than his not knowing. I will not put him through that — especially given his position in the church."

Thompson understood her logic, but still felt uncomfortable — he knew Mike, and now felt that he was a part of Aubrey's deceit of her husband. Thompson knew he had no choice — the law required that he respect his patient's medical privacy. "I understand, but I'm not happy about it. Here," he said, handing her a brochure on the medications that he would be administering to her on Monday, along with the itinerary for the nonsurgical procedure. "This is what you need to know about the meds and what to expect."

"I could practically write the script for this — after all the time I've spent at the Family Planning Center."

Despite her decision to leave her husband in the dark, Aubrey was still unsettled about the strategy. She was overwhelmed by guilt — feeling false-hearted. Mike took the Sanchez matter pretty hard and, despite the circumstances, he was just as upset about Father O'Connor suspending Aubrey's communion rites. Aubrey also knew that Mike planned on complaining about the matter to Monsignor

Norton — they were concelebrating a Sunday morning Mass. She wondered what the implications would be inside the walls of the rectory, once Mike raised the issue with the pastor. Aubrey felt for sure that there would be some sort of fallout for Father O'Connor's rash judgment.

Aubrey left Doctor Thompson's office and walked down the hallway to wait for the elevator. She glanced up to check the time on the clock above the elevator doors — she planned to stop off at the main offices of the Family Planning Center at Journal Square, which was in the center of the city and up the hill from the Downtown neighborhoods of Jersey City.

While riding the lift down to the lobby, Aubrey stuffed the brochures given her from Doctor Thompson into her pocketbook. She then began plotting her routine for Monday: she would head to the bank in the morning and retrieve cash from her safety deposit box in order to pay for her abortion meds — not wanting to create a record for the procedure by purchasing it with her family's prescription and health benefits plan. *No one will be the wiser.* After the bank, she would then head back to Doctor Thompson's office to pick up her meds.

Aubrey worked it out with Nikki Spencer for the use of the Spencer's summer shore house as the place where she would undergo her ordeal. The cover story to keep Mike from becoming suspicious was that Nikki would be hosting a sham *'girl's week'* at the Spencer's summer getaway home. Both of the girl's husbands were working, and Nikki's kids were visiting with her husband's parents in Vermont. All of that made Nikki's shore digs the best location where Aubrey figured that she could stealthily abort her fetus. Nikki and Aubrey did the *'girl's week'* routine every year at the Spencer's shore getaway, and Aubrey trusted that no one would suspect any ulterior motive. Aubrey and Nikki planned to leave Jersey City about midafternoon, before the late afternoon rush-hour traffic began to buildup.

Inside of her psyche, a deep-rooted fear overwhelmed Aubrey's every move — *what if, God forbid, Mike ever found out?*

Retrieving her car from the parking garage adjacent to the medical building complex, Aubrey slipped her *Blue Tooth* device over her ear then scrolled through the list of missed phone messages posted on her phone. She saw "Angela Sanchez" appearing twice. *Good God, something's up.* Angela's procedure was scheduled for Monday morning as well. Aubrey was becoming somewhat of a nursemaid to Angela, growing rather close to her since their first face-to-face at the Family Planning Center. As the teen's sole confidante, she looked upon Angela as a temporarily adopted daughter, and she tried to fill the family void that the girl missed at home.

While driving from out of Downtown and heading uptown towards Journal Square, Aubrey called the teen back. She could sense that Angela's anxiety and nervousness were heightening as the time drew closer for the procedure. Angela then expressed a personal request of Aubrey — she wanted her there, with her, while she underwent her abortion procedure. Aubrey at first resisted — to do so, would be an inappropriate protocol for her as a Board member. But Angela persisted, and Aubrey felt the girl's fragile state would only suffer further if she declined. Other, younger clients, on rare occasions had a family member accompany them on the day of the procedure, right up until the time that the client made their entry into the procedure room where the abortion would be performed. Aubrey gave in and consented to be there for Angela.

By the time she completed her rather lengthy chat with Angela, Aubrey arrived at the main offices of the Family Planning Center in Journal Square. She intended to make sure that everything was up to snuff for Angela's scheduled procedure. Doing so might have been a mistake for which she could have paid dearly. Aubrey kept a duplicate file of her health and insurance information inside the drawer file of her desk at the center. She intended to place a copy of the paperwork Doctor Thompson gave her in that file. The original would be destroyed after her procedure — she definitely wasn't taking the chance of stashing a copy in her home's family medical file for Mike to stumble across.

She brought the four pages of paperwork to the copy room down the hall from her office, then inserted them into the feeder tray of the master copy machine. She was distracted by the melody of *We Are Family*, hailing from her phone that she left in her bag back in the office. It signaled that Nikki Spencer was returning an important call that Aubrey earlier placed to her.

"Shoot!" Aubrey said, disguising an expletive. She left the papers in the feeder tray and hurried back to answer Nikki's call.

From the other end of the hallway, Cindy Stone scooted into the copy room unnoticed, watching as Aubrey scurried back down the hall the other way. Ironically, she needed to copy paperwork involving her case file on Angela Sanchez. As she prepared to use the machine, Stone noticed the papers in the feeder tray and picked them up to peruse. *Holy shit! The mother lode.* She quickly surmised that Aubrey left the papers there while she ran back to her office for a second. *So, Miss Prim and Proper, wife of the deacon, can have an abortion while the hypocrites in the rectory play dumb. They condemn the masses but not her.* Stone totally misread the situation. *This could be put to some interesting use.*

Stone worked quickly, replacing the papers in the feeder tray and hitting the machine's COPY button. The papers passed through the machine as it spewed out the duplicates. She retrieved the original papers and set them back into the feeder tray, grabbed the copies, and then tore ass out of the room and down the hall — back to her office.

The Sanchez file could wait. Cindy Stone now had what she needed.

Chapter Ten

Monsignor Norton peered through the nylon curtains hanging between the open drapes and the picture window of the parlor rectory. He just finished work on the parish financials and checkbook. Rain was forecast, and he was checking out the overcast sky from the vantage point of the large parlor window. His weather observation was suddenly interrupted by Father O'Connor popping into view, trudging along the path between the backdoor of the church and the front door of the rectory. O'Connor had just served the Sunday one o'clock Mass and was heading back to join the monsignor for lunch, as was their custom. The bite to eat was to hold their appetites over until dinner, usually served late on Sundays — an hour or two after the last Sunday Mass at five o'clock.

Norton was a bit miffed with Father O'Connor — Deacon Fitzgibbon assisted the monsignor at the eleven-thirty Mass and relayed the sentence that O'Connor handed down to the deacon's wife. Although O'Connor raised the topic of restricting Holy Communion for Aubrey Fitzgibbon, when he and O'Connor discussed the matter a few nights back, the priest never suggested he was actually going to impose the penance. Norton thought O'Connor should have told him.

He planned to take it a bit easier than he normally would on O'Connor, as he knew the priest was still shaken from an ordeal that he suffered at the hands of Rosalita Sanchez — Angela Sanchez's mother. High as a kite on drugs, Sanchez besieged the priest on the church steps as he greeted the parishioner's departing from the Friday afternoon one o'clock Mass. She yelled at the top of her lungs that O'Connor should mind his own business and leave her daughter alone. She threatened that if he interfered with her daughter's abortion she would sue him. After delivering her ultimatums, she hacked up some phlegm from her throat and spit it into O'Connor's face. Parishioners on the church portico stepped between the two, then other parishioners escorted Misses Sanchez off of the church property.

The incident humiliated Father O'Connor, who would not be over it for a while.

Ironically, without anyone's knowledge, it was Cindy Stone, Angela Sanchez's caseworker from the Family Health Center, who wound up the poor girl's mother and then egged her on to assault the priest. Stone led Rosalita to believe that unless she confronted O'Connor, her daughter's abortion could be jeopardized. This was before Stone discovered the *'mother lode'* later that same day. When Angela's mother tried to put the arm on Stone for a handout, in order that she could buy a fix to satisfy her drug habit, Stone negotiated her charity — she promised Sanchez a twenty spot if she had the moxie to spit into O'Connor's face. While Rosalita carried out her end of the deal for the bounty, Stone watched from her car, parked across the street from the church. She burst out into a fit of uncontrollable, ghoulish laughter as O'Connor tucked his hand beneath his vestment and fumbled for a pants pocket holding his handkerchief. He withdrew the cloth and wiped the mucous from off his face.

"Does that burn, Father?" Stone said to herself.

O'Connor ambled up the rectory porch steps and into the parlor. Norton greeted him, then they both proceeded to the rectory's dining room, just off the kitchen. Misses Cavendish, the elderly cook and homemaker for the priests, had just laid out an assortment of cold cuts, salads, and fresh corn rye bread on the dining room table. Sodas and an electric coffee percolator had been placed on the table as well.

"Misses Cavendish outdid herself today," Monsignor Norton said.

The priests sat across from one another — one on each of the long sides of the table. Then they said grace and began to dig into their lunch.

"Oh, by the way, Father, Deacon Fitzgibbon told me all about your little chat with Misses Fitzgibbon."

"Uh-oh. I mean, OH?" O'Connor knew that he'd been caught.

"Funny, I don't remember you saying that you were going to actually deny Misses Fitzgibbon her communion rites when we spoke."

"Oh…well…I think I did say so in a roundabout way, now that I re — "

"'Baloney,' Father." Norton lifted up a plate of *Schickhaus* bologna slices that he knew were O'Connor's favorite, poking some fun with his double entendre utterance.

The elderly priest took the dish, lifted some thin slices of the deli meat, and then set them down onto a slice of rye bread. "Well…I told her that she could still receive the sacrament from ye though. I told her that what I did, and what I said, did not apply for ye."

"Well they didn't ask for me to intervene for them, Father, but if they did, I would stick with your decision."

"Ye would?"

"Yes, I would, Father. I might disagree with you from time to time, but I respect your opinion and your years of wisdom. I know a forgiving soul like yourself would never administer a harsh penance without just cause."

"Ye do?"

"Oh, yes I do, Father. You see, I remember last year, when our parish adulteress, you know — Misses Malone — when she was going through her crisis…you were quite forgiving, in fact you were insistent about it!"

"Aye, I recall."

"Do you want to hear an odd coincidence?"

"How's that?"

"Misses Malone is the one who has been baking all of those delicious blueberry and apple pies that are being anonymously dropped off at the rectory every Saturday morning."

"Ye don't say." A sheepish, not so surprised look, crept across O'Connor's face.

"Yes, I do say, I do. So, you see, I know just how very forgiving you are, and how you would want for all of our parishioners to be treated the same. You know, *'you cannot play favorites with the people who fill the pews'* someone once said. Father, did you not know that it was Misses Malone who was baking all of those pies that we've been stuffing our faces with?"

Father O'Connor began to blush and wished to say nothing more on the subject, but he knew that he was cornered. *How did he ever find out that Misses Malone was baking those pies? It could be considered part of her penance. Perhaps, it's time to come clean.* "I knew. I figured that I'd just keep her busy baking so she'd have no time to be foolin' 'round with the married men of the parish, 'tis all."

O'Connor's response left Norton in wide-eyed astonishment. "Maybe you should have opened her a bakery."

"Aye."

A few bites and swallows of sandwiches later, Monsignor Norton spoke, "Oh — by the way, Father, I think that I better fill you in on some very bizarre behavior regarding a few of our high school students."

"Is that right, Father, and how is that?"

"Well, one of our unrulier cliques of students, Master Jason Nealon and his gang of friends, happened to drop by the rectory the other day and made a very odd request — they were looking for milkshake money." Monsignor Norton began to elaborate.

"Milkshake money?" O'Connor rolled his eyes, recalling the student of which Norton spoke and whom Sister Joseph

Eleanor, the high school principal, asked him to discipline a few days back. "What on earth for?"

"For beating up students who attend Saint Peter's Prep." Norton frowned and shook his head from side to side in a disapproving fashion. "Seems like they felt they were upholding the honor of Saint Aloysius by punching out the Prep kids. On top of that, they then thought that they should be rewarded for doing so, of all things. Of course, I told them that the Christian thing to do would be to *turn the other cheek,*' but then they told me something rather quite peculiar."

"Oh no…I mean, how's that?"

"They quoted scripture, the Old Testament in fact — I believe its *Exodus 21* to be precise. You know, *'an eye for an eye and tooth for a tooth'* and all of that sort of thing."

"Ye don't say."

"Yes, I do, I do say. I'll have to remind the good sisters to be less dramatic with the students in their Bible study classes. The students felt the scripture gave them the liberty for just hauling off and hitting any Prep student right in the nose."

"In the nose?"

"Oh yes, in the nose. You see, they claimed that because the nose is between the eyes and teeth, the scripture covered it. Remarkable deductive reasoning on the part of the students. …Don't you agree, Father?"

"Indeed, indeed," O'Connor tried to act surprised. "I certainly would not know how the *youngins* could be so misinterpretin' the scriptures."

"More 'baloney,' Father?" Monsignor Norton again dangled the plate of cold cuts in his hand.

"No more, 'bologna,' Father, I think I'm full of it,"

"What a shame. I thought we would have a delicious piece of Misses Malone's blueberry pie and then perhaps stroll on over to Lee's and wash it down with a nice *three-dollar* milkshake," he added, watching as Father O'Connor blushed even redder as he hung his head low. "Imagine, three dollars for a milkshake. Why, I bet the Jesuits are pricing the menu over at Lee's these days," the monsignor said.

Seconds later, Monsignor Norton concluded his sermon. "That *Tullamore Dew* bottle appears as if it will be collecting dust for a few more months, Father."

O'Connor just frowned, shaking his head from side to side in resentful agreement. "Aye," he muttered. Father O'Connor now had enough egg on his face to make an omelet.

Chapter Eleven

It was the early morning hours of the day following Angela Sanchez's abortion procedure...

Aubrey Fitzgibbon opened her eyes. Everything was a blur. *Where am I? What day is it? What time is it? What has happened?* Her fuzzy vision slowly came into focus. She identified the surroundings as that of her bedroom. Gradually, the memory of the day's events came back to her. She replayed those events — her past conscious hours — over again in her head. She recalled passing out on her feet during Angela Sanchez's abortion, and then finally coming to her senses in the recovery room of the abortion clinic. The doctors were forced to administer a mild sedative to Aubrey, in order to calm her nerves. They also reached out to her husband. Mike Fitzgibbon dropped everything at his law office and rushed over to the clinic. The doctors explained to him all that happened.

With the aid of an attendant, Mike escorted Aubrey out of the center and brought Angela along with them — the teen had been counting on a ride home from Aubrey. Mike switched into Aubrey's car, he would arrange to pick up his own car the next day. The drive from the clinic made for an uncomfortable ride — a church deacon transporting a teenager home after she just had an abortion. There were no words exchanged between the two. After dropping off Angela, Mike brought Aubrey home and put her to bed. Then he phoned Nikki Spencer to tell her the news — the planned *'girl's week'* would be put on hold. Nikki promised Mike that she would stop over the next day to keep an eye on Aubrey, so that he could go to work. Mike appreciated, and accepted, her offer.

Lying on her side and focusing her sights on one of the bedroom windows, Aubrey clutched her abdomen, thinking about the fetus growing inside of her. She could not shake free from thoughts of the lurid scene that she witnessed just hours before — the spectacle of Angela Sanchez's abortion. The sight of the being's face lying in the surgical tray, seemingly staring back at her, was indelibly imprinted in her memory. The Sanchez abortion would haunt Aubrey for weeks and months to come — she couldn't shake it. Aubrey felt that she played God by making the final decision to authorize the teen's abortion and terminate a life. In just a few short hours, Aubrey would have her own personal revelation — she was going to have a baby. She nixed the idea of having an abortion — it was her choice.

It was dark outside. The nightlight on the nightstand slightly illuminated the area in the vicinity of the bed. Aubrey pivoted her head on the pillow, checking the time on the clock sitting beside the nightlight. It was two-thirty in the morning. Aubrey slid a leg behind her and across the mattress top in search of Mike. He wasn't there. *Must be sleeping in the spare room so not to disturb me. The poor dear.* Aubrey should have been so lucky.

Mike Fitzgibbon's absence from his wife's side had nothing to do with his concern for her, and everything to do with his contempt for her. Upon their arrival home, Mike lifted Aubrey's *'girl's week'* suitcase from out of the car trunk and carried it up to the bedroom. Rather than rummaging through a set of bedroom drawers in search of a nightgown for Aubrey, Mike popped open her luggage to grab whatever nightgown that she packed for her trip. Instead of a nightgown, Mike found a nightmare. Lying on the very top of all the folded clothes was an information sheet from Doctor Thompson's office — the instructions and itinerary for Aubrey's then planned abortion. Aubrey had relocated the paperwork there from her pocketbook. The news knocked the wind out of Mike. He filled with rage. He wondered if her sickness resulted from actually being shook up over witnessing Angela Sanchez's abortion, or if, in fact, she had taken the abortion medicine, and that is what was making her sick. He wanted to shake his wife awake but resisted the urge.

Mike's anger soon melted into hurt — a very deep hurt beyond belief. His wife had betrayed his trust. It was the first time that he ever felt disgust for his wife. Aubrey could sense something was wrong between them the next day. She decided to light up his life with news of her pregnancy. When she told him, he let her have it with both barrels — excoriating Aubrey for dare considering an abortion and hiding that fact from him. Aubrey could tell the magic between them was gone. She felt cheap and dishonest. She had betrayed the good man whom she married — the man who so adored her. Aubrey feared that this would be one of those life changing events that could irrevocably wreck their marriage and permanently alter their relationship. One week, two weeks, a month — nothing got better. Mike felt nothing more towards his wife. He shared no joy in their expected blessed event. The Fitzgibbon children could sense something was wrong between their parents, but neither Mike nor Aubrey would let onto the kids just what.

Aubrey shared her plight with Nikki — the only one with whom she could find commiseration. She felt bad about weighing down her best friend with her burden. As her pregnancy progressed, Aubrey felt worse and worse, she wore it on her face and it showed in her physique — she looked sickly. She tired easy and was constantly exhausted. People took notice.

***

Aubrey Fitzgibbon wasn't alone in her depression, in the weeks that followed her abortion, Angela Sanchez slipped into a steadily worsening state of morose. She couldn't free herself from thinking about the child that she aborted. Angela became plagued by a case of the *"what ifs?" What if she had decided against the abortion? What if her child had lived?* She wondered about what her daughter might have become. She pondered the mother and daughter relationship they might have shared, but now would never know. Her only sounding board through all of the gloom was Aubrey, who despite her own problems, still made time for the teen and remained truly concerned about her condition. Aubrey and Angela saw a lot of each other. Aubrey made sure that the Family Planning Center's psychologist attended Angela as well. On top of all else, her mother's drug problem was adding to Angela's anxiety, and that was something that no one had control over. Angela wanted her mother out of her life in the worst way.

Angela could hardly wait for school to start in September, the change and diversion that she felt she needed. It so happened that her whacked out mother had blabbed about Angela's abortion to a not-too-closed-mouthed fellow druggie at her shooting gallery. *Loose Lips* then put the tale of woe out on the streets. Some of Angela's classmates at Dickinson High School found out about her ordeal and, kids being kids, they began to tease her profusely. She was embarrassed beyond belief, and it incurred another emotional setback for the teen. Unable to cope, she decided to take flight from her problems, never realizing that they would follow along with her — Angela ran away from home.

Angela's grandmother was brokenhearted, and Aubrey Fitzgibbon felt just as downhearted upon learning the news of Angela's flight. Aubrey felt a sense of guilt, feeling that her facilitating the abortion for the fragile girl was the cause of her running away. Even Angela's whacked out mother was shaken to the point of wanting to get sober. It was a tragedy.

To complicate the matter, a canister of sleeping pills was missing from the family medicine cabinet. Angela obviously had taken them with her. Everyone feared the worst but continued to hope and pray for the best.

Chapter Twelve

"Lift High the Cross," sang the Saint Aloysius church congregation. It was the recessional hymn of the Mass. Father O'Connor followed the altar servers in the procession out of the church.

O'Connor's baritone singing voice boomed out over the church's sound system, transmitted by the wireless microphone headset that he wore. His vocal rendition practically drowned out the choir and the organist, who were perched in the choir loft, opposite the altar end of the church. O'Connor exited through the front doors of the church, stepping onto the buildings front portico. He spryly pranced down the front steps; there he would stop to greet the congregants as they exited the Sunday ten-o'clock Mass and spewed onto West Side Avenue.

There was little time for O'Connor to enjoy his typical gabfest with the parishioners after the Mass — he was to be the guest speaker at the local Knights of Columbus council's brunch. The Knight's assembly hall was south of the church on West Side Avenue, at the southern end of Lincoln Park and across from the beginning of Harrison Avenue. He intended to hoof it over the four blocks once he changed out of his vestments. The September weekend marked the opening of the *NFL* season, so O'Connor knew that he would be keeping his routine short.

As he entered the Knight's council hall, O'Connor passed through the attendees, stopping to chit-chat with as many tables as he could. Slowly, he made his way towards the dais at the front of the room. He was trying to dodge as many of the hucksters pushing raffle ticket sales as he could. He noticed Deacon Fitzgibbon seated with his two children at a table alongside one of the walls. It struck O'Connor as odd that Aubrey was not there, then again, given that the topic of O'Connor's address would be abortion, he was a bit relieved that she wasn't.

The Grand Knight served as the master of ceremonies, and he dispensed with a short program before asking Father O'Connor to offer the benediction just prior to the brunch being served. The dais was served and ate first. O'Connor wolfed down his meal before being brought back up to the podium again to offer the keynote address. He was warmly received by the gathering — always a favorite among the community of Saint Aloysius parishioners, as well as the other parishes located in Jersey City, all of which comprised the majority of the Knight's council membership. As was his custom, O'Connor regaled the crowd with an assortment of jokes, loosening them up before broaching the more somber subject matter of his speech.

Segueing, O'Connor likened the raffle ticket hawkers at the brunch to a Las Vegas gambling casino, attempting to setup his final joke. "Ye know, there are some little-known facts about the Catholic Church in Las Vegas: There are many more churches in Las Vegas than there are Casinos. And, during Sunday services, some of the worshippers contribute casino chips instead of cash. Of course, they must be sorted into their respective casino chips by the archdiocese. Now, it comes to be, that a junior priest makes the rounds to all of the casinos, turning the chips into cash for the churches. And he, of course, is better known as the *Chip Monk.*" O'Connor's delivery made even the corniest jokes in his repertoire go over big.

O'Connor then launched into his ban-on-abortion rhetoric, saluting the Knights for their commitment and efforts to the anti-abortion cause. When he mentioned the Hudson Family Planning Center by name and singled out their misguided philosophy, he could see Deacon Fitzgibbon uncomfortably lowering his head. The Fitzgibbon children did likewise. Of course, as expected, O'Connor received a rousing ovation after his address. Then the crowd cried out for a tune, as O'Connor, for sure, knew that they would. Spying the church organist, Charles Baber, in the crowd, O'Connor asked him if he wouldn't mind accompanying him on the piano that was stationed alongside the wall beside the dais.

Baber obliged, taking a seat on the piano bench. "What'll be, Father 'O'?" he shouted back.

"I'll Take You Home Again, Kathleen, if you don't mind, *Maestro,"* O'Connor said. The room drew silent throughout the priest's moving performance. Hitting and holding the high notes of the song's coda brought the crowd to its feet, begging to hear more. *"The Town I Loved So Well,"* O'Connor directed to Baber — signaling him to play a moving Irish folk song about the town of Derry, Northern Island, which had been devastated in the rebellion against the British. There wasn't a dry eye in the hall when he finished, and he was rewarded for his effort with another thunderous standing ovation.

"Irish Lullaby," some in the crowd cried out, prompting O'Connor to sing what was considered his signature song.

But the priest's angina was kicking in, and he figured out a way to gracefully decline. "Come on now folks, this was a ten-dollar brunch and *Too-ra-loo-ra-loo-ral* is at least a fifty-dollar dinner song. 'Tis one that I only croon on special occasions. Now, be done with ye, and get on home to watch some football." O'Connor left the dais and kibitzed his way out of the hall, making his way back down West Side Avenue and returning to Saint Aloysius.

As he passed by the front of the church, he heard a woman's voice calling out to him in broken English. O'Connor turned around to see Angela Sanchez's grandmother, Maria Ramos, making her way towards him. The woman was in a glum disposition and her reddened, watery eyes indicated that she had been crying. She broke the news to O'Connor about her granddaughter's running away from home — he hadn't known. She pleaded with him to pray for her, and of course he told her that he would.

Then Misses Ramos grabbed O'Connor's hands and asked him for his help. *"Por favor,* Padre O'Connor, *por favor,"* she cried. Then, in a broken English which O'Connor understood, she asked if he would help her daughter Rosalita — who once, prompted by Cindy Stone, spit in the priest's face. Misses Ramos explained that Angela's running away had so devastated Rosalita, the woman now wanted to kick her drug habit and get herself straight. Her hope was that Angela might want to return home…if ever they could find her. Rosalita had a bed awaiting her at a much-touted rehabilitation and behavioral sciences hospital clinic in Florida. The clinic had a stunning success rate for its thirty-day program, but an unfortunately costly fee schedule that was out of the reach of Rosalita and Misses Ramos. She asked the priest for assistance, handing him a brochure they got from a doctor at the West Side Neighborhood Health Clinic.

O'Connor glanced over the brochure. He could almost still feel the stream of warm spit slowly dripping down his face that came courtesy of the woman whom he was now being asked to help. "I'll see what I can do, Senora. Stop by the rect'ry to see me on Wednesday."

Then Misses Ramos hit him up again, asking if he could help in finding them an apartment outside of the city housing project where they currently lived. She felt that drugs were too easy to access on the grounds of the projects, and if her daughter was ever able to kick her habit, she did not want her living in an environment where such easy access to drugs could provide a temptation. Again, O'Connor told her that he would see what he could do.

"Gracias, Padre." Misses Ramos departed with hope in her heart. O'Connor had a reputation for making the seemingly impossible a reality. A modern-day miracle worker.

O'Connor detoured his return to the rectory, instead, heading back into the church again. He strolled up one of the side aisles towards one of the smaller side altars. There he lit a candle in front of a statue of Jesus Christ revealing his Sacred Heart. O'Connor prayed to the Lord, asking to be shown a way that he could help Rosalita Sanchez — the woman who had spit in his face.

Chapter Thirteen

"Good to hear from you again, Doctor Thompson," Doctor Brian Friedman said, talking through the speaker mode of his office desk phone, so that he could use his hands to flip through the paperwork on his desk to which he would be referring. Friedman was Aubrey Fitzgibbon's internist and general practitioner; whom Aubrey's obstetrician asked to examine her. "She's certainly anemic. I've never seen a case this severe — her hemoglobin level is 8.2. That's bad enough on its own, but her hematocrit levels are below thirty percent, her ferritin levels are depleted, as is her serum iron, and she is deficient in folate and vitamin B12, to boot."

"I ran the same blood tests on her during the third week of August, and your numbers show that the condition is worsening. And, I prescribed her a hundred milligrams of iron per day. This is troublesome," Thompson advised.

Friedman flipped through a few pages of the laboratory analysis report on Aubrey's blood work, zeroing in on another of the test results. "Her reticulocyte count is below 80,000 milliliters — she's either slowly hemorrhaging somewhere, or her bone marrow is not producing enough red blood cells."

"I'm going to increase the dose of the iron supplement," Friedman alerted. "Is there anything else that you might advise?"

"Well…let's see how the increased dosage works — try doubling it. Confidentially, her heart and circulatory system are showing signs of stress. I'll be consulting a cardiologist. I'm going to be seeing Aubrey again next week, and if her system is still being strained, then we're both going to have to put our heads together and come up with a strategy,"

Friedman said. "In the meantime, let's make sure that she takes it slow and does nothing to exert herself."

"Agreed. Let's touch base after we both see her again," Doctor Thompson said.

"How's the baby doing?" Friedman asked.

"The baby's doing just fine. By the way, her ultrasound yesterday shows that it's a girl. The baby is okay — she's just sucking the life out of her mom."

Aubrey's appearance was indicative of everything her doctors had discussed. She was seventeen weeks pregnant. Her skin, lips, and nails were ashen. She was tired and weak and stricken with occasional dizzy spells that made her nauseous. She had trouble catching her breath, and she could detect her heart beating rapidly on occasion. On top of her infirmities, Aubrey was traumatized by the images that still haunted her after witnessing Angela Sanchez's abortion — images which she still could just not seem to shake.

Aubrey's husband and children were measuring her steady decline, living with it day by day. Aubrey had hardly ever been sick before. Her progressively worsening condition had them worried. If time heals all wounds, then when someone you were once head-over-heels in love with takes ill, the wounds heal even quicker. Despite his animus for Aubrey, still strong since learning of her attempted abortion, Mike Fitzgibbon emotionally melted, confronted with her worsening condition. His animosity fell victim to human emotion and sentiment. A good deacon, he put his faith into practice and forgave Aubrey for her deception. He had prayed on it and knew that God wanted him to be there for Aubrey. Mike Fitzgibbon also put up a good front for his children, but beneath the façade, he was deeply troubled by Aubrey's condition. Though he found comfort in his enchantment with Aubrey once again, he was scared to death that she was so ill.

***

"Good morning, Father Sean O'Connor," the class of first graders shouted at the tops of their lungs. The priest had just entered the schoolroom. The youngsters stood, then the boys bowed and the girls curtseyed — the polite manners instilled into all Saint Aloysius students by the Sisters of Charity. Father O'Connor and Monsignor Norton typically made impromptu visits to all of the grades in the grammar and high schools — mostly to the religious study classes.

"Good mornin'. Good mornin'. Good mornin' to you all, children," Father O'Connor greeted.

"We have been learning all about our religious Holy Days this week, Father O'Connor," Sister Marion Theresa, the religion class instructor told him. "We were just learning all about Easter."

"Ye don't say. Why, that is the most important day on the church calendar." O'Connor asked the class if anyone knew what happened on Easter.

A gazillion hands shot up into the air as each of the children vied to be called upon to answer his question first. Each child stretched up from their chairs, some kneeling upon the seats — all trying to help extend the length of their arms a bit higher and higher, practically pulling their feet out of their shoes, as if the one whose arm could reach the highest would be the one who would be called upon first. The hands began waving frantically about. O'Connor pointed to a small girl sitting in the middle of the class, prompting her to answer.

"Easter is when the Easter Bunny comes, and he leaves us candy baskets with chocolate and marshmallow chicks," the precious child answered.

"Well that certainly is so, but it's not quite the answer that I'd be lookin' for," O'Connor said, letting the tyke down gently. "Who else can tell us, what is Easter all about?"

This time O'Connor called upon a young lad from the back of the classroom. "It's when our moms and dads take us shopping for clothes and let us color Easter eggs."

O'Connor shook his head from side to side, looking over at the nun and rolling his eyes. "No, I'm afraid that's not quite the answer that I was looking for either. Who knows the answer? Who can tell us?"

Again, the hands shot skyward. This time, O'Connor picked a tiny young girl sitting in the front row. She promptly shouted out her answer. "Easter is when, Jesus Christ, our Lord and Savior, died for our sins, and then, and then — he came back to life three days later. And —"

"Right on the nose." Relieved, O'Connor continued, *"Whew.* Very good, Lass."

Then, the youngster spoke up again. Unbeknownst to anyone else, she had not finished giving her answer. "And then, Jesus came out of his cave. And then, he saw his shadow…and then, and then, there was six more weeks of the winter."

O'Connor's jaw dropped as his opened hand instinctively smacked his forehead, resting there while he shook his head furiously from side to side. *The little darlin' should have quit while she was ahead.* "I think, I'll be running along, I will." O'Connor turned and headed for the classroom door.

Sister Marion Theresa followed after him. "Are you leaving us so soon, Father O'Connor?"

"Pardon me, Sister, but to stay here any longer would be a test of me own faith," he whispered to her.

O'Connor headed back to the rectory — Maria Ramos was due to meet him there in a half an hour. He felt that through prayer he had been *shown a way* to help the family. When he arrived at his residence, he immediately went into the priest's office across from the parlor — on the other side of the first floor of the rectory. He picked up the parish checkbook from off of the desk that he and Monsignor Norton oft times shared in the office. He flipped through the pages, locating the sheet of the last check cut. He checked the balance — $25,541.24. *"Ouch!"* O'Connor mouthed aloud to himself. "This is gonna hurt." He flipped to the next to last page of checks, where he knew that Monsignor Norton had endorsed the blank checks on the page — resources for covering the payment of any parish emergencies that might occur in his absence. He grabbed a pen, then began writing out a ten-thousand dollar check to the name of the Florida rehabilitation and behavioral science center that was written on an index card which he had stashed away in his shirt pocket. It was the center where Rosalita Sanchez would be headed.

O'Connor thought to himself a minute, then he picked up the phone on the desk and called the Newark Archdiocese office, wanting to contact his friend, Archbishop Mario Scaponi. He planned to call in a chit with his lifelong friend by asking that the archdiocese cover the Sanchez rehabilitation bill for the parish. He knew that Monsignor Norton would hit the roof, otherwise. The Archbishop took his old childhood buddy's call right away. O'Connor mentioned that he wanted to come to Newark to see him about something — he did not want to explain the ten-thousand-dollar matter over the phone.

"You know, Sean, there is something that I have been meaning to talk to you about. I've been putting it off, but I am glad that you called," Scaponi said.

That comment troubled O'Connor — he sensed that it was possibly about a reassignment. *Time to be put out to pasture.* "What would ye be wantin' to see me now for?"

"I'd much prefer to see you in person, Sean. Besides, we have a lot of catching up to do. What do you say we kibitz over a game of golf? We haven't played in quite some time. I'll have the archdiocese office secretary check my schedule. Misses Harrison will fit it in, and then call you back to arrange a date. Give me a few weeks though — things are pretty busy here and I'll be heading away to a Catholic Bishop's Conference next week."

In person? For sure it's bad news — he's sending me off to the retirement home, he is. "That sounds good, Mario — I'll be waitin' to hear from Misses Harrison." O'Connor was a bit disappointed that the meeting would be a few weeks off. *I hope there aren't any large bills or expenses coming due for the parish in the interim.* He was not planning to tell Monsignor Norton about the check that he cut for Misses Sanchez's rehab, not until the parish was reimbursed by the archdiocese.

A short time later, Maria Ramos came by the rectory and Father O'Connor handed the check over to her. The grateful woman was overcome with emotion, crying hysterically and thanking the priest profusely. O'Connor told her that he was still working on trying to find an apartment outside of the housing projects where she, her daughter, and runaway granddaughter could relocate. He inquired about how much they could afford to pay in rent, so that he had some idea of what to be looking for. The rent they could afford didn't give O'Connor much to work with. He needed to find another ace in the hole, and it brought to mind another of his dear friends — Rabbi Martin Turner from Temple Beth-El of Jersey City.

Chapter Fourteen

A few days after cutting the check for Rosalita Sanchez's rehab, Father Sean O'Connor was hoofing it along West Side Avenue, paralleling Lincoln Park. He had just finished serving the nine o'clock morning Mass at Saint Aloysius. Arriving at the foot of Harrison Avenue, he crossed the street and trudged up the hilly block. Along the way, O'Connor passed by several apartment buildings that were owned by his friend, Rabbi Turner. Finally, he ascended to the top of the block and Kennedy Boulevard. Temple Beth-El sat at the boulevard's intersection with Harrison Avenue. Battling the pangs of angina, O'Connor took a breather, then marched up the steps of the synagogue and went inside. As he entered the foyer, he could hear the voice of Rabbi Turner, singing a canticle in Hebrew. It was just about at the end of the congregation's Morning Prayer and worship service.

O'Connor picked up a kippah, a customary religious skull cap, from out of a basket resting on a table in the foyer. Then he opened one of the many foyer doors leading into the worship hall. As he stepped inside, he fitted the kippah atop his head. He walked up the main aisle that divided two rows of pews and led up to the bihma, or front altar area. O'Connor quickly ducked into the next to last row of pews from the back. Rabbi Turner, leading the proclamation in song, noticed his friend's arrival. O'Connor planted his index finger on his chest, then he swung it back around, pointing it up at Rabbi Turner. He next tapped his four fingers in unison upon his thumb, up and down, several times. Rabbi Turner understood the pantomime — *you and I have to talk.*

Without missing a note or skipping a beat, the rabbi made the okay sign with his fingers and flashed it back in the direction of O'Connor. The congregation turned around to see whom Turner was signaling. Many did a double take, beholding the sight of a priest, wearing his collar and sporting a kippah, sitting in on their worship ceremony. Father O'Connor just smiled back politely. When the service concluded, Rabbi Turner announced his guest to the congregants. As they filed passed the priest on their way out of the temple, many of the worshippers acknowledged O'Connor with polite "Hellos," some sounding a bit bewildered.

"Don't' worry, I'm not convertin' at me age — I'm just here to see Rabbi Turner."

Some of the congregants kidded back and teased O'Connor, making light of the situation.

"If ye liked the *Ould* Testament, wait till you get a load of the 'New' one," O'Connor responded. A short while later, Rabbi Turner appeared, having changed out of his prayer shawl. He greeted his old friend with a giant bear hug, planting a kiss of respect on each of O'Connor's cheeks. "Father O,' a very longtime, no see."

The two religious figures' friendship was formed decades ago, borne out of calamities affecting both their houses of worship. When some row house fires displaced numerous Saint Aloysius Church parishioners while O'Connor was monsignor, Rabbi Turner offered them shelter in several of the vacant apartments in his buildings. Turner discounted the rents to further accommodate the families. A few years later, a fire in the Temple Beth-El basement kitchen spread out of control and destroyed much of the upstairs worship hall. Father O'Connor allowed the Rabbi's congregation to convert the school hall of the recently closed Saint Aloysius Academy into a temporary makeshift synagogue, until the repairs were completed to the Temple Beth-El building. It was a typical Jersey City story — neighbors looking out for neighbors.

Father O'Connor reciprocated Rabbi Turner's welcome, and then the two friends decided to go for lunch. They hopped into Rabbi Turner's Toyota Camry and drove to George's Fish Market on West Side Avenue, just across the street and down the block a short way from Lee's Luncheonette & Old Fashioned Soda Shoppe. They caught themselves up on the events of the many days that had passed since last they met, which was quite some time ago. Once they reached the fish market, O'Connor hopped out of the car and dashed inside to retrieve two lunch orders to go. This was a ritual between the men — they loved the delicious beer battered fresh cod fish and specially seasoned, crisp french-fries that were a staple lunch special at George's. The potatoes were fried in the same oil that the batter laden fish were cooked in, and the flavor was out of this world. Within a matter of minutes, O'Connor returned with two grease-streaked brown paper bags bellowing steam. The hot food flavored the air inside of the car, putting the two men's stomachs on alert as their digestive acids began to flow. A third bag that O'Connor toted carried two Cokes and the condiments for the meals.

Rabbi Turner continued down West Side Avenue for a few blocks, passing Saint Aloysius Church and turning into Lincoln Park. He continued driving halfway around a circle in the road that surrounded a magnificent fifty-foot tall park fountain — a gift from France to the city, dating back to when Frank Hague was mayor. The magnificent structure was a Jersey City landmark. Rabbi Turner pulled off one of the circle's spurs, drove several hundred feet more, and then pulled into the parking lot of the Casino in the Park — a restaurant and catering hall. They exited the parked car and fast paced it across the road to the park's huge lake, planting themselves on the same park bench that they had frequented for years. There, the pair shared many a lunch over time, typically accompanied by deep conversations about their different faiths. They had the gift of pleasant, late September weather, as the days of summer had finally dwindled down.

The two enjoyed a long and lengthy laugh, reminiscing about the time when O'Connor, at the last minute, convinced the rabbi to bailout the parish children's Christmas party by playing Santa Claus — the parishioner who was supposed to play Kris Kringle suddenly fell ill. With his rotund body frame, Turner was the logical perfect fill in — he didn't even need a pillow.

"I swear, Rabbi Turner, 'tis a scene that I will never forget — and I'll always bust me gut a laughin' when I recall ye a hollerin' *'Oy vey! Oy vey! Oy vey!'*" O'Connor held his sides as he was overcome by a fit of hysterical laughter.

Ducks patrolling in the lake took notice of O'Connor, arching their necks around to peer up at the laughing priest as they paddled by him.

The rabbi recalled the scene and chimed in with a deep belly laugh that reverberated around the area of the lake where they sat. Then Turner tried explaining his actions, as he always attempted to do each time the duo shared the retelling of the priceless moment in time. "I was so nervous, I forgot my lines: *'Ho! Ho! Ho!'* So, I had to adlib."

The two wiped happy tears from their eyes and finished off the fish and chips. Soon, it was time to get down to business, and Rabbi Turner asked his friend what had prompted his visit. Father O'Connor told the rabbi about the circumstances concerning Maria Ramos and Rosalita and Angela Sanchez — leading into their need for a living quarters outside of the housing projects. A new place for their family to live, Father O'Connor explained, would help give them a fresh start. He also told Turner about Angela running away from home, and then he asked the rabbi to remember her in his prayers, which Turner said he would.

"Consider it done, Father O'. Whatever rent they can afford, consider it done. God has led them to our doorsteps. Another O'Connor miracle, like in the old days."

O'Connor thanked his friend profusely as they concluded their lunch meeting. They tossed the empty, grease-streaked, brown paper bags and empty Coke bottles into a nearby trash receptacle. O'Connor told the rabbi that he would walk back to the rectory to work off the fish and chips. Then they warmly embraced each other again and headed off in separate directions.

A few paces into the trek back towards his car, Rabbi Turner turned around and called back out to his friend, "Father O,' I'll keep an extra apartment reserved…just in case."

"Just in case o' what?" a confused Father O'Connor called back.

"Just in case Monsignor Norton decides to put your rear end out onto the street when he finds out that you cut that ten-thousand dollar check for Misses Sanchez's rehab."

The two friends laughed aloud, still walking away from one another.

O'Connor couldn't let the rabbi top his wit. "In return, how 'bout I send the Temple over some of the extra statues from the church basement?"

The two men roared again with laughter as they departed from the park and each other.

Chapter Fifteen

There was a chill in the autumn air as Father O'Connor briskly treaded along the path to the rectory, blowing warm breath into his cupped hands. He had just finished serving the weekly seven o'clock morning Mass and was headed back to the residency for a hot cup of tea and a light breakfast. He retreated to the dining room where Monsignor Norton was finishing his breakfast and tightening up notes on his sermon for the nine o'clock morning Mass. Misses Cavendish handed O'Connor a piping hot cup of tea and took his breakfast order — an English muffin with butter and strawberry preserves.

"'Tis a cold mornin' out there, Father Norton," O'Connor said.

"Indeed, it is," the monsignor replied. "And it's probably going to be a lot chillier in here today — I've decided to have the rectory's boiler and water heater replaced, before the more frigid weather of the season really sets in. So that we don't have to go through some of those heatless nights again like last year. I was downstairs before, and some of those boiler pipes are starting to leak again. Misses Cavendish will be calling the plumber the first thing this morning."

A boiler and water heater? That'll cost a pretty penny. O'Connor gulped down some saliva, worrying that he would no longer be able to keep the monsignor from finding out about the ten-thousand dollar check that he cut. "Why be wastin' that kind of money — just have Mister Johnson take care of it." He was referring to Arnold Johnson, the parish and school's custodian, janitor, handyman and all else. "Besides, that'll cost ye an arm and a leg. It's best that ye save the money for a rainy day."

"I thought about it — that's exactly what I did last year. The checking account is pretty flush right now, so I'm going to replace those units while we can. I refuse to spend another winter's night sleeping on the den floor in front of the hearth. …Besides, Mister Johnson is just like every other parish handyman, you know — *jack of all trades and master of none.* No siree! This time, I'm gonna nip it in the bud. You never know what tomorrow may bring."

"No, ye certainly don't know what tomorrow may bring." O'Connor continued to struggle for a solution to his dilemma.

Monsignor Norton shortly left for the church, with ample time to prepare for his Mass.

Father O'Connor then sprang into action. "Misses Cavendish, hold up on callin' any plumber. Where is that *ould* toolkit of mine that I used to keep about the rectory?"

Oh Lord, no! Misses Cavendish thought. "I believe it's in one of the storage cabinets in the basement. But Father, you are surely not going to be tampering with anything down there, are you?"

"Sometimes, ye gotta just take charge." O'Connor headed down the basement stairs. "All I need to do is just tighten a few of the joints on those leaky pipes, 'tis all. The Lord will bless those who help themselves."

"But Father, don't you remember when you were monsignor here, and you tried to fix that leaking pipe in the church? You flooded the whole darn basement. Please, let me call the plumber," she said, calling down the staircase.

"Do nothing of the sort, Misses Cavendish, O'Connor is in charge." The priest's voice was muffled by the environs of the basement.

Misses Cavendish heard an assortment of creaks and clanks — cabinet doors being opened and closed. Then an enormous metal clanging — the toolkit emptying out on the concrete basement floor. She then heard several thunderous bangs and clangs, practically shaking the rectory. Misses

Cavendish brought her hands up to cover her ears. Then there was an enormous creaking sound interspersed with the resonances of Father O'Connor's grunting. That was followed by a colossal crashing sound, almost as if someone had dropped a drawer full of silverware on a kitchen floor. This time, the rectory did in fact shake. The crash was followed promptly by a gushing sound — like a torrent of water pouring over a waterfall.

"Mother Machree!" O'Connor yelled.

"Father O'Connor, are you all right?"

The gushing noise was now more profound. Then came the sound of footsteps plodding up the cellar stairs.

Squish. Thud. Squish. Thud. Squish. Thud.

Father O'Connor appeared at the top of the stairs, soaked to the bone and dripping wet — as if he just dove into a swimming pool with his clothes on. Every step he took squeezed more liquid out of his waterlogged loafers, oozing it onto the floor of the landing. Then Father O'Connor began to shiver.

"Father O'Connor!" Misses Cavendish's mouth hung wide open — she covered it with her hand. Then she headed for the basement stairs to assess the damage below.

O'Connor grabbed her by the arm. "Misses Cavendish, 'tis not fit for man nor beast down there. Ye had better page Mister Johnson — have him go down there."

The basement filled with water — a slew of broken pipes gushing water forth like geysers. Father O'Connor knew the gig was up — this would cost plenty to fix. He prayed quietly to God for finding a way that he would be able explain it all to Monsignor Norton, including the ten-thousand dollar check for Rosalita Sanchez's rehab.

*   *   *

Mike Fitzgibbon sat stone faced, riveted to what Doctor Friedman and Doctor Thompson were telling him as he sat in the latter's office. Aubrey was being attended to by a medical technician and a nurse, finishing up some testing in one of the examining rooms of the office suite that was located in the Medical Arts Building of the Jersey City Medical Center complex. The doctors ran down a litany of symptoms that their treatments, so far, had not helped. Her hemoglobin was still depleted and they were unable to locate any internal bleeding. Every category of Aubrey's blood tests continued to worsen. Her pattern of heart irregularities led the doctors to consult a cardiologist.

All odds were that the baby living inside of Aubrey was driving her anemia. "Let me be blunt, Mike," Doctor Thompson said. "Aubrey is going to have to be confined to bed. And we're putting her on oxygen — that will help to oxygenize her blood. The cardiologist is extremely concerned that her heart is being overtaxed. The rapid heartbeat and high blood pressure hasn't dropped in weeks — it's too much for the heart to take. We're limited to what medicines we can administer because of the pregnancy."

Doctor Friedman then interrupted. "Mike, we haven't addressed this to Aubrey yet, but you need to know — in order to prepare yourself. If the bed rest and the oxygen, and some of these other measures that we're going to prescribe don't work, then we're going to have to recommend — what I'm trying to say is — you see, if these symptoms persist — what we will have —"

"Spit it out, Doc," Mike said. He could tell the doctor was beating about the bush.

Friedman looked over to Thompson, who frowned while nodding his head up and down. He signaled for Friedman to continue. Friedman took a deep breath. "Mike if this doesn't work, we are going to recommend terminating the pregnancy."

The words broadsided Mike like a freight train, knocking the wind out of him again. He sat there in silence for a few seconds and took it all in, unable to respond.

"Given your position in the church, we thought it best to let you know. We can't let this fester, or else, we may come to a point in time when either the stress of the birth or an abortion procedure could be fatal. We need to act before her poor health prohibits us from using the procedure."

"The church has exemptions for abortions that are necessary for preserving the life of the mother, doesn't it, Mike?" Thompson asked.

Mike collected himself. He wasn't happy with the options. *The principle of double effect.*

"Church protocols are the least of my worries at this point — do whatever you must to save my wife." His decision overwhelmed him with guilt, but Aubrey was the love of his life whom he now placed first. The predicament confronted him with a crisis in his faith.

A moment later, Aubrey entered the office assisted by the nurse. She was twenty weeks pregnant. From the looks on the faces of the doctors and her husband, Aubrey could sense that something was far worse off than what they were telling her. She confronted them; but they lied better than her suspicions. Aubrey attributed her misgivings to paranoia. They told her about the new routine — confined to bed and twenty-four-seven oxygen. She was frightened. They also arranged for having the next round of blood to be extracted from her at home.

When she arrived home, she could read the fear in the faces of her children. Justin and Tracy watched as their once spry mom was carried in on an ambulance stretcher and taken up to her bedroom. Tracy lost it and ran to her room for a quiet cry. Justin buried his face in the parlor couch and began reciting prayers. The ambulance technicians assisted Aubrey into bed, then setup the oxygen and instructed Mike on its usage. They left him with extra canisters and handed him a business card with a phone number to call for replenishments.

Aubrey decided to position herself sitting up in the bed, with several bedroom pillows propping her up from behind. She adjusted the oxygen tank's nasal cannula around her ears, and then repositioned the air prongs that were in her nostrils. She picked up the TV remote from the bedside nightstand and began channel surfing — anything to distract her from thinking about her ordeal. Mike entered the room and placed a jug of ice water on the nightstand next to Aubrey's bed. He asked her if she wanted anything else. She told him "no." He left to fill the children in on their mother's new routine.

When Mike left the room, Aubrey picked up her cellphone and called Nikki — her great comforter. The two friends spoke for about an hour. They cried, had a few laughs, and discussed Aubrey's condition. As usual, Aubrey felt immeasurably better after her chat with her best friend. Nikki promised that she would be visiting Aubrey quite often, for as long as she would be laid up. After their conversation concluded, Aubrey slid her head back onto the pillows and closed her eyes, contemplating how saintly a friend she had in Nikki, which triggered tears of discomfort — feeling that, perhaps, she didn't deserve such a loyal friend.

***

Ahhhh Cheww! Father O'Connor's sneeze rocked the den of the rectory. Adorned in a tightly bound terrycloth bathrobe with towels stuffed in its V-neck opening like a scarf, O'Connor sat in his favorite easy chair. The chair had been repositioned directly in front of the blazing fire in the room's hearth. He was recovering from his plumbing job.

"Here you go, Father," Monsignor Norton said, entering the den and handing O'Connor a hot cup of tea that Misses Cavendish prepared.

"Did ye spike it with the creature?" the seasoned priest asked, sipping some down.

"I sure did — and that creature be named *Johnnie Walker.*"

O'Connor opened his mouth and let the libation trickle back into the teacup. "Egads! *Johnnie Walker?* Father Norton, have ye gone mad — that's a *Scotch* whiskey!"

"Consider it your penance for all that's gone on today."

"I'd rather be drinking water. And with a good bottle of Irish whiskey — *Tullamore Dew,* no less — gatherin' dust in the kitchen cubby. I feel like a traitor to me own kind."

"Well, I can get you that glass of water." Norton motioned to grab the teacup away from the senior priest.

O'Connor pulled the cup away from Norton. "No-no. That's all right, I'll take me penance like a man, I will,"

"And, after that little scheme of yours that you pulled today, they're going to need an archeological dig team to retrieve that *Tullamore Dew* from all of the dust that will be collecting upon it. Do you mind telling me what you were thinking in writing out a ten-thousand dollar check for a parishioner's drug rehab? What if everyone in the parish started lining up at the rectory door for ten-thousand-dollar checks?"

"'Twas for an emergency, I assure ye."

"Why couldn't you have just asked Misses Malone to bake you some extra pies and then organized a cake sale to raise the money?"

"She couldn't bake that many pies."

"Your friend the Archbishop will have your hide when he finds out."

"I'll be okay. It's you that I'm worried about. Ye see, I cut one of the checks from the back of the ledger — it's got yer signature on it."

Norton did a double take.

"Don't worry, I already have a plan to square it away with the Archbishop. He owes me a few favors."

"A few favors? I hope he has a sense of humor. And cutting the check on behalf of Misses Sanchez, no less — the woman who spit in your face. What happened to your Old Testament theory of an *'eye for an eye and a tooth for a tooth'* that you were preaching to the high school students who were punching out the Saint Peter's Prep kids — pretending that they were holding up the honor of our school? "

"Some bright young monsignor enlightened me to the wisdom of the New Testament teaching of *'turnin' the other cheek,'*".

"Ohhh!" Norton chuckled at O'Connor's reasoning. "So, now you're going to turn all of this around and dump it on me? ...Too bad your sudden affinity for the New Testament didn't kick in earlier this morning — like when you were in the basement giving your Old Testament rendition of *Noah and the Flood.* All that you were missing was an ark and several pairs of animals. You certainly had enough water. ...Too bad you're a bit rusty on your Moses — we sure could have used a parting of the seas while we waited for the plumbers."

O'Connor sheepishly hung his head, staring into his teacup. "I'm not quite the handyman that I used to be."

Norton did another double take.

"Monsignor Norton," a raspy voice from outside of the room called. Then a burly man garbed in work coveralls entered the den. A Brophy's Plumbing insignia was emblazoned on the vest of the work outfit. The man had responded to Misses Cavendish's call earlier in the morning, after Father O'Connor burst the pipes. The plumbing company replaced the pipes, along with the boiler and water heater as well. He handed Norton a slip of paper with the same Brophy's Plumbing insignia on its header. "Here's the bill, Monsignor — Mister Brophy discounted it because of the church."

"Be sure and thank him for me," Norton said, glancing down at the bill and then letting loose with a shrill whistle. "Hope your boss makes allowances for installment payments."

"I'm sure it'll be okay. Goodnight, now," he bid to the priests, exiting the den.

"Goodnight. Misses Cavendish will let you out. Thanks again for responding so promptly."

"Mind if I take a gander?" O'Connor asked Norton, holding his hand out for the bill.

Monsignor Norton handed it to him.

Father O'Connor looked it over, letting loose another equally shrill whistle. "I think ye best be lettin' me have another shot of penance, Father Norton. That plumbin' bill is enough to have the creature workin' overtime tonight."

"I think that I'll be pouring myself a shot of penance and joining you." Norton took the teacup from O'Connor and exiting the den.

Father O'Connor let out with another *Ahhhh Cheww* as Norton left.

Chapter Sixteen

Monsignor Norton and Deacon Mike Fitzgibbon carefully draped their vestments over hangers and returned them to the cedar closet in the church sacristy. The duo just served the nine o'clock weekday morning Mass. Mike Fitzgibbon was practically at a breaking point — Aubrey's condition was bearing down on him. Doctor Thompson and Doctor Friedman continued their twice weekly examinations of Aubrey at the Fitzgibbon home. She was now twenty-two weeks pregnant. They took more blood samples and continued talking to Mike outside of Aubrey's presence, telling him what they were going to tell his wife — they were recommending that she terminate the pregnancy. Because they knew that Mike was a deacon and a devout Catholic they were giving him the heads up.

Mike was now saddled with the unpleasant responsibility of convincing Aubrey to abort a baby she was committed to having. He wanted to line up as many ducks in a row that he could, in order to convince his wife to change her mind. A dispensation from the church, granting her indulgence for the procedure, was one of those ducks that he hoped to line up. Mike planned on confronting Aubrey with a powerful, high pressured sales pitch, once he resolved the matter regarding their faith.

"Do you have a moment, Monsignor?" Mike asked.

"Always, Mike," Norton said.

Mike filled Norton in on what was happening with Aubrey. He didn't let on about her earlier attempt to abort the baby she now carried — not wanting to needlessly embarrass his wife or complicate the matter anymore than it was already. The news shocked Norton; he was genuinely upset.

"Do you think she could be granted a dispensation from the church to end the pregnancy?"

Monsignor Norton thought for a second, then he answered Mike, looking him straight in the eyes. "Only the Archbishop can authorize a dispensation in such a matter. You'll need a strong written statement from the doctors. I'll have to write the request for you as the pastor — the Archbishop would not consider it otherwise. ...I'm so sorry that it's come down to this."

"Thank you, Monsignor. I'm sorry, myself, that it has come down to this."

"You know, Father O'Connor and Archbishop Scaponi have been best of friends since childhood — it might not be a bad idea to have him chime in on this."

Mike Fitzgibbon flared red. "Absolutely not! I would appreciate it if you kept this matter between you and me. I don't want Father O'Connor's nose in mine or Aubrey's business."

"Wow, I never realized that things have gotten so ugly between you and him. I thought — "

"Monsignor, what he did in terminating Aubrey's Holy Communion rite was overkill. He should have spoken to me first — given my position here. She was hurt, really hurt, by what he did — you have no idea how terrible she still feels."

Monsignor Norton tried to see if he could smooth things over between the deacon and O'Connor, but Mike stiffened his spine — he wanted no involvement of Father O'Connor in anything that concerned him or his family.

Then Mike let Monsignor Norton in on another decision that he was contemplating. "I'm thinking about taking a leave of absence from my vocation here. I'm starting to have doubts about my commitment to my faith."

"Mike, you're upset and under a lot of pressure — don't be making rash decisions under the strain. You're rushing to judgment."

"No, Monsignor, this has been a longtime coming."

Norton could see it in the deacon's eyes — the man wasn't sure of himself anymore.

***

With October past and Thanksgiving closing in, the trees that lined the fairways of the Bellville Golf Course in Essex County, New Jersey were nearly void of leaves. Some of the fallen leaves spotted sections of the course here and there. Across this landscape, two friends played a round of golf, sharing plenty of laughs along the way — as giddy as they once were in their high school and college days. They felt spry and young again, forgetting, for a while, the outside world and all the problems that it brought. Father O'Connor and Archbishop Scaponi regaled themselves with tales from their youth, recalling old friends and incidents indelibly seared in their minds and hearts. The golf match that they were playing was merely an excuse for their getting together to reminisce about *the good ol' days.*

Sinking a twenty-foot putt on the ninth hole, Father O'Connor clenched his hand into a fist and pumped it skyward, then he praised the Lord. Archbishop Scaponi dipped down and retrieved his rival's golf ball from the cup and tossed it back to him, then he replanted the flagstick.

"You're on fire, Sean," Scaponi said, as the two men ambled off the green towards their cart. They were a rare twosome playing, extended the courtesy of not teaming up with another pair of golfers because the course wasn't crowded this day.

"The saints are with me today, Mario." O'Connor said.

The men hopped into their cart, then Scaponi drove along the stone golf path that wound around the holes and layout of the course. He stopped at a snack shack that was tucked away behind some trees just before the 10th hole and which was aptly named, *The 9 ½th Hole.*

"How bad of a shellacking am I taking?" Scaponi asked.

"I've got ye by four strokes, so far, me friend."

"Looks like lunch is on me," Scaponi muttered, hopping out of the cart and heading towards the eatery. "Dog and a beer?"

"A dog and a beer 'll do just fine."

Moments later, Archbishop Scaponi returned carrying a cardboard tray holding two footlong grilled hotdogs with the works piled up a half inch deep upon them. In his other hand he clutched two frosty cold bottles of Coors Light beer, freshly drawn from a bucket of ice. Sitting back in the cart and resting the tray of hot dogs on the cart's dashboard, Scaponi handed O'Connor a beer. "So, what was it that you wanted to see me about, Sean?" Scaponi asked.

"Mario, I need a favor for me parish." O'Connor then went on explaining the entire matter concerning Rosalita Sanchez and his giving her parish funds to pay for her rehabilitation.

"Ten thousand dollars? Sean, have you lost your mind? What did Monsignor Norton say?"

O'Connor scrambled for words in his mind, articulating, what he felt, was a plausible alibi. He awkwardly tried to explain his reasoning for committing the money to Misses Sanchez, and how he prayed for guidance on the matter. He also explained how Monsignor Norton was none too pleased about what he'd done but supported his decision anyway. "That's me tale of woe, Mario. Please find it in yer heart to help cover the debt for the parish."

"For the sake of our friendship, I'll cover it. That makes for one heck of a month Saint Aloysius Parish has had. I've seen the last Archdioceses balance sheet — Monsignor Norton racked up a more than ten grand plumbing bill."

"Now, Mario, ye know how poorly put together was all of that plumbing in the rectory — Monsignor Norton had no choice in the matter."

Why not just use the parish maintenance staff to fix things like that? That's something they could handle."

131

"Nah. Ye know how parish maintenance men are — *jack of all trades and the master of none.* I betcha that the root of that very plumbing problem could be traced right back to a less than competent maintenance man," he added, crossing his fingers. He quickly meditated — *Lord, forgive me for this little white lie.*

"You know, Sean, I should not be sharing this with you, without first telling Monsignor Norton, but since you were once monsignor there, I guess, I will — the Archdiocese Council may be recommending to close Saint Aloysius High School next year. They are trying to consolidate schools throughout the archdiocese in order to save some money, and the high school's enrollment has been declining the past few years. Saint Peter's Prep seems to be the school of choice for young people. It seems that not so many kids want to go to Saint Al's."

"Egad! The high school? ...Surely, there's something that can be done. We can't let the Jesuits have a monopoly on educating Catholic kids in Jersey City."

"I'm afraid that resources are scarce, my friend. I knew that you would take this hard — you did so much in building up the school back when you were the pastor there. Unfortunately, Sean, we are in a bit of a spell where people aren't practicing their faith much anymore. The country is in as much of a decline."

"Aye," O'Connor agreed. "'Tis a sad state of affairs that our country is in, indeed."

"Just a cycle, Sean. We've been through a malaise like this before. Whenever our churches are strong so is our country strong. It's been that way since time immemorial. The church is the moral compass that serves as the fabric of society. People will turn back to the church again one day, and when they do, America will be all the stronger for it."

"I suppose yer right. I only hope it happens sooner rather than later."

"Until then, the church must do what it can to get by. We might not be able to afford so many Catholic schools for so few students. So, the kids in your school will be shipped over to some other archdiocese high school or follow the trend and go to Saint Peter's. Besides, what do you have against the Jesuits educating our youth?"

"Ahh, the Jesuits are nothin' more than an elaborate order of priests known for their innate ability to found colleges with great basketball teams, 'tis all that they are. They have a certain air about them, they do."

Archbishop Scaponi did a double take and chuckled at his friend's remark, then he bit into his hotdog again. A slug of beer later, he decided it was time to broach the tender subject that he told O'Connor he wanted to speak to him about in person. "Sean, I've got a bit of a problem that I need your help on. You know, we finally have a tremendous class of young priests who will be ordained at the beginning of the year — and there are just so few places open in our archdiocese for assignments. We need to make room for them in our churches or chance losing them to another archdiocese."

O'Connor took a dry gulp of air, then washed it away with a swig of beer. He didn't like the sound of what he was hearing. "Ahem," was all he muttered as Scaponi spoke, anxious for him to get to his point.

"Sean, I'll be frank — we need to free some room up at Saint Aloysius for one of our new priests."

"Now, Mario, ye can't be thinkin' of replacin' Monsignor Norton over that plumbing bill," O'Connor said, trying to lighten the mood. He knew his friend was offering him a save face, Scaponi did not want to force O'Connor to the shore retirement home for priests — he was hoping that he would volunteer to go.

Scaponi rolled his eyes at O'Connor's comic relief, trusting that O'Connor wasn't serious. "No, I'm not thinking of replacing Monsignor Norton. My friend, I need to make room for a new priest in the archdiocese — you know the score. If you tell me that you would like to stay on at Saint Aloysius…then for the sake of our dear friendship, I'll leave you be. But I'm asking for your help and understanding on this one. I need to know if I can free up room in Saint Aloysius before February, or else risk losing a new priest to another archdiocese."

O'Connor weighed the bind his friend was in, and the gift that Scaponi had already given him some years ago, by allowing O'Connor to go back to serve at Saint Aloysius. Scaponi stepped up for O'Connor big time then. "What if the Jersey City Saint Patrick's Day Parade Committee had me in mind for *Irishman of the Year* next year?" O'Connor was trying to buy some more time before accepting his fate.

"I know everyone on that parade committee, I don't think that will happen."

"What if I bribed them?"

"I've got a bigger wallet than you."

"Yer not just sayin' this and pullin' me leg 'cause I'm beatin' ye on the front nine, and ye now want me distracted before we play the back nine — are ye?"

Scaponi giggled, now knowing for sure that O'Connor was just playing with him. "No, Sean — I can whoop you on the back nine without resorting to any distractions."

There was silence for a few seconds as the pair of seasoned priests contemplated what they knew had to be done. O'Connor would make it easy for his friend. "Would we still be enjoying' our rounds of golf, at least every now and then, even if I were to retire?"

"Religiously. I wouldn't miss these classic outings for the world — I recapture my sanity and youth when we pal around out here."

"Well…then I guess I'll be a puttin' in me papers, and lettin' one of them young whippersnappers have the same shot that I once had in comin' to Saint Al's." O'Connor then made a stipulation. "But not a word about this to Monsignor Norton or anyone else at Saint Aloysius — I'll break the news to them about me retirin' as I see fit."

"Agreed. You are a true friend, Sean O'Connor — I don't think I could ever repay you for this."

A few seconds of silence followed. O'Connor was fast thinking — he couldn't leave *'I don't think I could ever repay you for this'* hanging out there unanswered. "Ye know, me *ould* friend, there is just one last favor that ye might consider doin' for me, before I leave dear *ould* Saint Al's."

Here it comes. I sure did put my foot in my mouth. Scaponi had no choice, he was a sucker for an old friend. "If I can help with something, I will."

O'Connor was thinking of Monsignor Norton's phone conversation that he overheard earlier that morning, while O'Connor passed through the foyer outside the office of the rectory. Norton was lamenting to his sister about his inability to get permission to continue his studies in pursuit of his doctorate — a lifelong ambition. He confided to her that he was terribly depressed. Around the parish, Norton always put up a good front — no one truly knew how down in the dumps he really was over his disappointment.

"Mario, I know that this is a tall order, me friend. But, I'm askin' that ye do me this one last favor…and then we're square. I would like fer ye to grant Monsignor Norton that sabbatical he's been askin' for in order that he'd be able to get his doctorate."

O'Connor had just put his friend the Archbishop over a barrel. Scaponi tried to talk O'Connor out of his request, but abruptly halted the attempt when O'Connor hinted that maybe he should not consider his retirement just yet. "Well…I guess we can work that out — it'll make room for promoting another well deserving priest to a parish pastor, and that will free up yet another spot for a new priest. You can let

Monsignor Norton know — tell him that it's your early Christmas present."

"No. No. I don't want him to know that I had anything to do with this, lest he won't take it. I tried on many an occasion to talk him into lettin' me bring the matter to ye — but he begged me not to. He's a very proud priest, Monsignor Norton is." O'Connor thought to himself a moment. "Ye know, on second thought — that could really save me a few bucks in shopping for a Christmas present for him this year. Can't ye just wait a bit and then tell him yerself around Christmas time? That's it. Just wait until Christmas, and then let him know that it was all me own doin'.'"

Scaponi just shook his head from side to side. The priests finished their lunch and resumed their round of golf. Somewhere along the back nine, the masterful O'Connor cashed in another favor for his early retirement — the Archbishop's commitment for a writ of absolution for Angela Sanchez, otherwise the poor girl would face dire church consequences for her decision to have an abortion. O'Connor made his case for Angela, and Scaponi agreed that he would grant her absolution if she was repentant when, and if, she returned home.

The golf game concluded with O'Connor edging out Scaponi by two strokes. The gleeful victor gently rubbed the victory into his friend as they retreated to the parking lot. Scaponi invited O'Connor to have dinner with him back at Saint Michael's Cathedral in Newark. O'Connor declined, informing Scaponi about his other dear friend, Sal Panetta, whom he had promised to visit later. O'Connor had been making frequent visits to the Panetta house to administer his friend Holy Communion, while the rest of the family kept a round the clock deathwatch on their dearly beloved.

Before getting into their respective cars the friends huddled together in the parking lot.

"Was good to see ye again, Mario. I look forward to the next time."

"Not as much as me — the next time, I'll beat you," Scaponi retorted. "By the way, Sean, please extend my special thanks to that Mister Ford. He came through again for the diocese Thanksgiving food pantry drive — donated and raised more than ten-thousand dollars' worth of food for some very needy families."

"I certainly will." O'Connor solicited the donation on behalf of the Archbishop's annual appeal. Ed Ford was the proprietor of Dohoney's Tavern which was located on West Side Avenue, within a few short blocks from Saint Aloysius Church. "The 'Faa' has a very big heart," O'Connor further commented, referring to Mister Ford by his nickname. "He's a good soul."

"Indeed, he is," Scaponi said. "Maybe you should have hit him up for the plumbing bill," he teased.

The two friends laughed.

"Seriously, the next time I'm up your way, I'd like for you to take me over to Dohoney's to meet Mister Ford, so that I can thank him in person."

"For sure I will, and believe you me, it's an introduction that ye'll never forget."

Instinctively, O'Connor and Scaponi extended their hands to each other. It was then Scaponi looked deep into his friend's face, taking account of all the years that had added up — measured by the lines and creases. Despite the ageless spirit of the friend whom he had just shared a round of golf with, Scaponi also noted the slower and unsteady gate to O'Connor's walk, and his occasional gasps to catch a breath of air. He knew that he had made the right decision to retire the priest.

The handshake broke apart, but before O'Connor began his retreat back towards his car, Scaponi had something else on his mind. "By the way, Sean, have you been in touch with your old army buddies?"

"We stay in touch, but we haven't gotten together since dear old John Santoro passed. The last planned get-together that we had was the one 'round Christmas time, years ago — the time when I introduced you to the gang. Me Lord…that was almost twenty years ago. Could that much time have gone by?"

Scaponi recalled the gathering that he attended during the Christmas holiday reunion. He was mindful of how being around his army buddies seemed to make O'Connor feel and seem much younger than he was. His reason for bringing up *O'Connor's Miracles* was to see if he could prompt O'Connor to get the gang of friends together once again. It might be just the medicine his old friend needed — the proverbial sight for sore eyes. "You guys seem way overdue for another reunion."

"Yer right, but that'll have to wait till after the New Year. Too much stuff on me plate right now."

"Well…think about it, Sean. Now I better be getting along before you start squeezing another few favors out of me."

The two men laughed aloud.

Later, driving back to Saint Michael's Cathedral, Scaponi laughed some more — thinking about all of the favors that O'Connor lifted from him that very day. *O'Connor miracles.* He was more than happy to help out his friend.

Chapter Seventeen

Alea iacta est — the die is cast. Her doctors finally told Aubrey Fitzgibbon to terminate her pregnancy or risk losing her life. She was twenty-three and a half weeks pregnant and she looked like death warmed over. None of the medical protocols improved her condition. Mike Fitzgibbon sympathized with Aubrey over the doctor's prognosis, and then relayed the news about Monsignor Norton's willingness to ask Archbishop Scaponi for a dispensation to proceed for an abortion. He presumed, of course, that Aubrey would come to the same decision, but instead he was greeted by pushback. Aubrey wasn't on board. In fact, she was indignant to the fact that the doctors, Mike, and Monsignor Norton — *all men* — were making choices for her and her baby.

Sick as she was, Aubrey was not giving in. Her *choice* was to fight tooth and nail for her child and give her a shot at life. The news was disheartening to Mike — in his mind she was committing suicide. He was sensitive to her deteriorating medical condition, concerned as to whether or not his wife had a state of mind that was rational enough for her to be capable of making such decisions. He kept pushing her towards the abortion solution, over and over — prodding, suggesting, and pleading. Aubrey's already shot nerves couldn't stand much more.

Mike moved in for another attempt at persuading her, confronting Aubrey as she lay in bed.

"Mike, drop it." Aubrey said, her voice sounding somewhere between shrill and a whisper. "This is my choice."

Mike lifted himself out of the chair positioned next to her bedside and then walked around to the other side of the bed.

He gently mounted the mattress and slid over to her, propping himself up with his arm, to face her. Taking her hand, he began to twirl the loose wedding band that hung limply around her finger.

"Brey," he softly whispered. "You are everything to me. Your children could not survive a day without you. This is not about anything else but my unending love for you. Call me selfish — anything you wish. I won't be able to go on without you. ...Please — have the abortion."

Aubrey adjusted the air prongs from the nasal cannula that attached to her portable oxygen unit. Her breathing was deep and labored. She straddled her open hands around her swollen abdomen "This child is every bit as much ours as is Justin and Tracy. I will protect her the same way that I've always protected them. I want your support on this — I don't want to be arguing with you every day over my decision. I need your prayers. You're too willing to give up. What's happened to your faith?"

"I don't think you get it. You're not going to save the child — you're going to kill the both of you. Please come to your senses. You have to save yourself."

Aubrey was becoming frustrated and the discussion was causing her already rapid heartbeat to increase its rhythm even more. Mike was to the point of tears and they streamed down his face as he came to the realization that Aubrey wasn't budging. He needed another strategy for convincing her to save her own life.

The clock was ticking.

***

Cindy Stone waited in her car, parked across the street from an apartment building on Jersey City's Harrison Avenue. The teenage kids from the housing projects told her that this was where she could find Rosalita Sanchez — the new digs that came courtesy of Rabbi Turner. Stone had no idea that

Rosalita had been away to rehab and had remained clean ever since. Stone was there to recruit Rosalita to carry out another of her dirty deeds, of course, in exchange for some cash to buy a fix. A half-hour later, Rosalita appeared in the apartment foyer. Stone peered at her through the iron grate glass doors at the entry way of the building. Rosalita was headed to the neighborhood grocery store — Schimenti's Market.

As she descended the front concrete steps of the building, Stone tapped her horn and flashed her headlights on and off. Rosalita, recognizing the car, walked over to the curbside driver's door and bent down. Stone handed her a copy of the paperwork for Aubrey Fitzgibbon's abortion.

"The *'Holy rollers'* gave your daughter a hard time over her abortion, but they kept their mouths shut about this. They're freaking hypocrites." Stone said. "Now we're going to have our fun — we're getting even."

Stone was ticked off about a protest march on the Hudson Family Planning Center, organized by the *Knights of Columbus Council* affiliated with Father O'Connor. It was triggered by word of mouth concerning Angela Sanchez's abortion, that spread throughout the Catholic community like wildfire.

Stone told Rosalita that the parish bulletins for the Sunday Masses were put out in the vestibule of the church about a half-hour before the seven o'clock morning Mass began. She offered to pay Rosalita twenty dollars to stuff the bulletins with three hundred copies of Aubrey Fitzgibbon's abortion paperwork. She whipped out a twenty-dollar bill and handed it over to Rosalita. "This is for now. There will be another twenty after Sunday's Masses."

Rosalita took it all in.

"I'll come by here Saturday afternoon — say three o'clock — and drop off the rest." Stone said.

Rosalita Sanchez stuffed the twenty-dollar bill in her pants pocket, then folded up the copy of Aubrey Fitzgibbon's abortion paperwork and pocketed it as well. "I'll see you here, Saturday."

Chapter Eighteen

Frank Sinatra's rendition of *The Way You Look Tonight*
boomed out from the practically antique stereo record player
in the den of the rectory. Father O'Connor was enjoying some
downtime, listening to the albums collection that he amassed
over the years at Saint Al's. A panting Monsignor Norton
entered the den, fresh out of breath from his jog up the stairs.
His attempted phone call to O'Connor failed because the
music drowned out the ringing phone. O'Connor did not even
notice Norton's entrance, nor hear him shouting his name
from across the room. He was lost in the music and gazing
into the dancing flames of the hearth.

For the moment, O'Connor was trying to forget about the
condition of his friend and church parishioner, Sal Panetta,
whom he had just visited. Hospice was at the house,
preparing Sal and his family for the inevitable. O'Connor
knew that he would shortly be returning to see Sal, this time,
in order to administer him the Last Rites. He told Sal's
family, in case of an emergency, they were to call him day or
night, at any time. He dreaded such a call and knew it was not
that far off.

Norton walked over to the stereo and twirled the volume
knob all the way down. "You think you have this loud
enough, Father? I don't think the folks passing by on West
Side Avenue can hear it."

Startled by the voice, O'Connor jumped up from his chair.
"Sorry, I was lost in the moment with Frank."

"Well, I sure could use your help in getting '*lost in the
moment*' in the rectory office. There are two visitors down
there, who are here because of your doings."

"Huh? Who's that?"

"Remember when you and I had that little disagreement about the young couple you decided to okay for *Pre-Cana?* ...You know — the couple I felt were too young to get married and that I tried to encourage to hold off for a year."

"Yes. Oh yes. Now that ye mention it — they do come to mind. Have they come by to ask that I baptize their first born? What a darlin' lovely couple!"

"No, I'm afraid not. They'd prefer to have an annulment."

"An annulment? Are they divorced?"

"No, Father — they are very confused. That's why I figured that you'd be the best suited to deal with them. Besides, I have to see Mother Superior and the good sisters at the convent. They want to show me some leaky pipes in the basement over there — they feel that they are entitled to a new boiler and water heater since we got the new ones in the rectory. I wonder, who might have put them up to that? But anyhow, while I run over to the convent — could you see if you might be able to get our two young friends back on the straight and narrow?"

"That I will, Father. But if ye would like, I could handle the good sisters."

"Whoa no," Norton said, trying not to laugh. "That might be a bit of a too expensive proposition for the parish. I think you've had enough of plumbing experiences already for this year."

Father O'Connor followed Monsignor Norton down the staircase and into the rectory office. There, Brittany and Darrin McCarey sat in the chairs stationed in front of the office desk. The monsignor reintroduced Father O'Connor, whom the young, handsome couple — each no more than twenty-four years of age — fondly recalled. O'Connor had joined them together in matrimony. Norton excused himself and exited the office, closing the door behind him. He looked up to the heavens and made the sign of the cross while shaking his head from side to side, darting off to the convent.

"Monsignor Norton told me that ye came by here to get an annulment," O'Connor said, taking a seat behind the desk as he ran his hand through his bushy white head of hair. "Might I inquire as to how long it's been since the two of ye were married?"

"Eighteen months, Father," the couple answered in unison. "You see we've outgrown each other," Darrin added.

O'Connor slapped his forehead with an open palm. "A full eighteen months and ye've outgrown each other. Mother Machree!"

"You see, Father, Darrin doesn't pay attention to me anymore," Brittany said.

"And she won't let me go out with the guys every now and then."

"Every now and then? You mean a couple of times a week," Brittany said.

The couple rambled on and on — bickering over trivial matters that now seemed monumental to the both of them.

"Now, now. Let's not be arguing here," O'Connor said. He picked up a book from the top of the desk — a priest's handbook. O'Connor flipped through the pages, pretending to be looking for something. "Let's see…annulments." O'Connor stopped at a random page, making up the text that he narrated. "Here we are — annulments."

O'Connor then began to explain that he would have to present their case to an ecclesiastical tribunal which would evaluate their request for the annulment. That certainly was true, but he then began to make things up as he went along, intending to turn the tables on the pleasant young couple sitting before him. O'Connor opened a desk drawer and pulled out several sheets of blank paper, divided them up and handed them over to Darrin and Brittany. Then he slid a canister of pens and pencils over to them.

"I'm going to need some information that yer gonna have to bring back to me," O'Connor told them, still putting on a ruse. "But first things first — when and where did ye first meet each other, might I ask?"

"That's easy, Father — at Lee's — sophomore year of high school, after a school dance. Britt was sitting in one of the back booths, and I went right over and asked her out."

"It was the same booth where you popped the question to me," Brittany said. She looked towards O'Connor. "That means that we were getting engaged."

"That's nice," O'Connor said. "Now, what I want ye both to do is to go over to Lee's, right now, and sit in that same booth. Then, I want you to put down on paper all of the things that ye both love about each other — what ye found attractive about each other over all of these years, excuse me, all of these months of marriage."

"What?"

"How's that?"

O'Connor pretended to be reading from the book again and, bluffing, he told them the information was required by an ancient church custom. They bought into it.

"Then ye have to list what type of family it was that ye had envisioned on raisin' up. How many children did ye plan to have? What were their names gonna be and what did ye hope they were gonna grow up to be? It's all for statistical data that the church needs to record — the Pope is a stickler for such details, ye know." He reached into his pocket, pulled out his wallet and slid out a five-dollar bill. "Now, ye both have a couple of burgers and malted milks at Lee's, it's on me."

"Father, burgers and malts cost more like ten bucks," Darrin said.

"Oh, Sorry." O'Connor reached back into his wallet for another five dollars. "They've raised the prices there since when I was first monsignor." He then told them that they would also need to assist him in a church endeavor shortly, and that they would have to make themselves available. They looked quizzically at one another.

"Wow. Getting an annulment is certainly a very strange ritual," Darrin said.

"Yer telling me, but I need yer commitment in assisting me with something — and it may be in the next few days or so."

They consented, looking all the more bewildered as to what was going on.

O'Connor had a trick up his sleeve. He escorted the young couple to the rectory door and then headed up the stairs — to the chapel on the second floor — to pray a rosary for them.

On his way up the stairs, Misses Cavendish intercepted him, informing the priest that Rosalita Sanchez stopped by to see him while he was attending to the McCareys. Misses Sanchez considered it an urgent matter and said that she would stop by later on. O'Connor was intrigued, *what could Misses Sanchez want now?*

***

Doctor's Thompson and Freidman were perplexed — both physicians, despite their best efforts, could not convince Aubrey Fitzgibbon to terminate her pregnancy. Now, they needed a *"Plan B,"* because it was obvious that Aubrey was committed to carrying her baby right up until birth, even if doing so could cause her death. Aubrey hoped for a miracle by which she could at least carry the baby to term, but even that was fraught with risk — by doing so, the odds were high that, by then, her heart would be so weakened that she would die during the birthing procedure.

In the interim, weekly blood transfusions were helping to maintain somewhat of an elevated iron content in Aubrey's blood. The treatments were at least buying Aubrey some more precious time, slowing down the anemia, but not curing it. Whatever was causing the medical anomaly was still unknown, and the only option the doctors had was to play for time. They had consulted medical experts from coast to coast — they, too, were just as baffled.

Huddled in Doctor Thompson's office, the medical team tried to put forward a strategy to deal with the problem. "When is the earliest possibility for your inducing labor and the baby still surviving?" Doctor Friedman asked the obstetrician.

"I wouldn't consider anything earlier than the thirtieth week of her pregnancy," Thompson answered.

"You're looking at about the fourth week of December. My God, she is so damn stubborn. I don't see her making it — her heart will never hold out that long,"

"We have to plot a strategy that keeps her in the game day by day. Each day is a victory. Let's maximize every possible measure that we can take — anything that buys us an hour, a minute, or a second."

Friedman thought a moment. "I think that she should be kept in the hospital the last three weeks prior to our inducing labor — that will be a critical timeframe for her body. If anything is going to give out, it will be then. Whatever the case may be, we are much better off dealing with it in a hospital. If only we can get her to hold on until then. I'm going to recommend that she be transferred to the hospital in early December."

Thompson nodded his consent. "I'll let the Fitzgibbons know what to expect."

The doctors concluded their meeting without mentioning what they felt inside — what their medical acumen told them — this was all just wishful thinking and planning, because Aubrey Fitzgibbon was not going to make it.

***

Cindy Stone sat staring out from behind the wheel of her parked car, peering into the foyer of Rosalita Sanchez's apartment building, just across the street. Her eyes occasionally glanced over to the digital clock on the dashboard — it was now 3:10 p.m.

Rap, rap.

Stone was startled from the sound of knuckles knocking on the driver's side window of the car. She turned her head to the side and saw black dress garb and a Roman collar. Finally, a face appeared — Father Sean O'Connor stared in at her. She sat paralyzed for several seconds, all the while trying to work up her nerve. *Screw him.* She opened the door and planted her feet on the sidewalk, standing within a foot of the priest.

"I'll be filling in for Misses Sanchez today. And I suggest that ye be paying careful attention to what I've gotta say."

O'Connor's benevolence to Rosalita Sanchez was paying dividends — she told him what Stone wanted her to do and showed him a copy of the medical protocol for Aubrey Fitzgibbon's abortion. O'Connor consulted Monsignor Norton, securing his assurances that he would not tell Aubrey or Deacon Fitzgibbon that they were now aware of Aubrey seeking out an earlier abortion. They then plotted out a strategy for dealing with Cindy Stone. Norton thought the woman was a witch for what she was planning to do.

"Do ye know, Miss Stone, 'tis a federal crime, it is, to be swiping someone's health records, much less to be passin' them around all over town. I suggest that ye destroy every one of those copies, because if they start showing up around town, I'll be signin' the police complaint against ye, *meself.*"

Stone was trapped in a corner with no way out. She was beaten, but it didn't mean that she couldn't get her shots in at O'Connor. "You and your church are nothing but hypocrites. You scorned a young girl for getting an abortion, but then bit your tongues when it came to the deacon's wife. You might have tripped me up today, but you will never shut me up from speaking my mind. Never." She raised her voice as she shouted. "I'm a liberated woman. Hear me roar."

"Ye'll pardon me, Miss Stone, but the only thing that I see roarin' before me eyes is an *arsehole.*"

Such an undignified response from a priest caught Stone off-guard. Her mouth fell half open. After a few seconds, she collected herself and let O'Connor have it, full blast. "DROP DEAD, old man!"

O'Connor could take a personal insult, but he felt that Stone slighted what he represented and believed in as a priest. For a second, the devil took hold of O'Connor as he uttered words that were like no others he had ever pronounced before in his life. "Miss Stone, in the language that only someone like yerself could understand — go and fuck yerself." *Oh, my Lord, where did that come from?*

Stone was shell shocked. This time, she felt her mouth fall completely open. She couldn't believe a man of the cloth had just cursed her out in such blunt terms. Tears welling up in her eyes, she hopped back into her car, started it up, quickly slid it into gear and sped off.

O'Connor was just as much in shock — he couldn't believe that he had fallen for the temptation to get back at Stone and, by so doing, had thus sinned most grievously. He wished he could call back his terrible words. He felt horrible. He fell for Satan's bait — succumbing to the temptation of demeaning his nemesis. "Me Lord, Jesus, please forgive me for what I've said," he prayed with an eye towards the sky. "I must confess. I must confess," he muttered, fast pacing it down the block towards West Side Avenue. Once there, he trudged north along the side of the street that abutted Lincoln Park, heading towards Saint Aloysius Church.

O'Connor knew that Monsignor Norton was hearing Saturday afternoon confessions for the parish, and he couldn't wait to relieve his conscience from the burden that it now carried. His face had turned beet red and he began to sweat profusely, not realizing that all of the commotion was taxing

150

his heart. His angina began acting up, responding to the rapid pace of his walk.

Arriving at Saint Aloysius, O'Connor entered the church and headed up the side aisle to where a line of parishioners sat in pews adjacent to one of the church's confessional booths. "Excuse me," he said to the congregants awaiting their turn to confess their sins, "but I have a bit of an emergency, and I need to be tellin' Monsignor Norton somethin' right away." As an elderly gentleman walked out of one of the confessional closets, O'Connor cut the line and slipped into the booth. As his knees touched down on the kneeler, the green light above the open door switched off and the red light switched on. A panel in the wall in front of the kneeler slid open. A dark opaque screen was revealed with Monsignor Norton's silhouette cast upon it.

Father O'Connor began, "In the name of the Father, and of the Son, and of the Holy Spirit. Bless me Father for I have sinned. It's been several weeks since me last confession and these are me sins."

The priest's brogue was a dead giveaway; Monsignor Norton knew right away that it was Father O'Connor. "Father O'Connor, you sound a bit stressed out — are you okay?"

"Monsignor Norton, I have sinned."

"Father, please tell me that you weren't trying to fix the plumbing in the convent."

"I only wish it was that minor."

"Please, tell me what's happened."

"Father — I'm too embarrassed. Do ye suppose that ye could give me penance and just take me word that what I did was bad."

"You know absolution doesn't work that way. It's called *'confession'* not *'hide and go seek.'*"

O'Connor summoned up his courage and then finally fessed up. "I said 'go and fuck yerself' to Miss Stone," O'Connor said, whispering low.

"I'm sorry, Father, I couldn't hear what you said. Could you please repeat it?"

O'Connor said it twice more, still too soft and low.

"Louder, Father, louder, I can't give absolution unless I know exactly what it is that I'm dealing with."

On his fourth repetition, O'Connor was so irritated that he shouted out what he said to Stone: "Go and — "

Unbeknownst to himself, his shout was clearly audible to the entire church, expletive and all. Loud enough to wake the dead.

Three senior ladies, sitting and praying in the pew outside of the confessional, lowered themselves onto the kneeler and pulled out their rosary beads. They made the sign of the cross and prayed to God for mercy. "That Monsignor Norton can really grate on poor Father O'Connor's nerves sometimes," one of the ladies said.

Several nuns preparing the altar for the weekend church services made the sign of the cross as well, and then murmured a short prayer to themselves. Mister Johnson, the parish maintenance man, replacing light bulbs in the archway over the side aisle corridors, nearly toppled from his ladder at the sound of O'Connor's utterance.

Back inside the confessional, Monsignor Norton was biting his cheeks, trying to keep himself from laughing. He felt a strange satisfaction in digesting what Father O'Connor was relating to him, but despite his morbid glee, Norton could tell that O'Connor was taking it rather hard.

"Now see what ye have gone and done — ye've caused me to say it again. That's now twice in one day! For sure I'll be spendin' sometime in purgatory for this. If me own mother were alive, she'd be washin' me mouth out with soap."

"Is that all, Father?"

"How's that?"

"Was there anything else that you said — I mean, you didn't leave anything out? …Did you, Father?"

O'Connor thought to himself. "Oh yes, I called her an 'arsehole' as well," he said, whispering the profanity.

"I didn't catch that Father, what did you say you called her?"

Twice more, O'Connor repeated the transgression. Then, on the fourth repetition, the frustrated priest shouted out, "Arsehole," which reverberated throughout the church.

Another row of elderly parishioners hit the kneelers in their pews and joined together praying a rosary. The nuns on the altar were startled again, quickly making another sign of the cross, followed by their muttering of another simple short prayer. This time, Mister Johnson was so jolted, he dropped a light bulb which crashed to the floor. Everyone in the church practically jumped out of their skin at the sound of the bulb smashing onto the hard marble church floor, resembling the sound of a gunshot.

O'Connor was just as alarmed inside the confessional. "Dear Lord, Almighty, 'tis Miss Stone comin' to shoot me and take her revenge."

Norton quickly thought of a way to ease the poor priest's anguish. "Father, for your penance say three Hail Mary's, three Our Fathers, and three Glory Be's. Then go over to the rectory and make a gift to yourself of that bottle of *Tullamore Dew* in the kitchen cabinet — just to settle your nerves," the monsignor said, still pleased that someone had finally put Cindy Stone in her place for the heinous act that she contemplated. He then told O'Connor to say his Act of Contrition.

O'Connor did a double take, but he wasn't about to clarify the penance and sentence handed down to him by Monsignor Norton. The *Tullamore Dew* would for sure wash the bad taste of the foul language from out of his mouth. "Oh, my God, I'm sorry for my sins...."

While Father O'Connor made his contrition, Monsignor Norton pronounced absolution, "God the Father of mercies, who through the death and resurrection of his Son has reconciled the world to himself and sent the Holy Spirit among us for the forgiveness of sins; through the ministry of the Church, may God give you pardon and peace, and I absolve you from your sins in the name of the Father, and of the Son, and of the Holy Spirit."

As O'Connor left the confessional to pray his penance, the congregants sitting in the pews turned their heads in his direction. O'Connor gave them a wink, a nod, and a wave.

"Just a wee bit of a problem with the convent plumbin', 'tis all," he said, trying to cover his tracks.

Chapter Nineteen

Father O'Connor lumbered up Gifford Avenue, on his way to visit Aubrey Fitzgibbon. He was able to convince Monsignor Norton that they were compelled to let Aubrey know about Cindy Stone's conduct, in order that she could deal with the witch of a woman from her end. O'Connor timed his visit while Deacon Fitzgibbon and Monsignor Norton were serving the eleven-thirty Sunday morning Mass. The two priests felt it best that the matter be addressed to Aubrey alone, in case Deacon Fitzgibbon wasn't aware that his wife had sought an abortion. They both agreed that it was none of their business to butt into the affairs of the household, unless asked. In discussing the Stone incident with O'Connor, Norton broke his confidence with Deacon Fitzgibbon and told O'Connor about the current crisis gripping the Fitzgibbon family — Aubrey's pregnancy and malady. Deacon Fitzgibbon kept Norton posted on his wife's declining health and Aubrey's refusal to save her life by opting for an abortion. Norton filled O'Connor in on all of it, wanting to let the priest know what he would be walking into.

O'Connor was startled by the news. He had no idea of what he would say to Aubrey — he planned to play it by ear. He felt awkward.

O'Connor huffed and puffed at the top of the staircase on the front porch of the Fitzgibbon home. He paused a moment to recapture his breath, allowing a sudden attack of angina to subside before attempting to enter the house. He had sympathy for Aubrey Fitzgibbon's situation as was related to him by Monsignor Norton — he had a new appreciation for this gutsy woman. Collecting his composure, O'Connor rang the doorbell and was soon greeted at the door by the two

155

Fitzgibbon children — Justin and Tracy. The carnage the family crisis was taking on the children was written on their gaunt and *cheerless* faces.

As they led the priest inside the house towards the staircase, Nikki Spencer came bounding down the steps, on her way to the kitchen. She was there on one of her many frequent visits to see Aubrey and help out. She and O'Connor made chit-chat, exchanging pleasantries for a few moments. Nikki then led the priest up the stairs and into Aubrey's bedroom.

O'Connor could not believe his eyes when he witnessed the appearance of Aubrey's condition. He put on his pleasant smile and made sure that she could not detect from reading his face how bad she looked. Years and years of praying at the bedsides of the sick and dying helped the priest to keep a poker face that could break a casino.

The bedroom was adorned with Christmas decorations that Nikki and Aubrey's children put up. A compact disc player on the top of a clothes dresser was playing Christmas carols. O'Connor was a bit bewildered, it was still before Thanksgiving.

Aubrey told O'Connor to just ignore the holiday décor, it was simply meant to keep her spirits up. Christmas always cheered Aubrey up — it was her favorite holiday. O'Connor understood, confiding to Aubrey that it was his favorite time of the year as well. O'Connor then turned the conversation onto his concerns about Aubrey's ill-health. Telling her that she would dominate his prayers. Aubrey's spoken words were slow and drawn out — she talked only as she exhaled the air that was fed into her from the oxygen tank. Her voice was soft and low.

With their chat now focused on her health, Aubrey had her guard up, feeling that at any moment O'Connor would be telling her that she would be permitted by church doctrine to have an abortion in order to save her life, and then spend the rest of his time trying to convince her to latch onto that lifeline. She decided to head him off at the pass, just in case. "Father, I hope you haven't come to lecture me about abandoning my child in order to save my life."

"Misses Fitzgibbon, I assure ye, that is not my intention. I admire yer faith and determination. Let me clarify something fer ye, if ye'll let me — yes, I'll be praying for ye, but for yer child too." Then he told her the true nature of his visit and began to detail the exploits of Cindy Stone.

Aubrey was astonished, hurt, and embarrassed. Tears began to roll down her face. O'Connor reached for a box of *Kleenex* on the bedside nightstand and handed it to her. He tried to comfort her, telling her that "No one ever needs to know, Lass."

Aubrey thanked O'Connor for his efforts on her behalf, but it didn't lessen the contempt she felt towards him for denying her Holy Communion. From Aubrey's mannerisms, O'Connor got the sense that she was merely tolerating his presence, and that she still resented him deep down inside. Then, Aubrey confided that her husband found out about her plans to have an abortion *after the fact.* She made sure O'Connor understood that Mike had not been aware of what she contemplated at the time; lest it be used against him in his position as church deacon.

The conversation then swung to talk about Angela Sanchez. O'Connor could sense the girl's ordeal was still eating away at Aubrey — who felt responsible, in part, for the girl's running away. "I cry every now and then when I think about that poor frightened child out there. It breaks my heart."

When the carol, *It Came upon a Midnight Clear,* played, it distracted Aubrey's attention, and she began to hum along to the Christmas hymn. She excused herself to O'Connor, telling him that it was her favorite Christmas holy song. He told her that he understood and, on that prompt, figured it was time for him to leave. He thought that his company was still not wanted, despite Aubrey's civility. "Well, I believe that it's time for me to be shovin' off, Misses Fitzgibbon."

"Well thank you for telling me about Cindy Stone. You might have been a fine detective had you not decided to become a priest." Aubrey thought for a second, and then, out of curiosity, she asked O'Connor why he did decide to become a priest.

"Me favorite uncle was a priest. Uncle Charlie or, rather, Father Chuck O'Malley — on me mother's side of the family. He was from East Saint Louis. I still remember me parents taking us down from Boston to visit him in New York — he was pastor for a spell at Saint Dominic's Church in the city, and then later on at Saint Mary's. That was quite a while back."

"So, it runs in the family."

O'Connor laughed. "I guess it does. Father Chuck had a tremendous influence on me. He also taught me to sing — Father Chuck was quite musically talented, he was. Always writin' songs."

Before he left, Aubrey asked O'Connor if he would do all that he could to help in locating Angela Sanchez. She felt as if everyone had given up looking for the girl, just accepting that she was gone forever. O'Connor promised her that he would, again sensing how truly concerned she was about the teen. He said his formal goodbye but was then left with a feeling as if he was leaving something left unsaid. Aubrey felt the same. The unsaid was the uneasiness between them because of O'Connor's imposed sanction — forbidding Aubrey to receive Holy Communion.

Preparing to leave, O'Connor said a short prayer over Aubrey, then he blessed and anointed her with the holy water that he carried in a small plastic container that fit inside his pocket.

He left the bedroom and descended the staircase, heading for the kitchen to say goodbye to the Fitzgibbon children and

Nikki Spencer. Nikki eased O'Connor into a kitchen chair and set a cup of coffee and a stack of pancakes down before him. Steam bellowed up from the hot cakes — just off the griddle. O'Connor offered little resistance. She then grabbed a breakfast tray holding Aubrey's breakfast and headed upstairs to deliver it to her friend. Justin and Tracy were just finishing their breakfast and stayed seated at the table.

"Did you give mom her *Last Rites?*" Justin asked.

"I most certainly did not. Yer mom is going to be just fine!"

"That's not what the doctors said."

"Nonsense. They're not the final say."

"Who is?" Justin asked.

"Certainly not the naysayers." O'Connor timed his answers between swallows of pancakes and sips of coffee. "She will be just fine. Yer mom just needs plenty more prayers, 'tis all."

"We've been praying awfully hard. But she looks worse and worse each day."

"Well now, there's a lot more to prayin' than just sayin' the words. And, the two of ye are in luck, because today I'm gonna share with ye the secret to prayer. You'll see the difference once ye learn the secret."

Father O'Connor finished his breakfast, and then shared with Justin and Tracy his treasured secrets to prayer.

Chapter Twenty

"This is our faith. This is the faith of the Church. We are proud to profess it, in Christ Jesus our Lord."

Father O'Connor prayed at the baptismal font of Saint Aloysius Church, conducting the Christening ceremony. He then directed the godparents to lower the baby boy and hover him over the open basin of water. O'Connor dipped his cupped hand into the basin, scooping out a palm full of water. "Is it your will that Ethan Connors should be baptized in the faith of the Church, which we have all professed with ye?"

"It is," the godparents responded.

"Ethan Connors, I baptize ye in the name of the Father," O'Connor said, pouring water over the baby's forehead. He then dipped his hand back into the font and scooped out more water. "And of the son," he continued, spilling the water onto the child again, who was now beginning to smile and cackle. O'Connor reached into the basin a third time to retrieve more water. "And of the Holy Spirit."

The priest then reached for a small golden vessel inscribed with the initials *S. Chr.* — *Sanctum Chrisma* — which contained the Holy Chrism, or consecrated oil, and anointed the baby's forehead. "God the Father of our Lord Jesus Christ has freed ye from sin, given ye a new birth by water and the Holy Spirit, and welcomed ye into his holy people. He now anoints ye with the chrism of salvation. As Christ was anointed Priest, Prophet, and King, so may ye live always as a member of his body, sharing everlasting life."

A few moments later, Misses Cavendish came bounding down the center aisle of the church. She was intending to deliver an important message to O'Connor that had just been called into the rectory. Cavendish knew that the priest would be finishing up the scheduled baptism and wanted to catch him before he wandered off to the Christening festivities. By now, O'Connor had concluded the ceremonial dressing of the newly baptized child in the white garment, and the lighting of the candles. He was almost finished administering the sacrament. He recited the *Ephphetha Prayer* while anointing the child's ears and mouth. Then he led the participants and guests in the concluding *Lord's Prayer.*

"What a well-behaved child," O'Connor said. He just laid back and smiled when I poured the holy water on him — for sure he'll be a lifeguard or a fireman."

Everyone joined in laughing.

Father O'Connor quickly glanced up towards the front of the church. During the baptismal ceremony, from out of the corner of his eye, he saw that the two Fitzgibbon children had entered the church and darted up the side aisle to pray in front of the Sacred Heart of Jesus. He wondered how they were doing and if they were praying the way that he taught them on the day he visited their home. The emotional toll that the family crisis was extracting from the teens was becoming practically unbearable for them.

Misses Cavendish approached Father O'Connor and pulled him to the side, relaying some most unfortunate news. Sal Panetta's family was just told by the hospice nurse that the good man was fast approaching his final hours. The family was requesting Father O'Connor to administer the family patriarch his Last Rites. O'Connor had been expecting this dreadful call ever since he paid his first visit in a long while to his dear friend — after Monsignor Norton broke the news to him about Panetta's ill health. Since that initial visit, O'Connor frequented the Panetta household quite often, praying with the family and helping them to cope and prepare for the inevitable. Unfortunately, the inevitable also consisted of arranging for Last Rites and a funeral, over which Panetta and his family wanted O'Connor to preside.

During his visits with Panetta, O'Connor also helped to reconcile an estrangement that befell Panetta and his eldest son, Sal Junior. When young Sal decided upon a career change, his new work took him across country and landed him on California's west coast, forcing him to uproot his wife and kids. Sal was opposed to his son's decision and advised him against moving. Unpleasant arguments ensued. Against, his father's advice, young Sal departed. The bitter sentiments from their disagreements lingered, and to his family's consternation, Sal began to slowly shut his son out of his life.

O'Connor saw that this family sore spot was eating away at his friend on the inside and tearing apart his wife's heart. Through his charm and cunning, O'Connor gradually brought Sal to the realization that it was wrong to shun his son. He got Sal to concede that the decision was suffering him as much as it was the rest of the Panetta family. "Life's too precious and short for holding onto grudges in order to make points," O'Connor said. "Turn the page, Sal. Yer missin' the love of a son and his entire family. My God, ye have another grandson that ye have never seen. We're talking about irreplaceable things here, Sal."

O'Connor managed to work his typical magic and, before long, the father and son were reconciled. In fact, in just the past week, the younger Panetta returned to his father's home to be with him in his final days. Sal Junior also arranged for his wife and new son to visit, in order that his father could finally get to see his new grandson, Mathew Panetta, whom he had yet to lay his eyes upon. When the family reunited in the parlor of the family home, Sal Panetta was filled with a swell of elation. His *cup* truly *runneth over* with happiness. He was so glad that his friend, Father O'Connor, rescued him from his own pride.

O'Connor told Misses Cavendish to head back to the rectory and prepare his *Extreme Unction* kit while he changed out of the baptismal vestments in the sacristy. He reached beneath his religious garb and pulled out his wallet, lifting out from it an old business card that someone once gave him, and on the back of which he had written two cell phone numbers.

"Misses Cavendish, these are the numbers for that nice young couple — the McCareys — they are expecting a call," O'Connor said, recounting the arrangement he had made with the young couple, when they came to him for marriage counseling. He handed Misses Cavendish the card. "Just tell them that I said it's time for them to help me, and that they should come to the rectory — at once — to pick me up. If there is a problem, let me know."

Within the span of a half-hour, O'Connor was sitting in the backseat of the McCarey's car, heading to the Panetta's home. On the drive over, O'Connor gave the couple their instructions — they were to help serve the family while he administered the sacrament. The McCareys would also have to babysit some of the grandchildren, while the adults and older children surrounded Sal Panetta in his bedroom when O'Connor administered the last sacrament.

Arriving at Panetta's home, Darrin pulled the car into the driveway; then the three exited the vehicle and climbed the porch. They rang the doorbell and were greeted by one of Sal Panetta's sons — it was Sal Junior.

Traditional religious protocol required that the family greet the priest at the door in silence and bearing a lit candle. They were not supposed to socialize with the priest — a bit difficult considering that Father O'Connor was like family. The Panettas were unfamiliar with the rigid custom and O'Connor let them slide, excusing the usual formalities and playing it by ear. Most of the family were gathered in the parlor. Sal's wife, Cora, and his daughter, Paula, were attending to him, along with the hospice nurse, in the upstairs bedroom. O'Connor introduced Darrin and Brittany McCarey, telling the family they were there to help them. There were a lot of red and watery eyes staring back at the priest and the

McCareys. Father O'Connor excused himself and, toting the sacrament kit, he headed for the upstairs bedroom.

In the bedroom, Cora greeted O'Connor with a hug and a peck on the cheek. She let out a long, deep sigh as they embraced. Panetta's daughter told her father that his friend, the priest, had arrived. Under the influence of morphine that the hospice nurse administered, Sal was numb and groggy, lapsing in and out of consciousness and coherence. He pivoted his head on the pillow that was propped underneath him, taking notice of O'Connor, who was busy laying out the implements that he would be using for administering the Last Rites. O'Connor placed them on a nightstand that was pulled alongside the center of the bed. Panetta smiled and whispered the priest's name.

O'Connor talked softly and calmly to Panetta while he continued to organize the articles from the kitbag, which he began placing onto a white linen cloth cover that he draped over the nightstand. He set down a crucifix, two candles which he lit, a portable communion carrier which he set upon a square white linen cloth, a corporal, a bottle of holy water, a hand linen, several pieces of palm, cotton balls, lemon slices that Misses Cavendish had cut up, a vessel containing *Oleum Infirmorum* (the Oil of the Sick), and a small basin which he asked Panetta's daughter Paula to fill with tap water.

O'Connor threw a vestment stole over his shoulders that draped around his neck and hung down in front of him like a long scarf. He directed Paula to summon the family members from the parlor. The adults and older children filed into the bedroom and surrounded Panetta's bed. O'Connor handed each family member a prayer sheet from a stack that he brought with him, so that they could follow along and recite the required responses. Then he began the solemn sacramental ritual.

O'Connor lowered the crucifix to Sal Panetta's lips. Sal kissed the cross, then O'Connor positioned it in Panetta's hands, resting them atop his abdomen. O'Connor began to sprinkle the room with holy water using the strands of palm. "Peace to this house," he said.

"And to all who dwell therein," the family responded, reading from the prayer sheets.

O'Connor continued his prayers and the family continued responding. He then asked the family to step outside in the hall for a moment while he heard Panetta's last confession. "It'll only take a moment," he told them. "Sal's been a very good boy."

The family filed out into the hall. O'Connor closed the bedroom door behind them. He then turned back towards his friend and stood beside him at the head of the bed. He could see the toll that Sal's hopeless battle to beat the odds had taken on him. "Sal, me friend, I can tell ye what everyone else is frightened to say to ye — 'tis okay to let go and move on, me friend. Yer race is done, and it was a magnificent one from start to finish. I am truly proud to have known ye, Sal. But now, ye can let go."

A grin and then a smile crept across Panetta's face. "I know, Father," he whispered. "I'm afraid though. And, I've been hallucinating — I'm starting to see all of my dearly departed family members and friends."

"They're just waitin' to lead ye home, me friend. 'Tis no different than bein' a baby in yer mother's womb again. Ye were comfortable there — and being born was just as frightening. Dyin' is no different. Yer just movin' onto what yer whole Christian faith is based upon — life everlasting through Jesus Christ. It's one long train ride, but there is no final destination along this spiritual journey — just plenty of stops along the way."

Panetta's smile broadened a bit more.

"*John* — ten, twenty-seven. Jesus said, *'Me sheep hear me voice, and I know them and they follow me; and I give them eternal life, and they shall never perish...and no one shall snatch them out of my hand.'"*

Panetta nodded his head, gratefully acknowledging God's word. Then something awkward popped into his mind. "Have you ever thought about how and when you would prefer to go, Father?"

"Oh, sure I have, Sal. We all do. I guess, if I had me druthers, I'd like to make me move on outta here 'round Christmas — me favorite time of year. That way, when I see everyone that'll be greetin' me at the pearly gates, they will be handin' me some Christmas presents as well. Hopefully, my time won't come until after we're done here, Sal — lest they'll be sendin' for Monsignor Norton to bury the both of us."

Panetta smiled again — almost laughing.

"I'm gonna hear yer confession now, Sal, then I'll be bringin' everybody back in. Now, don't ye be sneakin' off somewhere until I've the chance to hand ye the bill for all of this." This time, Panetta actually laughed. O'Connor continued. "Me friend, the last goodbye 'tis always the hardest one to say — I'm gonna miss ye. We can only take from this life what we have given away to others. Ye'll be pullin' into Heaven with yer arms full. God Bless ye for everything ye have done for Saint Aloysius Parish. Ye were a true friend, Salvatore." His salute completed, tears now streamed down the priest's face.

O'Connor heard Panetta's last confession, then he administered absolution before opening the bedroom door and allowing the family back in. O'Connor led them in praying the *Confiteor* with Panetta, who was trying to remember the words and keep pace with the priest. O'Connor reached for the communion carrier and took out the Holy Eucharist. After a round of ritual verbal volleys, O'Connor administered the sacrament to Panetta. "Body of Christ," he said.

"Amen," Panetta whispered, then he opened his mouth and accepted the bread of life on his tongue.

"O Holy Lord, Father almighty and eternal God, we pray Thee in faith that the holy Body of our Lord Jesus Christ, Thy Son, may profit our brother Sal, who has received it as an everlasting remedy for body and soul: Who being God, lives and reigns. Amen."

Down in the parlor, Darrin and Brittany entertained three-month old Matthew Panetta — Sal Panetta's youngest grandchild. Brittany held the baby in her lap while Darrin fed him a warm bottle of formula. Matthew smiled at his makeshift babysitters, who found the child adorable. When the bottle was finished, Brittany held the babe close to her bosom and gently patted his back until she heard Matthew burp. Darrin and Brittany took turns pacing about and rocking Matthew in their arms until he went to sleep. They felt an unexplained inner glow — a pleasing contentment — as they did. They then lowered the fast-asleep Matthew into his portable crib, setup in the downstairs bedroom.

When they returned to the parlor, Darrin and Brittany scanned the countless family photographs on the walls, the fireplace mantle, and the end tables in the room. The pictures were almost situated to capture the family engaging in events throughout the decades of their lives together. Sal and Cora's wedding portrait, the children's baptisms, communions, confirmations, and graduations. Family vacations, Christmas, and birthdays. Then the children's children. The hallowed images of the Panetta family members captured in each snapshot oozed out a love that transcended time and dimension. So powerful that Darrin and Brittany could not help but feel it. They stood in the awe and wonder of such love; so vivid in each frame of history that was captured by the photographs. Darrin and Brittany sensed the magic in the love that Sal Panetta bequeathed to his family through the years, a love that would stand as a testament to this good man for time eternal.

Upstairs, O'Connor asked the family to pray the *Lord's Prayer* as the *Unction* was administered. He took the vessel containing the Oil of the Sick, plucked in his thumb and anointed Panetta's eyelids while making the sign of the cross. "By this *Holy Unction* and his own most gracious mercy, may the Lord pardon ye whatever sin ye have committed by sight," O'Connor prayed. Then he took a cotton ball and wiped the oil off of Panetta's eyelids. He repeated the anointment, prayer, and cleansing on Panetta's ears, nostrils, lips, hands, and feet. Then he took the lemon slices and cleansed his own fingertips of the oil, finally wiping them dry with the hand cloth.

A peaceful feeling consumed Panetta's face — he was beginning to slip away.

O'Connor and the family continued with a few more prayers and responses, then the melancholy priest administered the Last Blessing. "May our Lord Jesus Christ, Son of the living God, Who to His apostle Peter gave the power of binding and loosing, by His most gracious mercy receive yer confession and restore to ye that first robe which you received at Baptism; and I, by the faculty given me by the Apostolic See, grant ye a plenary indulgence and remission of all yer sins, in the Name of the Father, and of the Son, and of the Holy Spirit."

"Amen."

"By the Sacred mysteries of man's redemption may almighty God remit to ye all penalties of the present life and of the life to come; may He open to ye the gates of paradise and lead ye to joys everlasting."

"Amen."

"May almighty God bless ye, Father and Son, and Holy Spirit."

The family chimed in once more for the final, "Amen."

"Precious Lord, take my hand. Lead me on, let me stand," O'Connor began to sing softly, wanting to comfort his friend and the family with a well-loved Gospel hymn. As he sang, he motioned with his hands to the family members, signaling for them to approach Sal so they might say their final goodbye. There was a special and fond embrace between Panetta and his eldest son, Sal Junior. The tears they shed flowed from pure love and the remembrances of all the fond times that were shared by fathers and sons. Past differences between them were now forgotten.

"Through the storm
Through the night
Lead me on to the light.
Take my hand, precious Lord, lead me home."

One by one the other family members said goodbye to their patriarch, then left the room and went downstairs. Sal's beloved wife, Cora, was the last to say goodbye. She took hold of Sal's hands, still cradling the crucifix, and squeezed them.

"When my way grows drear
Precious Lord linger near."

Sal opened his eyes one last time and found the love of his life looking back at him. "Thank you for everything, my love." His final words.

Cora leaned over, then she and Sal kissed for one last time. She ran the fingers of her other hand through his white thinning hair, whispering to him, "Goodbye, sweet love. Thank you for the wonderful ride, old feller."

Cora gently hugged her soulmate. Then, Sal Panetta slipped off into paradise, cradled in his wife's arms. There could be no more comforting a send-off. O'Connor watched and absorbed the tender moment, knowing that such a love could never culminate in death. He finished singing the hymn, which was as soothing to him as the Panetta family.

"At the river I stand
Guide my feet, hold my hand
Take my hand, precious Lord, lead me home."

Downstairs, the McCareys were in the kitchen preparing a pot of coffee. Once brewed, along a tray of premade finger sandwiches, they carted it back into the parlor for the family. They graciously served the family members, who were now comforting themselves with the tender retelling of stories and fond recollections of Sal Panetta. Darrin and Brittany enjoyed every tale that was told, almost wishing that they could have somehow been a part of this wonderful family.

Father O'Connor had some sandwiches and washed them down with a cup of coffee. When the McCareys brought out a coffee cake, he had a piece of that too. Sated, O'Connor bid his goodbyes to the family, especially to Cora, reassuring her that he would take care of the church arrangements. O'Connor would be serving the Funeral Mass and delivering the eulogy that he had already written in his heart. Sal wouldn't have it any other way.

Darrin and Brittany said their farewells, still feeling blissful from the warmth and love they experienced. They drove O'Connor back to the rectory, profusely thanking him for the unexpected pleasure of making the acquaintance of the Panetta family. Before exiting the car, O'Connor asked the McCareys if they had brought along the lists that he had asked them to compose — all of the things that they liked about each other. Brittany reached into her bag and Darrin reached into his backside pants pocket. They handed the lists over to O'Connor, who then handed back to each of them the other's list — so that they could discover what they loved about each other.

"Ye need to remember these things. So many times, 'tis easy for us to find fault with one another, and then forget to remind the people that we care for about why we really love 'em so. We sometimes fail to appreciate the daily events of our lives until they become cherished memories." Thinking about the young couple's marital discord, he said, "Ye have just left a family that were so desperately tryin' to hold onto what the both of ye are all too willin' to so easily throw away. …Think about it." O'Connor let the thought sink in, then he bid them goodnight and exited the car.

"Goodnight," they said.

As Father O'Connor walked away from the car, something told him to look back. Through the car's rear window, he could see Darrin and Brittany embracing and making out with each other. O'Connor looked up to the sky. *Thank the heavens above that they're married. Annulment me arse.*

Father O'Connor quickly made the sign of the cross.

Chapter Twenty-one

"Yes, that is very good news, Father O'Connor," Aubrey Fitzgibbon said.

Father O'Connor had just telephoned Aubrey from the Jersey City Police Department's Central Headquarters. The priest was delivering on his promise to Aubrey — making sure that the search for Angela Sanchez was stepped up and not forgotten.

"Tell Detective Cummings — Richard — that I said hello," she said.

Detective Richard Cummings was the lead police official heading up Angela's case. Cummings looked familiar to O'Connor, which was confirmed when he told the priest that he was a graduate from Saint Aloysius's Grammar and High Schools. O'Connor recalled the young sleuth, who practically set the school record for detentions back in the day. Aubrey Fitzgibbon's recalled Cummings as well — he was in her graduating class.

Tripping down memory lane, O'Connor kidded the detective about the amount of time he spent in the school jug, pondering if whether the school's patrol boys were now all criminals in juxtapose. On the more serious side, Cummings assured O'Connor that he would press even harder towards finding the runaway girl. He also promised that he would keep O'Connor constantly updated as the case progressed.

"Oh, by the way, Father — I'll be shoving off to the hospital at the end of the week. Doctor's orders. So, if you have any news, please reach me on my cell phone," Aubrey told the priest.

O'Connor inquired what was wrong.

"They say that they just want to keep an eye on me from close proximity. They tell me that the longer I survive, the greater are my chances of dying."

"Me doctors tell me something along the same lines, Misses Fitzgibbon — they say the longer that I live, the greater is me chances of dying of *ould* age."

The two shared a heartfelt laugh over O'Connor's off-the-cuff remark. A laugh that seemed to help void any lingering bitterness between them. Humor was still one of O'Connor's most powerful weapons — a gift from God, he insisted. They said their goodbyes and ended the conversation.

From the sound of her frail voice, O'Connor sensed that Aubrey's condition had worsened since the last time that he visited her. He was right. Aubrey was nearly thirty weeks pregnant and still in declining health. It was a small miracle that both she and the baby were still alive.

The next item on Aubrey's agenda would not be as pleasant. She told her children that she wanted to see them both that afternoon. Voices always inadvertently traveled from the downstairs to the upstairs of their family home, and throughout her ordeal, Aubrey kept herself well abreast of how her family was coping with her condition by the conversations that she overheard in her bedroom. Justin and Tracy also overheard what Aubrey's doctors told their father; they realized that their mom's prognosis was dire. Aubrey and Mike tried to shield their children from bad news, but the kids resented the charade.

Aubrey further learned that her decision to bring another child into the world did not sit well with her two children. She heard them tell their Father that they wanted nothing to do with their new baby sister if their mother died.

That scenario worried Aubrey the most. Sacrificing her own life and fighting so hard to save her child, only to have the poor soul abused and neglected by the very family that Aubrey would be counting on to help raise her. It was resentment borne from selfishness, and she intended to put the matter to rest with Justin and Tracy this very day.

"Hi, Mom."

"Hi ya, Mom."

Aubrey lifted her head off the pillow a bit to see Justin and Tracy enter the bedroom. They wore their happy faces like makeup — not wanting Aubrey to know their anguish. Aubrey stretched out her arms and opened her hands towards them. "Come, sit here," she said, easing them onto the side of the bed and grasping a hand from each of them.

Aubrey told them that she wanted to thank them for taking such good care of her, and for being so brave throughout her ordeal. "I'm so proud of both of you. You have been such valiant soldiers for me and your father."

The kids wore blank stares. Aubrey wasn't telling them what they wanted to hear.

"I want you both to know something — if I were sick and weak like this when I carried either one of you, I'd have done the same thing. Your new sister's life is just as precious to me. Now, I need a favor from the both of you."

The kids perked up a bit.

"Justin, have I not been there to help you with anything that was worthwhile in your life — including trying out for the football team?" Aubrey asked.

"Sure, Mom."

"Tracy, have I not done the same for you — including the endless arguments with Dad concerning your wardrobe?"

"Yes, Mom."

"I have tried so hard to support every one of your dreams. And, the times that I said 'no' to either of you — believe me — were for very good reasons."

"We don't understand why you're not saying 'no' this time," Tracy said, hoping, perchance, that she might be able to sway her mother's decision. "We love you. We want to still keep you. We don't want you to die." Her voice began to crack as a teardrop escaped from the corner of her eye.

"Now, now. You are burying me already. Let me tell you both something — your Mom is one tough lady. I won't be taken away so easy. In case you haven't noticed, I'm still hanging in despite what the doctors say. According to them, I should already be six feet under. I'm going to make it, kids. You both have to just keep believing and praying. But, trust me, I'm going to make it."

"And what if you don't?" Justin asked. What if it's God's will?"

The question threw Aubrey. "Justin, whatever do you mean?"

"Father O'Connor taught us his secret for having prayers answered, but when I asked him, *'What if they aren't answered,'* he told us that we should then assume that it's just God's will."

"And what did he say about God's will?"

"That we should just pray to accept it, and then someday we may come to understand why."

"He told us about God always opening another door right after he closes one," Tracy said.

"Yeah. Justin said, "it sure must be awful drafty up there in heaven with God running around closing and opening all of those doors."

Aubrey chuckled at Justin's remark and then thought to herself for a moment. "What Father O'Connor said is true. So, let's agree to accept whatever God's will is. ...I certainly like his odds a lot better than the doctors." She gently squeezed their hands. "Besides, I don't think God would have allowed your prayers to bring me along this far, only to let everyone down."

A glimmer of hope was enkindled Justin's and Tracy's spirits. They liked their mom's reasoning.

"But, I am going to ask you both to promise me something — just in case. I want you both to swear to me, that you will do what I ask. I want you both to honor me by fulfilling your promise. Will you do that for me? Will you? Justin? Tracy?"

The kids were overwhelmed with emotion, and they just nodded their heads in agreement.

Aubrey continued. "I want you both to help your father in raising your new sister. He's going to need plenty of support. And, I'm going to ask that you love her as much as you love me." Aubrey glanced towards Tracy. "She's going to need an older sister to help her pick out clothes and learn to be a lady — I don't want a daughter that's a tomboy." Aubrey looked over at Justin. "And, she's going to need a big brother to watch over her and keep her safe. Someone to make sure that her boyfriends treat her right. …When you look at your little sister, I want you both to think of me — that is how you will have me forever. She will be God's open door for you. …Now, do I have your word on this?"

"I promise, Mom," Justin said, leaning towards his mother and planting a kiss on her cheek.

"You have my word too, Mom." Tracy leaned towards her mother and kissed her on the other cheek.

Aubrey embraced them both, wishing that she could do so forever. Then she took their hands and placed them over her abdomen. "See, do you feel that — your sister is dancing with joy."

Tracy and Justin could feel their unborn sister kicking inside of Aubrey's uterus. They smiled, and for the first time, they were happy about the prospects of having a new sister. They were learning to be acceptant of whatever God would will.

Chapter Twenty-two

"Silent night, holy night
All is calm, all is bright
Round yon Virgin Mother and Child
Holy Infant so tender and mild
Sleep in heavenly peace
Sleep in heavenly peace."

The Saint Aloysius High School choir was practicing in the school's auditorium, preparing for their performance at the parish's traditional Midnight Mass on Christmas Eve. The church organist and choir director, Charles Baber, oversaw the rehearsal, playing through the planned program on an upright piano that the choir huddled around on the stage. Unbeknownst to anyone, Father O'Connor slipped into the auditorium to observe the rehearsal.

"That was magnificent kids," O'Connor shouted from the back of the huge hall at the conclusion of the hymn. "Brought a tear to me own eye, I might add." He made his way towards the stage.

O'Connor was already feeling a bit gleeful. While finishing dinner at the rectory, Misses Cavendish interrupted him for an important phone call. The call was from Aubrey Fitzgibbon. She asked O'Connor if he would stop by the hospital on the night before her operation to give her absolution. O'Connor was honored.

Of course, their conversation also touched upon the still missing Angela Sanchez. O'Connor still hoped against hope that something would turn-up shortly. Deep down in his soul he sensed that God would soon provide the answer to his prayer...perhaps, sooner than he than he thought. What

O'Connor didn't know was, at that very moment, Detective Richard Cummings was about to leave police headquarters and drive over to Saint Aloysius parish to personally deliver the final disposition of the Angela Sanchez matter to the priest. Cummings felt it best that he turned towards a man of God, especially in order to help him break the news about Angela to the others who were concerned about her wellbeing.

As he arrived at the stage, the kids in the choir greeted Father O'Connor with a chorus of hellos. All of them truly loved the old priest, who was practically a parish mascot to them. Baber greeted O'Connor as well, tinkling the piano keys with a few bars of *Hail to the Chief* as O'Connor made his upon the stage.

"Would you honor us with a song, Father?" Baber asked.

The kids then followed through, encouraging O'Connor to sing for them as well. They broke into a round of applause.

O'Connor was over a barrel. "Well, 'tis close to Christmas and ye've caught me in the holiday spirit," he said as the applause faded. He thumbed through a stack of music sheets that were strewn on top of the piano, picking out one that caught his eye. "Are ye familiar with this one at all, Charlie?" he asked, handing the song sheet to Baber.

"Pescador De Hombres, you've got it," Baber said, launching into the song's introduction on the piano keys.

O'Connor dove right into the song, captivating his audience with the emotion that he poured into his singing.

"Lord, when you came to the seashore
You weren't seeking the wise or the wealthy,
But only asking that I might follow.
O Lord, in my eyes you were gazing,
Kindly smiling, my name you were saying;
All I treasured, I have left on the sand there;
Close to you, I will find other seas."

As the song hit its crescendo, O'Connor signaled the choir to join in, this time singing the song in its native Spanish language.

"Señor me has mirado a los ojos,
Sonriendo has dicho mi nombre,
En la rena he dejado mi barca,
Junto a ti buscaré otro mar."

The melodic tune carried out of the auditorium and filled every empty hall and classroom of the vacant school building. It drifted out of the building and over the school grounds. The nuns in the nearby convent were drawn to opening their windows to catch the beautiful performance and free concert — like everyone else, they too loved when Father O'Connor sang.

The choir applauded the priest at the conclusion.

O'Connor returned the compliment. "That was just special, kids. Yer voices are angelic — the parish is blessed to have ye singin' for us. Ye know, when I was a lad, singin' with the Saint Bridget's Church children's choir back in Boston, the hardest part about singin' was just getting' through a song without a fistfight breakin' out."

The choir and Baber broke into a chorus of laughter.

O'Connor decided to spice up the tall tale even more. "The choir director always selected a lotta short hymns for us to sing. Singing a second verse was always risky. Such *rebel rousers* we were back in those days. Our choir was so tough, that whenever we hit a high note, they sometimes hit back."

The choir burst out in another fit of laughter.

"Oh, and by the way," he said, remembering something else. "Meself and Monsignor Norton are treatin' everyone to some pies tonight at Pompeii Pizza...after the rehearsal of course."

The choir broke into a round of applause.

"There is also one other thing that I stopped by to ask of ye — a sort of favor that I'd be needing. I'll be seekin' some volunteers for the night before Christmas Eve. …What time would ye be practicin' on that day, Charlie?"

"We have practice right after school, which should wrap up at about four o'clock."

"That'd be perfect timing." O'Connor went onto explain another of his schemes to the choir, which the teenagers were all too willing to oblige. Having secured their assistance, O'Connor bid them adieu, mentioning that he would head over to the pizza parlor to make arrangements for the festivities that would ensue after the rehearsal. The Christmas spirit was about.

But, before he could take leave, the choir prodded O'Connor to sing one more song. The request was unanimous — they wanted to hear *Irish Lullaby*. It was a song that O'Connor taught to generations of Saint Aloysius mothers for singing their babes to sleep. Every one of the grownup *babes* in the choir heard the tune sung to them several times over during the course of their lives. O'Connor could not wiggle out of this one — not after the choir agreed to help him carry out one of his schemes.

"Would ye excuse me, Mister Baber, I'll tinkle the keys meself on this one." O'Connor plopped himself down on the piano bench, interlocked the fingers of his hands and stretched them out.

"Me early Christmas present to ye all." Then he began pressing down upon the keyboard and sounding out the song's introduction. With his rendition of the Irish ditty, Father O'Connor touched the hearts of all, including the good Sisters of Charity who were still eavesdropping at their convent windows.

"Over in Killarney,
Many years ago,
Me mother sang a song to me
In tones so sweet and low.

Just a simple little ditty,
In her good ould Irish way,
And I'd give the world if she could sing
That song to me this day.

Too-ra-loo-ra-loo-ral,
Too-ra-loo-ra-li,
Too-ra-loo-ra-loo-ral,
Hush, now don't you cry!"

The choir softly chimed in, singing the final chorus with O'Connor.

"Too-ra-loo-ra-loo-ral,
Too-ra-loo-ra-li,
Too-ra-loo-ra-loo-ral,
That's an Irish lullaby."

O'Connor's rendition of the song was perfect. He decided to leave on that high note.

Several Christmas carols later, the choir joined Father O'Connor at Pompeii Pizza, just a short half block from the high school on West Side Avenue. For O'Connor, the party would be cut short by the unexpected entrance of Detective Richard Cummings. Monsignor Norton sent Cummings to the pizzeria, knowing O'Connor would be there.

Detective Cummings informed O'Connor about the final disposition regarding the Angela Sanchez matter. He had found her.

Chapter Twenty-three

Angela Sanchez was staying at the Covenant House in New York City — a shelter home for troubled teens. When she first fled Jersey City, she hopped on the *PATH* trains to New York City. Some of Covenant House's eyes and ears on the streets found her wandering about the city. They approached Angela and saved her from an undoubtedly, otherwise, cruel fate. The many prayers to God on Angela's behalf were answered — her Guardian Angel came through with flying colors.

Detective Richard Cummings, calling a lengthy list of shelters for runaways, stumbled onto Angela's whereabouts just the day before. Angela was using an alias, but Detective Cummings' keen knack for sleuthing assisted the staff at Covenant House in making the positive identification.

Angela still suffered from depression — a casualty of her ordeal. She told the Covenant House counselors that she did not want to return to her family, and she wouldn't tell them anything about where she lived. Angela was unaware that her mother cleaned up her act, and that she and Angela's grandmother were now living in a new apartment.

Detective Cummings sought out Father O'Connor to go with him to New York, thinking that the priest's collar would help in getting through any of the shelter's bureaucratic red tape. He also would need help in convincing Angela Sanchez to return home. The day after he broke the news about finding Angela to Father O'Connor, Detective Cummings knew he was in for an adventure. No sooner did he and O'Connor set out on their journey to meet with Angela Sanchez, when they took an abrupt detour.

At the priest's request, Cummings drove to the Hudson Family Planning office at Journal Square and parked. O'Connor exited the vehicle and headed for the entrance of the building with the detective in tow. They walked through the foyer into the reception area. A lone desk sat out in front of a wide-open, warehouse sized room that accommodated about twenty other desks — where the general staff were positioned. As the employees in the room took notice of a priest in their midst, the chattering fell silent. Garbed in his cleric's clothes, O'Connor stood out in a Family Planning Center like a brown pair of shoes worn with a black tuxedo. He asked the receptionist if he would be able to talk to Cindy Stone.

Situated in the midst of the employees, Stone heard her name mentioned and walked towards the front of the room. She had just returned to her job from a belated one-week suspension for her misconduct in copying Aubrey Fitzgibbon's health records. Additionally, Stone was now restricted from counseling clients and instead assigned to admittance — a position which would exclude her from handling any of the clientele medical files. Stone was lucky that she got off so easy — the Board wanted her fired. It was Aubrey Fitzgibbon, Stone's victim, who rescued her. A very charitable Aubrey thought that termination was too severe.

He's up to no good, Stone thought to herself as she sized up O'Connor, making her way towards his direction. *What does he want to do now — punch my lights out?* "Yes?" she asked in a harsh, coarse voice; careful not to step too close to the priest.

"Miss Stone," O'Connor said, raising his voice loud enough for the entire office to hear. "I wanted to apologize for cussin' ye out a few weeks back. Me behavior was uncalled for and I'm sorry. If ye can't find it in yer heart to forgive me, I can understand why. Just, please, don't be holding it against me church or me religion — I take full responsibility for me actions. I'm truly sorry."

Stone's jaw dropped. She was caught completely off guard by O'Connor's expression of regret. She stood there in shock. O'Connor's soft apology almost broke her bones. The priest's humility hurt Stone worse than his cursing her out. She remained speechless.

"Good day, I have to be leaving", O'Connor said. He turned around and retraced his steps back out of the building. Detective Cummings trailed after him, returning to the parking lot. The inquisitive second nature of the detective caused him to interrogate the priest about the apology. O'Connor told him the story about what Stone and his confrontation with her. He spared no details.

"My gosh, Father, do you really think that she was owed an apology? I mean, what she did was practically unforgivable. I'd say that she pretty much had it coming to her."

"Me son, the older ye get, the more ye'll realize that there's nuttin', absolutely nuttin', that cannot be forgiven. Perhaps it's our own mortality that makes forgiven' one of the most powerful actions a person can take. When we forgive others, we grow ourselves."

Cummings allowed O'Connor's sermon to sink in, remaining quiet while he drove himself and O'Connor through the Holland Tunnel and over to Covenant House in New York City.

Chapter Twenty-four

The girl appeared meek and humble. She was blanketed in insecurity, lacking the confidence to look anyone in the eyes who knew about her past. Observing her, Father O'Connor knew right away that his work was cut out for him. Detective Cummings, ably assisted by one of his like counterparts from the New York City Police Department, was able to cut through plenty of typical, bureaucratic red tape in order to get O'Connor an audience with the teen. Covenant House higher-ups were also loath to say 'no' to a man of the cloth.

Angela Sanchez was reluctant to meet with anyone who had intentions of taking her back home. Surprisingly, she consented to meet with the priest, whom she had avoided prior to undergoing her abortion. In a small reception lounge, O'Connor pulled his chair in closer to the couch where Angela sat.

He struggled to get her to talk — she was confining her conversation to one-word answers and nodding or shaking her head. She never lifted her head to face the priest. O'Connor told her all about the changes that had taken place since she fled — her mother successfully rehabbing and her family's new digs. That news seemed to make a bit of a dent as Angela began opening up. When O'Connor told her how concerned Aubrey Fitzgibbon was about her condition, the girl lit up like a Christmas tree and opened up even more. She stopped staring at the floor, now focusing her sights on Father O'Connor and beginning to engage in conversation.

Angela asked how Aubrey was doing, and O'Connor gave her the glum news — within days, she would be induced into labor in an effort to save her life and the life of her child. Because of her anemia and weakened heart, the doctors now gave less than favorable odds as to whether or not Aubrey would survive the procedure. Angela became deeply upset. The teen insisted on meeting with Aubrey before she was forced into labor. That made O'Connor's job of trying to convince her to return to Jersey City a bit easier. He promised her that he would make sure that she would see Aubrey.

The obstacles for Angela were now fear and her inability to overcome her self-stigmatization. O'Connor plied another tact. "Ye know, Lass, what I'm gonna say to ye now is not gonna make much sense. Right now, it'll seem a bit over yer head, but as sure as the *sun 'll* rise tomorrow, one day, yer gonna say to yerself, *'By golly, ole Father O'Connor was right.'*"

Angela perked up. O'Connor had aroused her curiosity. Outside the open door to the room, leaning up against the wall in the corridor, Detective Cummings perked up as well. Eavesdropping on Angela's and Father O'Connor's chat, he too was curious as to what O'Connor was alluding about.

"Angela, nobody is promised a problem free life. Everyone, at some time or another, has to deal with a problem — they're a part of yer life. And for sure, when trouble lands at yer doorstep, the problem yer facing might seem to be the size of a mountain. But in time, after yer able to overcome it, and when ye have the chance to look back, that same problem will only seem to be the size of a pebble. Trust me, Angela, the only reason yer feelin' so glum is 'cause yer so darn young, and ye don't yet realize that ye have yer whole life ahead a ye. This is just a bump in the road, Sweetheart — 'tis all that it is."

O'Connor was connecting — what he was saying was seeming to make sense to Angela. "It wouldn't matter if ye were to run from here to Timbuktu, when ye gotta a problem, it never stays where ye think ye have left it, child; 'tis gonna always keep after ye until ye finally confront it. Runnin' away only increases the distance from the solution to yer problems,

Lass. The best way to escape from yer problems is to solve them."

In the hallway, Cummings began to think about his own teenage daughter, and how he might have taken her for granted whenever she brought up, what he considered, trivial matters to him. He now had a better appreciation for how those small difficulties might have seemed like the end of the world to her. He committed himself to paying better attention to his daughter's concerns in the future.

"And, Lass, ye have plenty of life ahead a ye — school, proms, graduations, maybe college, marriage and a family. Ye seem to be givin' up an awful lot for not dealin' with what yer goin' through right now. I'll tell ye this, there's not a child in this entire buildin' who would pass up the chance for a carin' family, and a new home to go back to, if they were fortunate enough to be in yer shoes."

Angela thought it over. *It can't hurt to try.* She did miss her mom and her *Abuela.* She was also looking forward to seeing her friend Aubrey Fitzgibbon again, especially now that she knew Aubrey was in crisis. Angela told Father O'Connor that she was willing to have a go at it. It brought the first smile of the day to the tired priest's face. But there was still another unsettling problem that was bothering Angela, and taking O'Connor's advice, she decided to confront it there and then. "Father, will God forgive me for what I did?"

O'Connor smiled. "Of course, Angela — that's what our faith is all about. That's why Christ died on the cross — the forgiveness of all of our sins. That's why he rose again — the redemption from our sins. May I have the honor of grantin' ye absolution? The Archbishop has already givin' ye his blessing."

Angela was relieved, she really treasured her religion despite her fall from grace. She thought of something else. "One last thing, Father, I really sounded off on some of my classmates who insulted me — I was so hurt that I lost it and cursed them out. I used words that I had never uttered before in my life. May I be forgiven for losing control?"

"Indeed, ye may." O'Connor then crossed his fingers and slipped them behind his back so that Angela could not see them. "Child, ye need to learn self-control when confronted with such circumstances. Never allow temptation to take ye over and cause ye to be cussin' out people who may provoke ye. Self-control, Angela." O'Connor thought of his incident with Cindy Stone and then looked skyward, as if he were asking God to cut him some slack.

Angela Sanchez was feeling like her old self for the first time in a long while. She, O'Connor, and Detective Cummings then headed to the Covenant House central office to locate Angela's counselor and begin the protocol procedure for dismissing a client. Angela could hardly wait to see her family and Aubrey Fitzgibbon again.

Father O'Connor could taste sweet victory on his tongue. It helped to remedy the bitter aftertaste left from his apology to Cindy Stone earlier that morning.

Chapter Twenty-five

Comfy-cozy back at the rectory, Father O'Connor sat in the den, nestled deep into the cushions of his favorite easy chair. Deep in thought, he stared into the dancing flames of the wall hearth, still savoring the pleasures of the fine dinner that Misses Cavendish earlier served. A Nat King Cole Christmas album played on the stereo phonograph, setting the mood for the Christmas holiday season.

Standing in the second-floor foyer of the rectory, Monsignor Norton peered in at O'Connor from the doorway of the room. He spied the worn-out look on the priest's face. Norton knew all about the tough day O'Connor had been through — hopping over to New York City to retrieve Angela Sanchez and apologizing to Cindy Stone. He knew the latter had to be a real chore for the prideful priest.

Walking into the room, Norton maneuvered two rock glasses filled halfway to the top with *Tullamore Dew.* "Father, Misses Cavendish told me that you forgot to take your nightly heart medicine," he said, raising one of the glasses in the air, then handing it over to O'Connor. "Here it is, *'a wee bit of the creature,'* as you would call it," Norton said, impersonating O'Connor's Irish brogue. He then eased himself into the empty chair across from his colleague. "Tonight, I thought that I would join you — if only to salute you. That was a magnanimous gesture you made today — apologizing to Miss Stone. Cheers! Here's to you, Father O'Connor."

Norton extended his glass towards O'Connor's glass, who then extended his glass towards Norton's. The two glasses clinked together, then the priests lifted the salute to their lips and sipped down some of the *Tullamore Dew* in a fitting tribute.

"You look a bit glum tonight, Father. Something got you down?" Norton asked.

O'Connor conceded that something did have him feeling lowly, then he expressed his concerns about things possibly not working out for Angela Sanchez. He was worried that she might not adjust, and then explained all that was entailed in order to just convince her to return home. "I hope I haven't let the poor girl down."

"You let anybody down? Forget it, Father. Angela Sanchez will be another one of *O'Connor's miracles.* You wait and see. She'll come around."

O'Connor nodded in agreement, hoping that Norton was right.

"And, by the way, Father, that nice young couple — the McCareys — dropped by today."

"Oh?"

"They've set a church record for booking a baptism so early — and they want you to administer the sacrament to the baby that they're expecting. They're another O'Connor miracle." The monsignor began to chuckle.

O'Connor remembered the couple dropping him off at the rectory on the night that Sal Panetta passed — he had the vivid memory of turning back to wave goodbye, only to catch sight of the McCareys through the rear window of their car...as they were making it with each other. "They'll probably be naming the child, *Buick,*" O'Connor said.

The remark left Monsignor Norton befuddled.

"You know, Father, you are quite a lucky guy, I'm the monsignor here but everyone wants you. You name it — christenings, weddings, last rites, confessions and Mass — everyone wants Father O'Connor. You are really loved by the people of this parish. I only hope that, someday, I can become just half the kind of priest you are. ...You want to laugh,

Father? I wish I had a nickel for every time that I've run across a mother in the parish strolling or rocking her baby to sleep and singing *Too-ra-loo-ra-loo-ral*. They should pay you the royalties for that song. The good sisters were talking about how you were singing it the other night — with the choir at practice. They were so thrilled." Norton took a sip from the rock glass. "Father, I've been the third monsignor to succeed you at Saint Aloysius, and you are still the standard by which we were all measured. I've learned a lot from working with you here, and I'll be forever grateful."

O'Connor was now feeling like a million bucks, and between the sips of *Tullamore Dew* and Monsignor Norton's compliments, his cheeks resumed their rosy red hue. "Ye know, Tim, in all me years as a priest, a monsignor, and now a priest again, this was me most enjoyable experience. That's mostly due to ye — yer the most unselfish person I know. Ye always find a way to make other people shine. Yer a wonderful monsignor."

"You really think so? I only wish the Archbishop felt the same way — maybe then I'd get that sabbatical."

"Father Norton, yer *wish'll* come true someday — sooner than ye think. Keep a suitcase packed." O'Connor thought maybe he'd gone too far with his hint. He didn't want to spoil Monsignor Norton's Christmas surprise. In fact, Archbishop Scaponi called O'Connor, just a few days earlier, to reconfirm that he would be sending out a letter to Monsignor Norton, informing him that he would be given leave to attend Georgetown, in order that he could pursue a course of studies for attaining a doctorate degree.

During the same phone call, Scaponi also confirmed arrangements for his visit to Jersey City the following day, in order for O'Connor to finally make the Archbishop's introduction to Ed Ford, the proprietor of Dohoney's. Scaponi wanted to thank, in person, the generous soul whom so overwhelmingly supported the diocese food pantry drive each

Thanksgiving. He also wanted to present Ford with a small Christmas present as a token of his appreciation.

The priests enjoyed a few more of Nat King Cole's Christmas nuggets, including the classic *The Christmas Song;* occasionally, they sang along. Before retiring for the evening, Norton brought up the subject of Aubrey Fitzgibbon's condition. The monsignor spoke to Deacon Fitzgibbon earlier and the man was a mess. The doctors tried to prepare him and his family for grim news — a baby girl Christmas Eve morning, but the loss of his wife in the process. There is no way they thought Aubrey's already weakened heart could survive the trauma. Deacon Fitzgibbon was already planning the final arrangements for Aubrey, asking Monsignor Norton if he would preside at her funeral.

Father O'Connor practically hit the roof. "There's a real pillar of faith."

Monsignor Norton knew that O'Connor would be stopping by the hospital to see Aubrey Fitzgibbon and hear her confession the next day, on the eve of her procedure. "Will you be giving her *final* absolution, Father?"

"Absolutely not! I expect Aubrey and child to both pull through. I'll not be runnin' a white sheet up the flagpole and surrenderin' on me own faith."

Monsignor Norton smiled — that was the O'Connor he so much admired. He said goodnight and headed for bed.

Father O'Connor listened to the rest of the Nat King Cole album, then he headed for the rectory chapel where he prayed for Aubrey and Angela, asking for God to deliver a miracle.

Chapter Twenty-six

Father O'Connor trudged along on West Side Avenue, tipping the brim of his flat cap to practically every passerby that acknowledged the legendary priest's presence. The whole of Jersey City knew Father Sean O'Connor — he was royalty. O'Connor made his way past Lee's, heading north, crossing Fairview Avenue. On occasion, he would dip his head behind the turned-up collar of his overcoat, using it to break the frigid wind that blew down the avenue, in order to keep it from freezing his face. It was sunny for now, but the forecast was calling for precipitation, and the cold temperature was dictating that it would be the season's first snowfall. As his foot touched down on the curb at the beginning of the sidewalk, he looked up ahead, toward a marquee that jutted out from a building down the block — *Dohoney's Tavern* it read.

O'Connor was on his way to meet his lifelong friend, Archbishop Scaponi, to finally make his introduction to Ed Ford. The priest was a little leery about the impromptu calendar date — only arranged a few days earlier by Scaponi. This day was also O'Connor's birthday, and he knew that his old friend was well aware of that as well. He remained suspicious about whether Scaponi had something else up his sleeve.

Out of nowhere, just up ahead, Archbishop Scaponi popped into view. He was coming from the opposite direction, having just stepped out onto the sidewalk from the parking lot adjacent to the tavern. The two clergymen caught sight of each other, grinning the smiles that typically accompanied the greetings of two close friends. Scaponi reached the front door of the tavern first, and he waited there for O'Connor. They greeted each other with a handshake, shoulder pat, and verbal pleasantries. Scaponi then pushed open the tavern door and held it ajar while he motioned for O'Connor to enter first.

"For he's a golly good fellow.
For he's a jolly good fellow..."

The loud and off-key singing startled O'Connor, who instantly knew that Scaponi had set him up. It took several seconds for the priest's eyes to adjust from the bright outdoors to the dimly lit tavern's atmosphere.

"...For he's a jolly good fellow,
Which nobody can deny..."

As soon as his eyes were able to focus, O'Connor could recognize many of the patrons standing alongside the bar and hoisting up a drink in his honor. Many in the crowd were Saint Aloysius parishioners. *Dohoney's* had an assortment of some of the most fascinating Damon Runyonesque type characters for clientele, all of whom knew Father O'Connor.

"Happy Birthday, Father O'Connor," shouted a boisterous and plump man who stepped up to greet the priest — it was Ed Ford, *Dohoney's* proprietor.

Mister Ford put together the spur-of-the-moment welcoming after Archbishop Scaponi called to tell him that he and O'Connor would be stopping by to say hello. Scaponi had also leaked the news about O'Connor's birthday to Ford.

Simultaneously, Archbishop Scaponi and Ed Ford took hold of Father O'Connor's arms and shoulders, guiding him toward the crowd.

"Ye two big stinkers," O'Connor said. One at a time, he looked his two friends dead in the eyes. "I should a known that the two a yer were up to no good. Egad."

"Job well done, *Faa*," Scaponi said to Ed Ford, referring to him by the nickname that the tavern owner preferred for people to call him. Nicknames were as common as alcohol in Jersey City taverns. You were truly a nobody in the tavern scene until somebody tagged you with a nickname.

The Faa and Archbishop Scaponi led Father O'Connor through the gauntlet of well-wishers, gradually making their way toward the backroom of the tavern — the dining area of the establishment. Along the way, O'Connor was the recipient of well wishes from the likes of notable Dohoney's patrons such as Shoe's Hughes, Fat Mac, The Hampster, Mister Nice Guy, Putty Face Malone, Mac-off, Murph the Surf, Wacky Willie, Beef-O, Blackberry Brandy Bob, and Applejack Schnapps Joe. These were characters who could, literally, fill the pages of books — an author's story for another day.

Reaching the back end of the bar, Scaponi and Ford maneuvered the birthday boy up the two short steps that led up to the dining area. The crowd start singing *Happy Birthday* to O'Connor. As he entered the dining room, the eyes of the celebrated priest were drawn to an occupied rear table. Father O'Connor did a double take. His heart skipped a beat as a rush of emotion swelled up inside of him, a reaction triggered by his sudden recognition of the faces seated at the table looking back at him — the surviving members of *"O'Connor's Miracles."*

Scaponi watched his friend's reaction to sighting his old army buddies. "Happy Birthday, Sean," he said. Scaponi had arranged the whole thing. The remaining trio of *"O'Connor's Miracles"* were happy to oblige the Archbishop's invitation, combining the reunion with a short New York City pre-holiday vacation with their wives. The wives were busy holiday shopping across the Hudson River in the city, while their husbands awaited regaling themselves with old war stories over lunch.

The Faa grabbed the attention of the young waiter who would be serving the table — a Saint Peter's College student making some quick cash by waiting tables during the school's winter break. "Patrick," Ford addressed the waiter, "the tab for this table is on the house."

Happy tears streamed down O'Connor's face as he reached the table to greet his old friends. He felt young again. The army pals politely teased each other, immediately beginning to recall the trials and tribulations of their hitch with Uncle Sam. The comrades snacked their way through beers and sandwiches on their stroll down memory lane. They spoke fondly of their fellow soldiers, some of whom had passed. When they finished lunch and ordered coffee, Archbishop Scaponi excused himself from the table — he had to get back to Saint Michaels' Cathedral in Newark. He was merely a spare tire at the gathering. O'Connor also excused himself for a moment, wanting to escort Scaponi out the back door of the tavern that led to the parking lot.

"Thank you very much for this, Mario. Yer a wonderful friend. I can never repay for gettin' us all together again." O'Connor said, referring to his army buddies.

"It was my pleasure, Sean. It made me feel good just to be a part of it," Scaponi thrust out his hand.

O'Connor reciprocated.

As the handshake was about to break apart, Scaponi gripped O'Connor's hand a bit tighter, not allowing it to retreat. He extended his other hand and clenched the priest's forearm. It was an odd moment, almost as if the man of God had sensed something. "Sean, you have always been and remain a good friend. The Lord has truly blessed me by giving me the gift of your friendship. Until the next time, my friend…may God bless you and keep you safe."

The wonderful sentiment was an uplifting gesture that was heartfelt by O'Connor. He nodded his head in appreciation.

Scaponi smiled across at his friend. O'Connor smiled right back at him. The handshake broke apart, but the bond between these two friends, who had grown old and supported each other since their early childhood days on the streets of Boston, would last an eternity.

O'Connor returned to the dining room of Dohoney's and regrouped with his miracles. After endless cups of coffee, the most solemn part of the reunion ensued, when they recalled the fateful date in December 1967 at Bien Hoa Province, Vietnam — the day that they were wounded and faced death. The day that they were rescued by a Chaplain of the 199th Infantry Brigade — Father Sean O'Connor.

The end of this mixed-emotion recollection was graced by a reverent silence — a moment for the gathering to reflect on how close they all came to death. A moment to count their blessings and be thankful for the benevolence of God's grace. This was the last that they spoke about the old army days. The conversation next resumed with talk about their families. Tyrone Williams reached for his phone and then his wallet, producing pictures and photographs of his wife, children, and grandchildren. Barry Freeman and Mike D'Andrea did likewise. They circulated the photos around the table.

As he viewed the family photos of his friends, O'Connor became overwhelmed with emotion again. Something had finally dawned on him — none of these families would exist had he not decided to act above and beyond the call of duty on that fateful December day so long ago. O'Connor was having his George Bailey moment. Listening to the stories of how the families had progressed throughout the years, made something very clear to O'Connor — he certainly wasn't irrelevant. The living proof was right before his eyes — none of this was possible had he not taken the daring action of rescuing his comrades back in Vietnam.

The reminiscing was over and the passing time reminded the former soldiers that they had to be heading back to meet their wives in New York City. Father O'Connor also planned to make some stops before his visit to Aubrey Fitzgibbon. The friends exchanged goodbyes and Christmas wishes with Father O'Connor, then they prompted their young waiter to take a group snapshot with each of their iPhones. Before they departed, Mike D'Andrea asked Father O'Connor to bless the gathering. O'Connor graciously consented. It would be the same blessing that O'Connor had bestowed upon them during their final discharge from the army — a famous Irish Blessing that he had used throughout the years.

"May the road rise to meet ye. May the wind be always at yer back. May the sunshine warm yer face, and the rain fall soft upon yer fields. And until we meet again, may God hold ye in the palm of his hand."

Chapter Twenty-seven

Alone, inside the non-denominational chapel of the Jersey City Medical Center, Deacon Mike Fitzgibbon knelt down and prayed, trembling as he wept. He was so much of a mess at the time that he wouldn't dare let his wife see him in such a condition. Having just left Aubrey's room in the intensive care unit, Mike was trying to compose himself before checking in with her again. He didn't hear the chapel door open, nor notice the figure of the man who slipped inside, Father Sean O'Connor.

When he signed in at the reception desk of the hospital, the clerk told the priest that Aubrey's husband was praying in the chapel. O'Connor stepped inside the pew and knelt beside the deacon. Mike looked over and frowned. O'Connor sensed that he was unwanted company.

"Me friend, I know that we have not always been seein' eye to eye, but please give me but just a second of yer time. Ye look like a man who has lost all hope. Ye've lost hope, because ye've lost yer faith. Mike, ye need to know that there are no hopeless situations — only people who feel hopeless in their situation. Ye need to learn the secret to prayer, me friend."

Fitzgibbon said nothing at first, but finally, he caved. "And, what might the secret to prayer be, Father?"

"I'd thought *ye'd* never ask. Ye gotta believe, Mike. Ye gotta believe. Ye can't be prayin' to God for Aubrey to pull through in one breath, and talkin' to the undertaker in the next breath. Ye gotta know that she's gonna get better. And ye have to pray to God with that firm conviction already soldered in yer heart. Belief — that's the secret."

"And who said that's the secret to prayer?"

"Christ, himself, ye dummy. Luke eleven, *'So, I say to ye: Ask and it will be given to ye; seek and ye will find; knock and the door will be opened to ye.'*"

O'Connor recalled another scripture. "Mark eleven, *'truly I tell ye, if anyone says to this mountain, 'Go, throw yerself into the sea,' and does not doubt in their heart but believes that what they say will happen, it will be done for them.*

Therefore, I tell ye, whatever ye ask for in prayer, believe that ye have received it, and it will be yers.'"

Mike let it all seep in. He felt a calming influence overpower him. He couldn't wait to pray with faith as Christ had taught. O'Connor's stock was rising with the deacon. Then, Mike asked the jackpot question, "What is God's purpose for making someone suffer through all of this?"

"That's somethin' that no one can answer, Mike. Just know that sometimes God writes straight with crooked lines, me friend. When the Lord reaches down to take somethin' from yer grasp, he's not doin' it to punish — he's merely opening yer hands to receive somethin' better. Be sure of one thing Mike — for the sake of ye and yer whole family — the will of God will never take ye to where the Grace of God will not protect ye. Only trust in the fact that He shall have the final word. He is the way and the truth and the life. ...Tend to yer scriptures, Deacon."

Mike pondered the wisdom of O'Connor's words. "Thank you, Father, for your inspiration."

"Just do me a favor, Mike — pray a little bit more here, and then cancel the undertaker. Yer gonna have a Christmas to always remember, along with yer wife and a new daughter."

His words of wisdom imparted, the priest stood up and walked out of the chapel, leaving behind him a rejuvenated Deacon Mike Fitzgibbon, who finally saw the light. The deacon realized that the animus he had been feeling towards

Father O'Connor was misplaced — the priest was truly a benevolent soul.

O'Connor headed back to the hospital reception desk to retrieve a bag of goods that he left there — some surprises that he brought along with him for his visit with Aubrey Fitzgibbon. He caught the elevator and headed up to the intensive care unit. When the elevator doors swished open, O'Connor stepped across the corridor towards the ICU. He pushed open one of the double doors leading into the unit and stepped inside. There was a nurses' station sitting in the center of the room. Doors to the individual rooms surrounded the station. Monitors displaying the vital signs of the unit's patients were set inside the back panel of the nurses' station. Toting his overcoat in one hand and his bag of goods in the other, O'Connor trudged over to the two nurses manning the command center, preparing to announce himself.

After a brief exchange, the nurses pointed Father O'Connor towards ICU Room 4. The priest made his way over to the large door of the room, pushed it open and walked inside. A reading light on the wall over the bed illuminated half of the room. Outside the large window of the room, the December sky was already dark. The streetlights from below cast some brightness in through the window. A light snow had begun to fall. Without a driving wind, the snowflakes drifted to earth like feathers.

Father O'Connor's eyes quickly fell upon Aubrey, lying in her bed. She was staring out the window watching the snowfall. Aubrey looked ashen and old to O'Connor, far worse than she looked when he visited her at home. She was breathing with the assistance of oxygen, but O'Connor saw that it was even a struggle for her to suck air through the prongs of the cannula in her nostrils. O'Connor cleared his throat, trying to grab her attention.

Aubrey slowly turned her head on the pillow, focusing her eyes in his direction, she saw a silhouette standing in the dark shadows on the far side of the room. Father O'Connor slowly stepped forward until he was illuminated by the reading light.

"Father O'Connor," Aubrey said in a barely audible whisper.

The sound of her weak voice alarmed the priest. He had tended to hundreds of parishioners on their deathbeds over the course of his priestly duties and, unfortunately, to him, Aubrey looked like she fit the part of one not long for the world. "Good evenin' to ye, Misses Fitzgibbon," O'Connor said. He planted a pleasant expression on his face so Aubrey could not tell how badly that she looked.

He reached into his bag and pulled out a two-foot tall Texas cactus rose in a planter. There were six buds sprouting from the plant that had yet to bloom. O'Connor could see the pleasant surprise lit up Aubrey's face.

"A cactus rose — my favorite flower," Aubrey whispered. "You remembered, Father."

"Indeed, I did," he said, holding it out in front of her from the side of the bed. "I'll put it on the windersill, so that it might be gettin' a bit of sun in the morning," he said, making his way over to the window. Facing the window, he pulled out a LED flashlight from his pocket and flashed it on and off several times. After returning it to his pocket, he turned back around towards the bed.

"Father, thank you for finding Angela."

"Have you spoken to her?"

"She called today, but I was asleep when she did. My husband filled me in on your trek over to New York to get her. Thank you."

"Mike? How did he know?"

"Monsignor Norton filled him in."

"O Holy Night! The stars are brightly shining, It is the night of the dear Savior's birth."

The singing filtered into the room from the streets below. The Saint Aloysius High School Choir were huddled two floors beneath the window of the room, there to serenade Aubrey Fitzgibbon. Father O'Connor's grand scheme of course — the one that he arranged with the choir during their practice that he attended. The sounds of music brought a smile to Aubrey's face.

"'Tis the high school choir that's come to give ye an exclusive performance, Misses Fitzgibbon."

"Oh, they sound wonderful. What the *Christmas Spirit* will inspire people to do."

"More like what the *Pompeii Pizzas* that fill a teenager's empty belly will get them to do."

Aubrey appeared to not understand what he meant.

"Fall on your knees! Oh, hear the angel voices! O night divine, the night when Christ was born."

They enjoyed a bit more of the choir's concert, then Aubrey reached over and tugged Father O'Connor's sleeve. "Father, I'm so upset that I may not live to see my child." Tears began to stream forth from her eyes. "To come this far and have to wonder what she will look like. It's not fair." The only thing that kept Aubrey from breaking down completely was the difficulty she had drawing her next breath. "I overheard my doctor tell the nurse that he didn't expect me to make it."

"Misses Fitzgibbon, don't ye dare be givin' in to despair after havin' come all this way. Ye need to fight to hold onto yer life and the life of yer baby. Fight with everything that's in ye. Ye can do it, Misses Fitzgibbon, ye just gotta believe that yer gonna pull through and fer sure ye will. Just as sure as the buds on that cactus *rose 'll bloom*." O'Connor pointed to the plant. Then the priest stared Aubrey straight in the eyes and professed his faith in God to her. "The doctors shall not have the final word, Aubrey — 'tis yer lord and savior that will. You must believe that, Child!"

"I believe, Father. I believe."

"Maybe this could help a bit." O'Connor reached into his pocket and pulled out a thin necklace chain with his Celtic cross ring dangling from it — the one that she so much admired and complimented when he visited Aubrey at her home. "This Celtic cross ring that me mother gave me has always brought me good luck from God. I swear to ye that it's sainted. Please keep it with ye when yer givin' birth to yer baby tomorrow." The priest unfastened the clasp on the chain, then placed it around Aubrey's neck and refastened it.

"Truly He taught us to love one another, His law is love and His gospel is peace."

"Oh, Father O'Connor, thank you. Are you sure it's all right?"

"I'd be honored to have ye wearin' it."

"Father, I have to tell you — on the day that we had our little quarrel, you said something to me as you left — something that's stuck with me ever since. It's helped me to carry on. I think about it all of the time. Do you remember? Do you remember what you told me, Father?"

"Misses Fitzgibbon, I'm so full of malarkey at spells, that 'tis hard for me to remember all that I have to say from time to time. I'm afraid that I've a gift for too much of the *blarney* at times."

"You told me that *'where God breeds life there will always be hope.'* That's what you said, and you're so right. You're so right, Father."

"Might I ask what name ye have chosen for yer child?" O'Connor asked, trying to inject an optimistic spin into the conversation.

"I've chosen Stefanie — it was the name Angela had chosen to call her baby, if — "

"That's sweet of ye."

Aubrey was out of breath. O'Connor could tell she needed a chance to collect herself. They remained quiet for a moment or so, enjoying the choir's rendition of *Hark! The Herald Angels Sing.* O'Connor kept a steady eye on Aubrey's breathing, waiting until it wasn't as labored.

"Misses Fitzgibbon, would ye like for me to hear yer confession?"

Aubrey smiled again and nodded 'yes.' She was about to take a load off her conscience and liberate her soul. About to finally rid herself of the dirty little secret that had been eating her up for almost a year. It was why she called the rectory and requested for O'Connor to hear her confession. Aubrey made the sign of the cross and began to confess her sins. "Bless me, Father, for I have sinned." Tears began to flow again. "I have sinned terribly…and I want to get this off of my chest." She sobbed and sucked in a deep breath of air from the respirator. "My God, I've betrayed two people whom I dearly love. And, if they ever found out, I'm afraid that I would lose them forever." Aubrey's sobbing intensified. "I need your help, Father. I'm troubled and I don't know what to do. I'm frightened by what I might have to do."

"Calm down, child," O'Connor said. He reached down and took hold of her hand, squeezing it tight. "Slow. Slow. Take it easy. I promise that I will help ye make all things right. Now, just find some strength and tell me what is wrong."

Aubrey collected herself, at least to the extent that she could talk between sobs. The tears continued rolling down her cheeks. She took in several deep breaths and began to spin her tale of woe to the priest. She closed her eyes tight, as if it would help her to clearly recollect the history of the events that she was now confessing. Aubrey began by explaining how, earlier in the year, she and Mike joined their close friends since high school, Nikki and Matt Spencer, for a weekend at the couple's shore home.

The ritual weekend getaway, a few weeks before Memorial Day, was an annual event for the friends, ever since the Spencers first bought the home. She and Mike always helped the Spencers get the home ready for the summer, but there was time for some fun too.

"Matt Spencer and I were always close. Ever since high school, if he had a misunderstanding or argument with Nikki, he'd call me for advice to help him patch it up." Aubrey paused to swallow. "I often got the feeling that Matt found me attractive, ever since the first time we met. He was always flirting with me — in a kidding around sort of way. It was nothing serious."

A queasy feeling began to well up in O'Connor's stomach. He was uncomfortable about where Aubrey's story was headed.

"In time, I came to realize that Matt really wasn't kidding — he actually had a serious crush on me. Over time, that crush built itself into an infatuation. I didn't see it coming, and when I finally did, I said nothing. I was, in some sick sort of way, I guess, flattered by the attention. I enjoyed it. I said nothing, damn it. I was so damn vain, I said nothing! I am as much to blame for what happened."

O'Connor braced himself as Aubrey's narrative turned uglier and uglier. Neither he nor Aubrey were now mindful of the tender Christmas hymns filling the air from the Saint Aloysius High School choir on the street below.

Aubrey went on to explain that after they worked helping to spruce up the Spencer's summer shore house all Saturday morning, by midafternoon, they decided to kick back and relax with a few bottles of wine. "Mike was planned to cook his special pasta dish and sauce for dinner. Nikki needed a few things from the store, so she drove Mike there in order for him to get whatever he would need to cook dinner. Matt and I stayed back at the house to set the table and prepare a salad."

She explained to O'Connor how the effects of the wine left her feeling giddy and uninhibited. After setting the table and making the salad, Matt began to flirt with her. She allowed it. Her failure to resist, enticed him to continue. "It happened so suddenly. We reached for each other's hands. We stared into each other's eyes. He moved his mouth towards mine. I moved mine towards him. Our lips met...then our passions took over."

Aubrey sobbed profusely now and gasped again to catch her breath.

"Easy, child. Easy," O'Connor said in a soft voice.

"We moved to the couch and stripped down," Aubrey said, her voice breaking. "We made love. I enjoyed it. When we were done, we dressed and said not a word to each other. In fact. I can't remember us saying anything more to each other for the rest of that weekend. I pretended to have a headache after dinner, and then went right to bed. Mike joined me shortly. We went back home early the next day." Aubrey placed her free hand over her swollen abdomen. She looked up into O'Connor's eyes. "This is Matt's baby. I know it!"

"Why are ye so sure that it's Matt's?"

Aubrey went onto explain that while she and Mike shared an active sex life, he hadn't gotten her pregnant since the birth of their youngest child, Justin — fourteen years ago. It was only after her tryst with Matt Spencer, as luck would have it, that she became pregnant.

"Does Matt Spencer know that he maybe the father?"

"No, Father. No one else knows about this yet, besides you." Aubrey opened her eyes and looked O'Connor straight in the face. "No one even suspects. That's why I wanted the abortion. Nikki suspected the pregnancy, but she knew how much that I was also into my career — that's why she bought the story that I concocted about why I wanted the abortion. Nikki never doubted me. My God, what have I done?"

O'Connor's face had turned ashen. Aubrey's tragic tale had finally cleared up for him the mystery about why she first sought to have the abortion. He pondered all that Aubrey had just confessed. "Misses Fitzgibbon, I never asked ye this before, but now I need to know — why did you decide to have the baby? Especially after knowing that ye were risking yer life."

Aubrey peered into O'Connor's eyes. "It was Angela Sanchez. She asked me to be with her when she underwent her abortion procedure. I never realized how gross the procedure was up close — not as tidy and neat as they explain it to you. It was so horrible that I passed out. What I witnessed that day stuck with me. Afterwards, I was overwhelmed by guilt — how could I choose to have another innocent child suffer the same fate because of my sin? The thought haunted me. I couldn't live with myself. Then I remembered your words, *'where God breeds life there will always be hope.'*...Those words haunted me."

Silence filled the room. Aubrey and O'Connor reflected on her confession. The choir took a short break from their caroling. O'Connor broke the quiet to address the fear of what he knew that she was pondering — her penance. She had explained to him how she worried that her penance might entail coming clean to her husband and Nikki. O'Connor empathized with her concern and he carefully weighed the options.

As the years-wise priest pronounced her penance, he stilled Aubrey's fears. "Yer acknowledgin' yer sin to others would serve no purpose but to hurt the innocent. Yer having to live with yer own hurt in silence, and havin' it hauntin' ye fer the rest of yer long life, will be penance enough. Though, there may come a time when the truth of all of this might have to see the light of day. Ye'll be the Solomon who'll have to make that decision, Misses Fitzgibbon. In the meantime, I want ye to keep prayin' the Our Father, the Hail Mary, and the Glory Be for the rest of the night as part of yer penance."

A sense of peace befell Aubrey. She now poured out tears of relief. "Thank you, Father O'Connor. God Bless you."

O'Connor then told Aubrey to pray an *Act of Contrition* while he administered absolution. "God the Father of mercies, through the death and resurrection of his Son has reconciled the world to himself and sent the Holy Spirit among us fer the forgiveness of sins; through the ministry of the Church may God give ye pardon and peace, and I absolve ye from yer sins in the name of the Father, and of the Son, and of the Holy Spirit."

"It came upon the midnight clear,
That glorious song of old,
From angels bending near the earth,
To touch their harps of gold."

"My favorite of all Christmas carols. Would you sing it with me, Father?"

"I'd be delighted." O'Connor cleared his throat as he prepared to add his voice to that of Aubrey and the choir.

"Peace on the earth, goodwill to men
From heavens all gracious King!
The world in solemn stillness lay
To hear the angels sing."

Aubrey got as far along as she could with the song until she was out of breath again. O'Connor sensed that she was weakening. He reached into his pocket and pulled out a portable Eucharist carrier.

"Would you like to receive Holy Communion, Misses Fitzgibbon?"

Aubrey's face lit up. "Can I, Father?" She was ecstatic.

O'Connor popped open the lid of the carrier and lifted out one of the hosts inside. He then recited a short prayer. "The Body of Christ, Aubrey," O'Connor said, holding the host up before her.

"Amen," Aubrey responded, she then opened her mouth and accepted the entrance of her savior into her temple. She began weeping with joy again, closing her eyes while in blissful contemplation. A moment later, she opened her eyes back up, then glanced out the window once more, watching the endless assortment of huge snowflakes continue to float down to earth from the sky. It was like peering into a giant snow globe.

"The snow is beautiful," she whispered. "Is it sticking?"

"Fer sure it is. And beneath that blanket of winter snow rests the roses that will bloom in spring. They'll be a bloomin' in tribute to ye, Misses Fitzgibbon. Now just lay yer head back and rest, child. …Fer sure, yer a saint, Aubrey Fitzgibbon. Close yer eyes and count yer blessin's while the silent stars pass by. We who live in God's grace may be hurt, but we are never truly damaged."

Aubrey smiled. "Thank you for restoring my faith, Father." Her compliment made the priest who struggled with his relevance feel like a million bucks.

O'Connor watched as Aubrey closed her eyes. He began to back away from the bed and toward the door. He raised his right arm and hand and made the sign of the cross over Aubrey, pronouncing a silent blessing as he did.

"Too-ra-loo-ra-loo-ral,
Too-ra-loo-ra-li,
Too-ra-loo-ra-loo-ral,
Hush, now don't you cry!"

The choir's rendition of the song stopped O'Connor dead in his tracks. Aubrey opened her eyes at the sound of the soothing melody.

"Those little stinkers," O'Connor muttered, "they'd be singin' me song."

"Sing it to me, Father. Sing me the *Irish Lullaby.*"

O'Connor could not deny Aubrey's plea for a curtain call. He began to sing to her that *simple little ditty.*

"Too-ra-loo-ra-loo-ral,
Too-ra-loo-ra-li,
Too-ra-loo-ra-loo-ral,
That's an Irish lullaby."

Father O'Connor backed away from the bed toward the door again, never skipping a beat of the song. Aubrey watched as he disappeared into the dark shadows on the other side of the room. She heard the door open and close, and then Father O'Connor was gone. But only for a second. Aubrey heard the door open again and she saw a silhouette moving toward her from out of the shadows.

"Misses Fitzgibbon," Father O'Connor said. "I almost forgot yer Christmas present. Merry Christmas, Aubrey. God Bless, ye."

The silhouette moving towards Aubrey was slowly illuminated by the reading light over the bed. It was Angela Sanchez. Aubrey was speechless — her eyes and face said it all. Happy tears streamed down her face and Angela's as well. O'Connor watched the scene — he wouldn't have missed this moment for the world.

"Too-ra-loo-ra-loo-ral,
Too-ra-loo-ra-li,
Too-ra-loo-ra-loo-ral,
That's an Irish lullaby."

O'Connor retreated towards the door, opened it again, and then slipped out. He looked back to watch as Angela and Aubrey embraced until the closing door slowly eased shut and eclipsed them out of his sight. Father O'Connor would then walk all the way home, savoring the glimpse of their reunion with each and every step along the way.

Making his way back to the rectory, Father O'Connor drifted along with the snowfall through block after block of the Saint Aloysius Parish neighborhoods. The city took on a peculiar silence during the snowfall — the sound of nothingness. The good priest appreciated the respite from the usual sirens and traffic noise. The snowfall seemed to amplify that silence. The only sound that could be heard was the crunching of the fluffy snowflakes underfoot with each footfall that Father O'Connor put forth.

He was caught up in the serenity and beauty of this silent night, appreciating the glistening of porch Christmas lights and decorations underneath a steadily, deepening, blanket of snow. He recalled cherished memories on each of the streets he passed through; fond remembrances in every one of the homes. Homes where parents would soon be busy setting presents underneath Christmas trees for their children, all in anticipation of the wonders of Christmas morning. These were neighborhoods and homes that were steep in O'Connor's miracles. On and on trudged the priest, without a single pang of angina — he hadn't felt this good in years.

Then Father O'Connor recalled the family photos of his army buddies that he viewed earlier in the day. Families that God, through *O'Connor's Miracles*, made possible.

Father O'Connor sensed the Spirit was within him. He was more alive and relevant than he had ever felt before in his life. He knew, and he trusted in God, that everything was going to work out all right for Aubrey Fitzgibbon and Angela Sanchez.

Chapter Twenty-eight

"Monsignor Norton, its half past six and Father O'Connor hasn't come down yet," Misses Cavendish said, alerting the pastor. The monsignor sat behind his desk, catching up on yesterday's mail. "He's going to be late for the seven o'clock morning Mass. Shall I go up and wake him?"

Monsignor Norton thought for a second, then looked over towards the housekeeper, who straddled the doorway between the foyer and the room. "No," he told her. Norton knew about the long hours that his elderly colleague had put in the past few days. "He came in very late last night. He hit every creak on the steps. ...Good thing that he's a priest — he'd never make it as a cat burglar. Let him sleep. I'll cover for him at the early Mass. Besides, we'll be concelebrating the Christmas Eve Midnight Mass, and he'll be putting in another long day. Let him rest, and just wake him up in time to cover for me at this morning's nine o'clock Mass. We'll switch."

He rose from the chair and fumbled through the papers piled in the inbox on the desk, where Father O'Connor usually stashed his sermon notes. He would deliver the sermon that O'Connor intended. Close to the top of the pile of papers, he found the sermon notes with a notation across the top — *Christmas Eve morning Mass*. He glanced them over, recalling the homily well — it was one that O'Connor frequently repeated throughout the years, typically on the days preceding Christmas. A rendition of an *Irish Blessing* from an unknown author. *Perfect.*

Alongside the inbox, Norton observed more of the unopened mail stacked up in a pile. The noticeable script on the envelope at the top of the stack caught his eye — it was prominently emblazoned with the seal and letterhead of the

Archbishop. He stuffed it inside the vest pocket of his jacket and proceeded towards the rectory front door, grabbing an overcoat from the coatrack. Outside, a brisk winter wind greeted him. Pellets of rock salt crunched underneath Monsignor Norton's shoes as he stepped.

Inside the sacristy of the church, Monsignor Norton quickly took a glimpse at the gospel reading for the Mass while he dressed, and then he quickly glanced over Father O'Connor's homily again. The still pleasant aroma of stale incense lingered into the sacristy from the altar area. Norton checked his watch — five minutes before the start of Mass.

The letter from the Archbishop crossed Monsignor Norton's mind. He opened the sacristy cloak closet door and retrieved the document from the jacket pocket where he stashed it. He opened the envelope and slid out the letter. He began to read it.

Adrenalin pumped through his blood system like gasoline in a fuel injection engine. *What a speed rush.* Archbishop Scaponi's letter explained that he had a change of heart — he was granting Monsignor Norton his sabbatical to attend Georgetown on a scholarship for attaining his doctorate. At the bottom of the letter in his own handwriting, a personal note: *Chalk it up to another O'Connor miracle. Good luck. Will be in touch soon — to work out your transition. Merry Christmas — Archbishop Scaponi.*

That old son-of-a-gun. God bless you, Father O'Connor. A tear of joy loosened itself from Norton's eye and trickled down his cheek, but he had little time to ponder his good fortune, as Mass was about to start.

Monsignor Norton stationed himself behind the altar servers. The lead altar boy stepped forward and yanked on the cord hanging outside the doorjamb between the sacristy and the altar area, clanging the altar bell that signaled the start of Mass. They proceeded out onto the altar. Norton bowed and kissed the altar top, then moved off to the side of the Holy platform — by the celebrants' chairs. He greeted the congregation, made the sign of the cross and began the Mass. He noted that it was being said for a special intention — a successful medical procedure for Aubrey Fitzgibbon.

"Grace to you and peace from God our Father and the Lord Jesus Christ," he prayed, initiating a series of responses and invocations from the assembly. As an altar server opened the *Order of Mass* and held in front of Norton to read, the monsignor glanced out over the congregation. His gaze was drawn to the empty organ and choir balcony hanging over the rear of the church. For a second, he thought he saw Father O'Connor standing in the loft and signaling to him by flashing the okay sign with his hand. Norton closed his eyes and shook his head, then peered back up at the balcony again — he apparently mistook a coatrack with several choir gowns hanging from it for Father O'Connor.

***

On the other side of town, several city neighborhoods in the distance, Aubrey Fitzgibbon was moments away from her birthing procedure. A team of nurses and hospital attendants prepared to transport her into a specially prepared operating room of the Jersey City Medical Center. They had already prepped Aubrey in several stages: the night before they started her on a Pitocin IV drip — an oxytocin used for inducing labor contractions — and then inserted prostaglandin suppositories into her vagina. By a little after six-thirty in the morning, Aubrey's water had broken. All this time, Aubrey remained on a steady flow of induced fresh oxygen to help ease her burdened breathing.

Aubrey's delivery team and cardiologists went over procedures and protocols for practically any situation that could develop given her fragile condition. As the orderlies and nurses moved Aubrey out of her room, she smiled when she saw that several of the buds were in bloom on the cactus rose that Father O'Connor left.

They wheeled Aubrey to the patient elevator, then into the operating room equipped with cardiology instrumentation for her special birthing procedure. The room reeked of a pleasing antiseptic aroma. Her two doctors and a cardiologist waited. The anesthesiologist administered a solution to numb her but not put her out. She would have to assist the birth by pushing her baby out of her womb during the delivery process, if all else went according to plans. Aubrey slipped into a pleasant high from the anesthesia, truly feeling no pain. She could swear that she saw father O'Connor standing beside her singing the *Irish Lullaby*.

The nurses and medical technicians connected her to the medical equipment to monitor her vital signs. They also switched her over to the operating room's oxygen supply. Then they lifted her legs into the stirrups at the end of the operating table. They finished not a second too soon, as Aubrey immediately went into labor. Above the operating table, the beeps sounding out and the jagged lines registering on the cardiogram screen, increased as the labor commenced. The grim expressions on the doctors' faces showed their grave concern. The delivery was just starting and already her heart was under stress.

Aubrey's gynecologist told the nurses to move Aubrey out of the leg stirrups and onto on her side — a position that would tax the heart less during the procedure. He then told one of the nurses that she would have to hold and elevate Aubrey's topside leg until after the baby was born. Thompson stepped up to the operating table, positioning himself in front of the womb. The birth was in process as the head of the baby appeared in the vaginal opening and then slowly slid out. Thompson held and guided the child with his fingers, glancing up at the cardiogram screen — the blips and wave lines were now going crazy, at a critical intensity.

"Push, Aubrey, Push," Thompson said, trying to get the baby's shoulders through the constricted opening.

Aubrey's heart was thumping like a bass drum. She gasped for air, but kept pushing and straining. A few moments later, her head fell limp as she lost consciousness. The bleeps from the cardiogram became a steady monotone and a flatline spread across the monitor. Blood pressure readings descended to zero and her complexion began changing from a sickly pale white to an ashen grey blue.

***

Monsignor Norton finished the gospel reading and began to addressed the congregation. Looking out over the gathering, he noticed the Fitzgibbon children — Justin and Tracy — sitting in a center front pew. They spent the previous night at the Medical Center with their Dad — comforting Aubrey and praying in the hospital's chapel the way that Father O'Connor taught them.

"Now don't be panicking — Father O'Connor and I are switching Masses this morning, but I do have the sermon that he was intending to deliver. Knowing how loyal you are to his homilies, I wouldn't dare have you sit through the drudgery of one of mine."

The congregation responded with polite laughter.

Norton glanced down at Father O'Connor's prepared homily. "You'll remember this 'ditty' as Father O'Connor would call it." At the bottom of page, he noticed a handwritten note — *Ask congregants to stay after Mass and offer a D.M.C. for Aubrey.*

Knowing what that meant, Norton asked the congregation to stay after Mass and pray the Chaplet of the Divine Mercy for the special intention of Aubrey Fitzgibbon. He then introduced the sermon by saying, "Father O'Connor writes, that on the days leading up to Christmas, children get busy making out their Christmas wish lists — filled with the toys and gifts that they are hoping to receive. We, too, begin to make our own wish lists — the things, other than toys, that we are all hoping for in the coming year. Not to be cheated out of this tradition, Father O'Connor made his own list of Christmas blessings that he was wishing for each and every one of us. This is a blessing from the *'ould'* country, which he hopes that each and every one of you will treasure. He writes:

"I wish for you not a path devoid of clouds, nor a life on a bed of roses — not that you might never need regret, nor that you should never feel pain. No, that is not my wish for you. My wish is that you might be brave in times of trial — when others lay crosses upon your shoulders. To be strong when mountains must be climbed and chasms are to be crossed; when hope scarce can shine through. That every gift God gave you might grow along with you, and let you give the gift of joy to all who care for you. That you may always have a friend worthy of the name — whom you can trust, and who helps you in times of sadness. A friend who will defy the storms of daily life at your side.

"One more wish I have for you. That in every hour of joy and pain, you may feel God close to you. This is my Christmas wish for you, and for all who care for you. This is my hope for you, now and forever."

Monsignor Norton said nothing more and walked back toward the altar, bowing before the tabernacle, then sitting down in the chair reserved for the priest saying the Mass. He allowed the congregation a short time to ponder the sermon and reflect on Father O'Connor's message to them.

***

Aubrey Fitzgibbon's heart did not beat for a full thirty seconds.

Doctor Thompson looked behind him, over toward where Doctor Friedman and the cardiologist stood, observing the procedure and whispering to one another. One of the medical technicians made a move for the defibrillator paddles, but froze in place, remembering the protocols that they went over before the procedure began — *the defibrillator could not be used in the case of heart failure as long as the baby was in the womb or still attached to the umbilical cord.* The cardiologist stepped up to the table and directed the nurses and technicians to roll Aubrey's limp body on its back. Doctor Thompson continued attempting to gently slip the baby's shoulders out of the womb. He had managed to free one arm and he was now working on the other.

Doctor Friedman pushed the heart specialist aside and placed a step platform on the floor, adjacent to the operating table, signaling for the doctor to step up on it. The cardiologist stepped onto the platform and began cardiac massage — furiously pumping down on Aubrey's breast area with one hand draped over the other. The same flatline and monotone continued.

The cardiologist stopped the CPR massage for a second, repositioned his hands, then began pumping furiously again. He took a glance down towards Doctor Thompson, who was still working the baby free. "Hurry, Doctor, hurry, or it will be too late."

All eyes in the room were locked on Thompson when a *beep* sounded from the monitor, then another and the flatline turned jagged. More blips followed along with a set pattern of peaks. The numbers on the blood pressure began ascending. Audible sighs of relief filled the room. Aubrey was back, though not out of peril. The blips soared up again — her heart was beating even faster than before. Her blood pressure was soaring. A stroke was imminent.

Doctor Thompson had by now freed the infant from the womb. He called for a clamp and directed the nurse to cut the umbilical cord while he held the baby. As the nurse severed the lifeline, the blips flatlined again on the screen — Aubrey's heart gave out. Within a matter of seconds, the cardiologist administered CPR compressions again. Thirty seconds, One minute. One minute and a half. Nothing. Flat line, no beeps.

Doctor Friedman's eyes scanned another monitor over the operating table, the EEG readings. "There's still brain activity."

Unconscious, Aubrey slipped into a surreal dream state.

Doctor Thompson and a neonatal team of two nurses and two technicians attended to the newborn. An incubator was wheeled over to the operating table, then the nurses wiped down the baby while Thompson used a suction tube to siphon mucous from out of the neonate's nasal passageways. Once clear, the child cried out. It was a healthy wail. Thompson looked the newborn over for any deformities and then quickly checked the infant's senses. "One healthy baby girl ready for the incubator."

The nurses placed the baby in the incubator and wheeled it away.

Aubrey's subconscious dream episode placed her in a tunnel with a bright white light at its far end. She was floating in air, moving towards the direction of the light. She could see the outline of many people up ahead — silhouetted by the blinding light. She realized she was carrying something in her arms — a metal hospital tray with the remains of Angela Sanchez's aborted fetus. The dead eyed stare of the fetal corpse looked back at her.

She couldn't loosen her grip on the metal tray, it seemed to be adhered to her hands. The blinding light became overpowering, impossible to look at, but she heard something behind her, singing, as clear as a bell — Father O'Connor crooning the *Irish Lullaby*. There was another sound chiming in with the singing — the cries and wails of a baby and the whine of what sounded like an ambulance siren.

"Hand me the paddles." The cardiologist yelled. A technician flicked the switch on the biphasic defibrillator and rolled it towards the table, then he dismounted the paddles

220

and handed them to the cardiologist. While the cardiologist grabbed the paddles, the technician peeled off the seal on the gel pad fitted over the contact surface area — the lubricant served as a conductance for the electrical charge.

The neonatal team moved the baby away from the operating table. The heart specialist called, "CLEAR!" The medical personnel attending to Aubrey took a step back from the table. He positioned the paddles — one underneath her left breast and one over the ribcage on the right side of her body. He pressed down hard with the paddles and then squeezed the handles to deliver the jolt.

Aubrey's body practically leapt up off the table, then quickly fell back down. No response from the cardiogram. The cardiologist resumed CPR compressions for another half minute, then recalled the defibrillator paddles back. "CLEAR!" he shouted, then jolted Aubrey again. It was futile — there was no change. The cardiologist resumed the CPR compressions for thirty seconds more. Shaking his head, he gazed at Doctor Friedman, who raised his index finger skyward, signaling one more time.

***

"May the Good Lord bless and keep you — in the name of the Father, Son, and Holy Spirit," Monsignor Norton said.

"Amen," the congregation said.

The Mass was over, but not a soul left the church. The entire congregation was staying to pray the Divine Mercy Chaplet for Aubrey Fitzgibbon.

Monsignor Norton retreated to the sacristy and grabbed a kneeler, which he then carried out and set down before the altar. He knelt down, made the sign of the cross and began to pray, "You expired, Jesus, but the source of life gushed forth for souls, and the ocean of mercy opened up for the whole world. O Fount of Life, unfathomable Divine Mercy, envelop the whole world and empty Yourself out upon us."

Amidst the prayers, the sounds and echoes of rosary beads, colliding with the wooden seatbacks of pews, resonated throughout the church. The calloused hands and fingers of some laborers, the soft and tender hands and fingers of homemakers and housewives, the smooth hands and fingers of high school students, and the arthritic hands and fingers of many seniors, all worked their way through the five decades of the rosary beads, imploring Jesus Christ's benevolence and his blessing upon Aubrey Fitzgibbon.

***

The cardiologist hovered the defibrillator paddles over Aubrey Fitzgibbon again. It had now been four and one-half minutes since her heart stopped beating for the second time. The heart specialist didn't hold out any hope but didn't let his sentiment show. He would carry out the charade of attempting to revive Aubrey for the sake of her family.

Doctor Friedman glanced up at the EEG monitor again — there was still brain activity. Then something made him look over at the ECG monitor still flatlining. Something draped over the corner of the screen glistened, reflecting the bright lights of the operating room. It was Father O'Connor's Celtic cross ring hanging from a chain, placed there by one of the nurses at Aubrey's request.

Doctor Friedman noticed something else — the blood pressure display in the lower right-hand corner of the screen was showing rising numbers. He looked back down at Aubrey; the ashen gray color was fading "What the hell?" Friedman said aloud.

"CLEAR!" the cardiologist shouted out.

"HOLD IT!" Friedman yelled moving towards the operating table and reaching with his arm between the cardiologist and Aubrey. He picked up the end of a wire from the ECG monitor that had detached from the sensors recording Aubrey's heartbeat — dislodged during CPR.

Doctor Friedman reattached the wire and, instantly, the beeping resumed as the blips began jumping up and down across the screen. The cardiologist told the anesthesiologist to administer a mild sedative — he didn't want Aubrey's heart to start racing again.

Still in the unconscious throes of her dream, Aubrey turned from the white light and headed back down the other end of the tunnel, toward the sound of a baby's cries and Father O'Connor's singing. The tray that held the carcass of Angela Sanchez's aborted fetus was gone. Then Aubrey could hear other voices — the chatter of those attending to her in the operating room — but she was still too groggy to awaken.

The medical team realized that if Aubrey Fitzgibbon pulled through, they had all just witnessed a miracle. A nice story to tell their families and friends later during their Christmas Eve gatherings.

***

Misses Cavendish rapped her knuckles on Father O'Connor's bedroom door. "Father O'Connor," she called, "are you up, Father O'Connor?"

There was no answer.

Misses Cavendish rapped the door harder, raising her voice. Still no response. She glanced down the hall at the bathroom door — it was open, but the light was out. *Not in the bathroom.* She turned knob, eased the door open, and then stepped inside. She was taken aback by a stiff cold draft. The bedroom window was wide-open and the chilly winter air poured in.

Misses Cavendish would be the first to know — sometime in the early morning hours of a snowy Christmas Eve, Father Sean O'Connor passed onto his heavenly reward. He had a peaceful smile on his face, almost as if to acknowledge that he had gotten his *'druthers'* — as he had expressed to Sal Panetta — *the Lord had called him home on Christmas.* Before retiring for the evening, O'Connor managed to fulfill for one last time his routine ritual of rummaging through the wooden chest that held his Medal of Honor and other memorabilia, and then praying again for *O'Connor's Miracles* and their families. He also took the time to write a letter to Archbishop Scaponi that he sealed in an envelope and left on top of his dresser.

Misses Cavendish summoned Monsignor Norton. Choking back tears, Monsignor Norton prayed over his colleague and friend, then gave a quick blessing before calling the undertaker to come and collect the body. Monsignor Norton next called O'Connor's closest friend, Archbishop Scaponi.

***

About the time that Misses Cavendish discovered Father O'Connor's body, Aubrey Fitzgibbon regained consciousness and was resting back in the intensive care unit of the hospital. Her husband stood by her bedside, rekindled in his faith, thanks to Father O'Connor. They rolled Stefanie's incubator beside the bed, so that Aubrey could see her new daughter before the sedation induced her to doze off. Tears of joy streamed from her eyes and down her cheeks. A sudden case of the *"what ifs"* occurred to her — the other scenario *if* she had chosen to abort the fetus way back when. That seemed so unthinkable now, especially in the face of her new infant child.

Aubrey and Stefanie were the last of Father O'Connor's earthly miracles.

Chapter Twenty-nine

The wake for Father Sean O'Connor in Saint Aloysius Church took place between Christmas and New Year's Day. Archbishop Scaponi, Monsignor Norton and other priests who were his friends or mentored by him — ten in all — concelebrated the Funeral Mass. Deacon Mike Fitzgibbon participated in the ceremony as well. O'Connor's coffin was draped with an American flag at the direction of Archbishop Scaponi and the priest's remaining family members — in recognition of his valiant service to his country.

Thousands came to bid O'Connor a final farewell — a multitude of family, friends, past and present parishioners, and residents of Jersey City. The crowd filled the church and spewed out onto the sidewalk and into Lincoln Park. West Side Avenue, in front of the church, was completely congested. There were other priests and nuns with whom he served, a Congressman, the Mayor, councilmen, and even an Honor Guard dispatched from the armed services. But mostly, there were the common, ordinary, everyday folk that O'Connor loved so well — the *O'Connor Miracles.*

Archbishop Scaponi gave a wonderful eulogy, filled with stories of Father O'Connor's life that brought the congregation to tears as well as fits of laughter. He recalled O'Connor's service to his country, something of which the modest O'Connor never mentioned. "This is my prerogative," Scaponi told the crowd. "It's my way of getting even with my dear friend for all the razzing that he always gave me. But, by God, the man deserves the recognition; and his story deserves telling, if only to inspire the rest of us." He then invited Monsignor Norton to say a few words. Norton likewise gave a tender eulogy about the man that he grew to admire and respect. Finally, Scaponi called upon one of O'Connor's army pals, Barry Freeman, to read the inscription on Father O'Connor's Medal of Honor citation. At the conclusion of its reading, the crowd stood and applauded spontaneously.

Before the crowd started to exit, Scaponi told them that Lee's Luncheonette and Dohoney's Tavern would be providing a repast for the crowd to attend at the end of the Mass. He thanked the proprietors of the establishments for their generosity, adding, "Thank goodness they decided to pick up that tab. After Father O'Connor hit the diocese up for that rectory plumbing bill a couple of months ago, we didn't have the money to pay for a repast." The whole crowd laughed aloud again — the tale of the beloved priest's exploits that day were now parish folklore. Father O'Connor would have approved.

Then, the honorary pall bearers — the remaining members of the original O'Connor's Miracles, Rabbi Turner, and two soldiers in Army dress uniforms who accompanied the military honor guard — rolled the coffin down the center aisle of the church on its carrier, heading towards the exit doors. Charlie Baber and the choir sang the recessional hymn. Father O'Connor slowly departed his beloved Saint Aloysius Church for the final time.

"When Christ shall come, with shout of acclamation,
And take me home, what joy shall fill my heart.
Then I shall bow, in humble adoration,
And then proclaim: 'My God, how great Thou art!'"

At the end of the aisle, the pallbearers lifted the coffin off of the carrier and maneuvered it through the vestibule doors, then through the outer church doors, finally, stepping onto the church portico. They rested the casket upon a makeshift platform setup there. Two tenfold flanks of bagpipers and drummers, clad in Irish kilts, were stationed on opposite sides of the church portico. The musicians blasted out *Amazing Grace.* Everyone sang along.

There may have been a few voices singing off key, but there was not one dry eye in the crowd. As the bagpipers wrapped up, the honorary pallbearers lifted O'Connor's coffin from the platform and began to descend the church stairs, heading toward the hearse. As the coffin was carried slowly through the crowd, hands reached out to touch its sides — a final farewell gesture to the priest that everyone loved. Monsignor Norton must have sensed something was missing, so he opened his mouth and began to sing the Irish Lullaby.

"Too-ra-loo-ra-loo-ral,
Too-ra-loo-ra-li,
Too-ra-loo-ra-loo-ral,
Hush, now don't you cry!"

Archbishop Scaponi joined in, as did Charles Baber and the choir, who had just descended the church balcony to join the throngs outside the church. The spontaneity of the complement spread, and in a matter of seconds the entire entourage packed onto West Side Avenue, inside of Lincoln Park, and all around the church belted out the tribute to O'Connor at the tops of their lungs. The singing radiated throughout the surrounding Jersey City neighborhoods, echoing through the city streets.

"Just a simple little ditty,
In her good ould Irish way,
And I'd give the world if she could sing
That song to me this day."

Slowly, the pallbearers trudged on through the throng as memorable faces from O'Connor's past reached out to touch his coffin. Angela Sanchez and her family, Sister Eleanor

Joseph, Sister Marion Theresa, and others of the good Sisters of Charity said their farewells. Many of the high school's students were there to say goodbye, including Jason Nealon and his gang of ruffians. Misses Cavendish and Mister Johnson of the parish staff said so-long, as did Doctor Friedman and Doctor Thompson, who knew all about the priest who so inspired their patient. Standing beside the doctors were Aubrey Fitzgibbon's children, Justin and Tracy, who came by to represent her. Still in the hospital recuperating, Aubrey took O'Connor's passing pretty hard.

The family of the recently baptized Ethan Connors, as well as the family of the recently deceased Sal Panetta, also stopped by to pay their respects. Misses Malone, sizing up the men in the crowd, came by. Ed Ford, proprietor of Dohoney's Tavern, and the proprietors of Lee's Luncheonette, Lee Burke and his son Lenny, were there as well. Nikki Spencer and her husband Matt, along with Brittany and Darrin McCarey, came to see O'Connor off. Detective Richard Cummings made it a point to be there; and, surprisingly, so did Cindy Stone.

As the pallbearers stepped off the curb at West Side Avenue, and then onto the street where the hearse was parked, they passed by Police Officer Bernard McCarthy, who was assigned to the funeral to work crowd control. McCarthy had managed to sneak inside the church to catch the Funeral Mass, before resuming his post again. He noticed a young teen stretching out his arm from behind a wooden police horse that was serving as a barrier. The lad was trying to touch the flag draped coffin with his hand. McCarthy took a second glance at the youth and recognized him — it was Griffin Reilly, the boy that O'Connor rescued from McCarthy's intended arrest earlier in the year. O'Connor had stayed in touch with the youth and his grandmother ever since that day, making sure that Griffin stayed on the straight and narrow.

McCarthy approached the teen. "Griffin," he called. "How are you doing, son?"

The voice startled Griffin, who had to convince his grandmother to take him to the funeral of the priest who so touched his life. Griffin focused in on the mountainous man in the cop's uniform and recognized the patrolman.

"Officer McCarthy, I'm doing fine, Sir. How are you?"

'Sir'. How polite remains the lad. O'Connor was right about the kid. I'm glad I didn't run the poor boy in that day. "Crouch down and scoot under the barrier, Griffin," McCarthy said, motioning with his hand for Griffin to step away from the crowd and onto the street where O'Connor's coffin was passing by.

Griffin followed McCarthy's direction.

"Go ahead, touch it," McCarthy said, pointing towards the coffin.

Rushing over to the coffin, Griffin stuck his arm between two of the pallbearers, resting his hand atop the American flag that was draped over the casket. "Thank you, Father O'Connor," he said aloud. "Thank you. I'm somebody! I'm somebody!"

When he finished his tribute, a teary-eyed Griffin stepped back from the coffin and retreated back behind the barrier. McCarthy reached out to give the lad a hug. Father O'Connor would have been beaming.

The pallbearers finally reached the hearse and slid O'Connor's coffin into the back of the shiny black vehicle. The hearse pulled away slowly as the police detail eased back the crowd that was standing in the street, in order to give the driver an opening. The vehicle was headed toward a Catholic cemetery for priests and nuns in Metuchen, New Jersey — for a private burial ceremony. Archbishop Scaponi and Monsignor Norton would later drive there to preside over the ceremony. On a distant cemetery hill, a lone bagpiper would play *Danny Boy.* Then an Army bugler would blow out *Taps* when they lowered Father O'Connor into his grave.

The crowd on West Side Avenue began waving goodbye, continuing to do so until the hearse drove out of sight, almost as if they thought that Father O'Connor could somehow see them. They continued singing their tribute.

"Its melody still haunts me,
These many years gone by,
Too-ra-loo-ra-loo-ral,
Until the day I die"

Other words from Archbishop Scaponi's eulogy struck a chord with the crowd — words that would linger forever inside the hearts and souls of everyone who heard the tribute that he paid to his dearly departed friend. Words reminding the gathering about the roads that people like Father O'Connor traveled down during their lives — roads that were lined with triumphs and losses. "Each joy and every heartache, as well as the acquaintances made along a soul's earthly journey, blend and culminate to mark the words and music of life's lullabies. People live and people die, but the lullabies that they write on the pages of their lives are what they leave behind for the rest of the world to sing."

Scaponi's sermon had captured the sentiment that Father O'Connor came to realize as he trudged through his dear Saint Aloysius neighborhoods, one last time, during the Christmas Eve snowfall; "Relevance is not measured by time, nor sustained by perseverance. Relevance is measured and sustained by the impact of the lives that we lead, the deeds that we do, and our humanity to our fellow man."

When the hearse was gone, the crowd began to slowly disperse.

The Saint Aloysius church bells sounded out the midday hour, signaling to the parish, and all others within earshot: *life goes on.* The crowd attending the repast at Dohoney's heard the bells. They promptly hoisted their drinks into the air, toasting the priest one last time. The clanging church bells would remind all who so loved Father O'Connor of the most important lesson that he left with them — *"where God breeds life there will always be hope."* A relevant lesson for all eternity.

The sage priest's truth would outshine his fame.

Rest in peace, Blessed Father Sean O'Connor, who preached the Gospel of life.

"Too-ra-loo-ra-loo-ral,
That's an Irish lullaby."

A Word From the Author

During his visit to Ireland a half century ago, shortly before his assassination, President John Fitzgerald Kennedy stated, "It is that quality of the Irish — that remarkable combination of hope, confidence and imagination — that is needed more than ever today." How endearing were President Kennedy's words, especially in light of the events transpiring in today's world.

I was born and raised in the predominantly Irish-Catholic neighborhoods of Jersey City, New Jersey's West Side and Lincoln Park districts — also known as the Saint Aloysius Parish neighborhoods. I was blessed to share the customs, heritage, stories and lives of so many who befriended me. An Irish Lullaby is my personal tribute to the friends and families of my childhood and the old neighborhoods — fabulous people. The book is also an expression of gratitude for my Catholic faith. To me, the old Jersey City neighborhood was the greatest place on earth where a kid could grow up.

Somehow, Saint Aloysius Parish became the center of our lives—everything seemed to flow from the church. Each parish that comprised our midsize city was like its own small-town America. For the purpose of heightening the enjoyment and nostalgia of the reader, I took the customs and values of 1960 parish life and transformed them into the modern-day timeframe in which the story takes place. Likewise, many of the settings and locations from the 1960's Jersey City [some which no longer exist] are also recreated for the modern timeframe of the story.

Particularly important to note, is that when reading the depiction of the clergy in the story, the culture and mores of 1960's clergy are being portrayed. The priests in the story are an amalgamation of the characteristics of the priests that I had known while growing up. Older priests were more conservative and younger priests were somewhat more active in social politics, such as speaking out against the Vietnam War that was raging at the time. The priests then, more so than at any other time that I can recall, really involved themselves in the community issues of the parishes to which they were assigned. In today's PC world, these characteristics may seem to be a bit more politically incorrect or unpolished than in the 1960's era for which they were suited — but they are genuine.

Particularly noteworthy is the backstory of the main protagonist, Father Sean O'Connor, and his service as a chaplain during the Vietnam War. It is based on the war record of Chaplain (Captain) Angelo J. Liteky of the 199th Infantry Brigade, who earned the Medal of Honor for his heroic and extraordinary exploits on December 6, 1967 while serving in the Vietnam War. Chaplain (Captain) Angelo J. Liteky's war record is authentically portrayed in the story.

After his service in Vietnam, Liteky left both the Army and the Catholic priesthood and became a peace activist. In 1986, he renounced his Medal of Honor by leaving it in an envelope at the Vietnam Veterans Memorial in Washington. The National Park Service recovered Liteky's medal, and it is now on display at the National Museum of American History.

The provocative abortion scene that opens the novel is based upon medical research and the interviews of medical professionals and personnel. It was a labor of intense care and thought— rewritten and edited over and over, until I felt it was right. It is controversial and gut-wrenching, but it is factual. It is presented, as the reader will discover, not for the sake of being gratuitous, but to rather invest the reader in the story that follows— it heightens the drama and the value of the reading experience.

The discussions by the characters in the book concerning abortion comprise prolife and prochoice viewpoints publicly expressed by modern-day advocates of those positions.

I also want to express my grateful appreciation to Judy Katz and Mark Malatesta, two writing coaches and friends, who have helped me to seriously hone my craft; and a special thanks to Kris Millegan of TrineDay Publishing, who gave launch to my writing by publishing my first book. Special thanks also to Augie Torres and Al Sullivan, journalists and hopefully future authors, for their insightful and helpful critiques of my manuscripts, before they were marketed.

I also wish to extend my gratitude to Dr. Gene D. Robinson, the head of MOONSHINE COVE PUBLISHING, for his faith in this story, along with the true grit to publish a story with such controversial a subject matter.

And, of course, my heartfelt thanks for the many family and friends who continue to enjoy and encourage my writing. Now, back to work on my next manuscript...

CPSIA information can be obtained
at www.ICGtesting.com
Printed in the USA
LVHW091230090521
686913LV00005B/1135